Rejected Writers
Take the Stage

Center Point
Large Print

Also by Suzanne Kelman and available from Center Point Large Print:

The Rejected Writers' Book Club

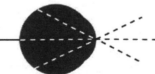

This Large Print Book carries the Seal of Approval of N.A.V.H.

Rejected Writers Take the Stage

A SOUTHLEA BAY NOVEL

Suzanne Kelman

CENTER POINT LARGE PRINT
THORNDIKE, MAINE

The text of this Large Print edition is unabridged.
In other aspects, this book may vary
from the original edition.
Printed in the United States of America
on permanent paper.
Set in 16-point Times New Roman type.

ISBN: 978-1-68324-548-3

Library of Congress Cataloging-in-Publication Data

Names: Kelman, Suzanne, author.
Title: Rejected Writers take the stage : a Southlea Bay novel /
    Suzanne Kelman.
Description: Center Point large print edition. |
    Thorndike, Maine : Center Point Large Print, 2017.
Identifiers: LCCN 2017028894 | ISBN 9781683245483
    (hardcover : alk. paper)
Subjects: LCSH: Women librarians—Washington (State)—Fiction. |
    Book clubs (Discussion groups)—Fiction. | Female friendship—
    Fiction. | Large type books.
Classification: LCC PS3611.E464 R46 2017 | DDC 813/.6—dc23
LC record available at https://lccn.loc.gov/2017028894

To my grandfather, Leonard Frederick Shelley, and my grandmother, Joyce Diana Shelley. Though neither of you will ever get to read this book, your influence is on every page. Thank you for your abundant steadfast love, your unequivocal way of seeing humor in everyday life, and your unflinching support that was the heart and soul of our family.

Chapter One

FROZEN YETIS &
SCOTCH TAPE SHENANIGANS

Karen, the Southlea Bay library manager, approached the door with her keys and stopped short before announcing through a clenched smile, "Doris alert."

I looked up in a panic and caught a glimpse of the most infamous resident of our small town, Doris Newberry, peering at Karen from under the "Reading Is Fun" decal affixed to the window. She was standing atop the library steps, looking akin to a demented yeti. Clothed from head to foot in icy, wet fur, she wouldn't have looked out of place at a Moscow drinking festival.

From behind the library desk a few feet away, I allowed a curse word to slip out.

Karen giggled at my outburst. "Let's hope that isn't one of the phrases our preschoolers will be learning in the story corner with Ruby this morning."

Turning the library sign from "Closed" to "Open," Karen acknowledged with a smile the ram waiting to charge and fogging up the window.

Karen placed her key in the lock. Doris's nose

was practically pressed against the pane as she stomped from foot to foot. Her bizarre appearance was so disconcerting that the mothers of fearful small children had moved across the street to await the opening of the library from a safe distance.

As Karen unbarred the door, the frozen Attila the Hun stomped in, and her menacing presence domineered the whole space as she surveyed the room.

"Janet!" snapped Doris pointedly. She was not one to clutter her speech with pleasantries. "I want to speak to Janet. It's urgent."

"Good morning, Doris," said Karen cheerfully, appearing not at all intimidated by a large, overbearing woman squeezed behind crocheted buttons and beaver fur.

Karen pointed toward the counter.

Reflexively, I dropped to the floor.

"Of course, Doris. Janet is just over . . ."

Karen stopped short because the space that seconds before had contained me, a cursing Janet, was now empty. Yep, Doris Newberry could have that effect on folk in this quaint Northwest island town. The words "Doris Newberry" worked faster than "abracadabra" to create disappearing tricks all over Southlea Bay.

From the floor, I chided myself. What was I doing? I was a grown woman. This was absurd.

What had possessed me to drop to the floor like that? There was nothing down here that could have needed my attention, and if I just popped up now, I would look ridiculous. In the five years I had lived in Southlea Bay, I had found I was constantly doing things that I wouldn't have dreamed of doing during my first forty years of living in California. When my husband and I had decided to move to a rural island community in Washington State five years ago as we headed toward our later years, I had images of cooking classes, quilting bees, and ice cream socials. Instead it often felt like being on the lam in some sort of witness protection program. I was always thinking on my feet as I navigated my way through all shades of crazy that is small-town life. Once mistaken for a Jaclyn Smith lookalike, I had noted that my chestnut-brown hair had started to gray the day after I arrived in this "quaint" Northwest town.

I observed the scene from a crack in the welcome desk. Doris trudged to the counter in her thick, knee-high sheepskin boots as a trickle of protective parents holding bewildered offspring rushed inside, heading toward safety of the Wind in the Willow children's section.

"Where?" said Doris gruffly as I continued to watch her peer down at Karen from below the brim of whatever dead animal had been thrust unceremoniously on her head.

9

Karen followed her stare with a quizzical look.

I suddenly had an idea. If I could get to the office, maybe I could pop up in there and walk out as if I had just gone to fetch something.

"She was just here," Karen said, making her way back behind the counter, where she caught sight of me crawling on my hands and knees toward the safety of the office. Karen grinned mischievously. "Now, where could she have got to?" she questioned in a singsong manner as she playfully opened drawers and looked under piles of stacked library books.

Doris pursed her lips, her piercing expression communicating clearly that she was unimpressed with Karen's lack of sincerity.

I caught a glimpse of Doris as she stood on her tiptoes and glared over the top of the counter, probably just in time to catch the tail end of me as I tried to scurry on all fours through the office door.

"There you are, Janet," she boomed, totally oblivious to the Laurel and Hardy comedy skit that was unfolding right in front of her. "What are you doing down there?" she inquired belligerently.

Caught in my act of escape, I stopped dead in my tracks and hastily picked up something from the floor.

"Tape," I said quickly as I leapt to my feet. "I needed to pick it up."

Doris stared at me with obvious irritation. And then, as if to stress the point, I waved a fuzzy piece of tape I had ripped from the carpet.

I could tell Karen couldn't resist a playful tone. "Oh yes, we have a lot of problems with that here at the library, you know. Tape sticking to the carpet."

I felt the heat spread across my face as I continued my ramble. "It's not good for it, you know. Tape, that is."

With great ceremony, Karen took the piece of tape from me, adding with mock reverence, "Thank you, Janet, for doing us that great service." We both turned to Doris.

Doris looked from one of us to the other—two frozen-faced, smiling mannequins, Karen holding the tape aloft like a prize. She didn't look convinced by our shenanigans, but apparently unperturbed by the needs of the library carpet, she plowed ahead.

"Janet, if Karen can spare you from tape duty, I have something I need to talk to you about. Something that is very urgent. Very urgent indeed."

I looked at Karen with pleading eyes. "Karen, do you need me?"

"Absolutely not," stated Karen in a tone of great assurance. "I think we can spare you for a while from protecting our world from Scotch tape strips."

11

And with that, Karen turned on her heels and headed for the office, flashing me an impish grin as she left.

Doris leaned across the counter toward me, as if ready to divulge a secret, and a whiff of smelly, wet dog arrived before her words did.

"Need a meeting over at the Crab. Usual booth, usual time."

I stared at her wordlessly. Doris had this way of making everything sound as if it were a matter of state security. And what did "usual booth, usual time" mean? Meeting Doris at the Crabapple Diner had resulted in me going on a crazy cross-country road trip with Doris and her band of rejected writers.

I was going to nip this idea in the bud before it could spring a petal. I was not bcing dragged into another wacky race, no siree. Since the trip, I had grown to love all the ladies of Doris's group— and I was an honorary member—but there would be no more crazy escapades with Doris Newberry. That had been my only New Years' resolution this year.

I played for time.

"Sorry, Doris, you know I would love to, but we are really busy here today."

Then, as if to emphasize my point, I shuffled purposefully through the never-ending pile of books stacked on the counter, studying each title with great intensity.

I could feel Doris's expression boring into me as it changed from urgent to incredulous.

"But this is of paramount importance," Doris spat out, emphasizing the word "paramount" as if that word alone would incline me to throw the books in the air and run to our local diner.

I tried again as Karen arrived back at the counter. "I'm really sorry, Doris. It's just not possible."

"Karen," said Doris curtly, "I was hoping to talk to Janet here over lunch at the Crab about something imperative, but—"

I finished Doris's sentence for her. "I was telling Doris we are too busy today."

A mischievous look crossed Karen's face as she raised her hand. "Nonsense. If this is imperative," she said, nodding at Doris, "of course we can spare her. I'm sure Janet will be happy to join you for lunch."

Doris lit up like a firework. "Perfect," she boomed. "See you at one, then, Janet. It will rally all the girls to see you there. Serious things to talk about, delicate things of the utmost importance." She punctuated her sentence by slamming down a meaty, fur-gloved hand on the counter, causing a white-haired little old lady waiting behind Doris to jump out of her skin.

Then, without further ado, Doris marched out the door in a flurry of fluff and fur, ready to gobble up her next victim.

13

I turned to Karen, my mouth agape. "What are you doing to me?" I cried desperately.

"Oh, come on," said Karen, her eyes dancing with the excitement of it all. "Where's your sense of adventure? Aren't you just bursting to know what's so 'imperative and important'?"

"Not really," I responded. "You might have forgotten, but I've been down this rabbit hole before, and as I recall, there were plenty of mad hatters and very few tea parties. I have no desire to follow that crazy white rabbit dressed in a dead beaver anywhere it is going."

"Me neither," added the little old lady, who was now at the counter. "Doris Newberry once talked me into going on a cross-country skiing expedition with her years ago," she continued. "We were lost in the mountains outside Leavenworth for two days with nothing but a blanket and a whole bunch of pots and pans she had taken with her. It was the longest two days of my life, and my knees still aren't right."

I looked at the frail old woman with the earnest expression that pleaded with me not to go and tried to imagine cross-country skiing with Doris.

Karen tapped my hand. "Got to live dangerously, and I love doing that through you."

"Thanks," I said. "You're a real friend."

14

Chapter Two

HOCKED-UP HIPPIES &
CARROT WARS

An icy wind sliced its way down Main Street, taking hold of the candy-striped awning of the local florist—All Stems from Here—and sending pink scalloped edges up into a frenzied, freestyle cancan. The wind's chilling presence reminded all residents of Southlea Bay that, though spring was around the corner, the lion of winter was still roaring with a vengeance.

Flora sank her frigid cheeks deep into the collar of her thick sage-green velvet jacket as she wrestled with the door of All Stems from Here with one hand and swiped away strands of wispy blonde hair from her mouth with the other.

The door finally gave way, and overhead a bell tinkled as she plowed into a pile of Easter flyers already stacked behind it. The store always received a lot of catalogs when wedding season was just around the corner, but this year there seemed to be more than ever. As she turned to close the door, she glimpsed a character wearing what looked like a floor-length fur coat moving at a brisk pace up the middle of Main Street.

Shaking her head in disbelief, Flora gathered

15

up the stack of mail, wondering who would have the courage to wear such a thing on their politically correct little island. Meandering to the counter, she searched through the mail for her favorite Victorian flower catalog. As she shuffled through the pile, a cream envelope with large round writing and her name on it emerged from the heap.

Her heart skipped a beat. It was from Dan. She hurriedly dropped the rest of the mail onto the counter and focused on his letter, precious in her hand. Her mind raced with all it could say, all it could mean, and she couldn't help but squeal as she ran her fingers over the soft cream-colored paper.

Her first desire was just to tear it open and devour every word. But she wouldn't. She had already decided exactly what she was going to do when he had hinted at sending her a letter at work. She would put it aside and wait until her lunch. Then she would make a pot of her favorite Earl Grey tea and climb the rickety stairs to sit outside on their little balcony. No matter how cold it was, she would sit there and look out across the bay, savoring every word he had written to her.

The bell over the door jangled again, forcing Flora from her reverie. She slipped the letter quickly into her pocket as Gladys Binkley, the Crabapple Diner's oldest and most unceremonious waitress, stumbled into the shop.

Flora took in what she was wearing with surprise. The cold weather sure brought out the oddest of wardrobe choices from her fellow Southlea Bay residents. Over her cheery Crabapple uniform, Gladys was enveloped in a monstrous blue afghan, and stretched over her knobby knees were thick brown ribbed tights and chunky burgundy knit leg warmers. To complete her mismatched ensemble, a tatty-looking green scarf was wrapped multiple times around her neck and ears. She made a beeline toward the counter, her curly brown hair a windswept mass of wired wool and her now-fogged glasses perched on a face that looked as if it had eaten grumpy for breakfast.

Not bothering to pull down her knit muffler to speak, she glared at Flora through the fog. "My cactus is dead!" she spat out through icy, green scarf. "The one you sold me. It's dead!"

Then she continued on her own little rally. "I told people everything dies in my house. It's the kiss of death on living things, that place. Plants, animals, people. In fact, anything that needs to suck in oxygen to survive just keels over in my den of destruction."

Then, peering over the rim of her glasses, she fixed Flora with a beady stare as she added with a powerful assurance, "There's something in the walls, you know. It was built in the sixties, when builders were all hocked up on lead-based

17

paint. It's just a mew of plastic and asbestos and a whole heap of other hippie crap, no doubt." Her eyes narrowed. "My module's been murdering things for years. I think I'm only still alive because I'm too ornery to die."

Flora nodded nervously as Gladys started to parade around, flicking her scarf in front of her as if she were conducting an orchestra.

"But people said, 'Buy a cactus, Gladys. Nothing can kill a cactus. Cacti can survive anything.' So, I bought a cactus."

She stopped conducting and hitched up her saggy chest as she delivered her next line with gusto. "Well, it's dead. So, what are you going to do about it?"

Flora blinked behind her pink frames and said nervously, "Cacti are usually pretty resilient. They live in the desert, you know."

Gladys scowled. "They may be able to make it through the perilous temperatures of the Sahara, but they're just not hardened enough to tackle hippie plastic and asbestos. So I need help."

"I could give you your money back?" said Flora.

"That doesn't solve my plant problem though, does it? I need something fresh and clean to soften up the jagged edges of that death trap. Got anything hardier?"

"Hardier than a cactus?" mused Flora thoughtfully. "I don't think so, but why don't you

18

look around and see if there's anything that you think might work."

Gladys huffed loudly, then sank her hands deep into her pockets and slumped around the shop, poking various plants and mumbling to herself.

The phone rang. It was one of the flower suppliers Flora needed to complete an order. Just as she was finishing with the details, she noticed Gladys was back at the counter, a prize clenched in her bony fist.

"I found something," she said triumphantly and then held up her "catch," a long string of plastic ivy that trailed back behind her. "But there's no price on it."

Flora hurriedly put down the phone. A horrible heat spread across her cheeks. "Where did you find these?" she asked, flustered.

Gladys was jubilant. There was no way to calm her enthusiasm. "Over there," she said as she held her treasured hoard high in the air. "You had it hiding in the front of the shop."

"Do you mean in the window display?" asked Flora. A horrified thought was rising in her chest.

"Yes." Gladys's eyes danced, and for the first time that morning, a grin crept to her lips. "I had to move a whole bunch of Easter crap to get to it, but don't worry about me. I managed to crawl into the window all on my own." Then, as if admonishing a small child, she added, "How is anyone supposed to find what they need when

you've hidden it like that? It's no way to sell things."

Flora stepped from behind the counter and scooted toward the window. She couldn't help but let out a tiny yelp as she took in the full extent of the aftermath of Cyclone Binkley.

Just moments before, what had been Bunny Heaven, an Easter oasis of hills and brooks magical enough to rival any of Beatrix Potter's greatest achievements, was now ground zero. Watership Down had just been well and truly depth-charged.

Flora took in the whole sight. Bunnies and baskets were tossed hither and thither, their fluffy little tails poking out from under pots and plants like casualties of some horrendous carrot war. And all around them, scattered like luminous linguine, were large heaps of shredded pink Easter grass that left a stringy trail all the way to the counter.

Flora found her voice, though it was more of a squeak than a speak. "That greenery is—was—part of our Easter display, Gladys. We can't sell it to you. We need it for the window."

Gladys snorted. "This is what I want. You're a shop, aren't you? Don't you want to make money?"

The doorbell tinkled again, and a mother and her young daughter walked in and started looking around.

Flora acknowledged them and then turned her attention back to Gladys. "But we use this plastic greenery all year-round. It's an important foundation of our display."

"It's the perfect thing to hold up to my asbestos hoarder. I'd like to see the walls of doom kill this stuff. How much do you want for it?"

She wasn't going to leave without a fight, Flora thought as she eyed her customer, whose face was set like a wall of wrinkled concrete.

Flora caved. "Why don't you let me talk to the owner and see if we can order some plastic greenery in for you? She'll be in later. I can ask her then."

Gladys's eyes twitched through the clearing fog of her glasses, and she growled in a low tone, "So I can't take this home now?"

Flora answered softly, "It's just not mine to sell you."

Flora picked up one end of the greenery and tried to ease it over the counter. With dogged determination, Gladys pulled back, and for a minute, Flora thought she wasn't going to let go. Flora gently but firmly tugged back, but Gladys hung on even tighter. The two of them locked eyes like a pair of strays fighting over a string of sausages.

Eventually, with great theatrical bravado, Gladys flung the greenery down with disgust. "Weird kind of a shop that doesn't sell stuff.

You're not going to be in business long like that."

"Come by later," continued Flora. "I'm sure Mrs. Bickerstaff will be happy to figure something out for you."

Totally miffed, Gladys wound the scarf tightly around her head like a bandage and shoved her hands into her pockets. Her muffled voice once again fought its way through. "I've got the lunch shift at the Crab. I'll be back around four to see what you've decided." Her eyes narrowed.

"Perfect," said Flora, the relief obvious in her voice.

And with that, Gladys sulked despondently toward the door. She nudged the mother and daughter as she passed, tapping a bony finger on the mother's arm. "Make sure you find things in here they're actually selling, and don't get your heart all set on anything until you're sure they're willing to part with it."

The bemused mother nodded weakly, then continued to admire the potted spring bulbs she had in her hand.

"I will be back!" Gladys threatened over her shoulder, a formidable terminator in mismatched wool. Then, with a jangle of the bell and a crash of the door, she was gone.

Flora tucked the plastic greenery under the counter and hoped it wasn't going to be a Gladys

Binkley sort of day. Then she remembered the letter from Dan and felt her stomach flip-flop. Nothing, not even a horde of Southlea Bay's most eccentric residents, was going to dampen her spirits today.

Chapter Three

BEAR TRAPS & BULLDOZERS

Lottie Labette perched awkwardly on the very edge of her window seat, chin high, back straight, and legs crossed stiffly at the ankle. Being old-school from the South, she had never sat comfortably in her life. Still in her starched cotton nightgown and with her hair bound neatly in blue curlers held in place by a pink net, she sipped her peppermint tea as she stared out her window. Normally, there was an incredible 360-degree vista of the Puget Sound, but this morning, all that greeted her was a heavy, drifting fog. She was mesmerized by the stark, icy blandness, the mood dramatically enhanced by the eerie echoes of a distant ferry horn signaling far offshore.

Raising the delicate china teacup again to her lips, she took a sip and sighed. The sitting and sighing were the tail end of a long-established morning ritual that included a full hour of prayer and reading her Bible and then, if the weather permitted, drinking peppermint tea while seated on one of the wrought iron patio chairs with the little tapestry seat pads her momma had made. Today was far too cold for the patio, so

she did the next best thing, which was to sit on their prim red velvet window seat instead. She sighed because she didn't like the way her body was starting to feel and had informed her twin, Lavinia, on numerous occasions, in no uncertain terms, that aging was killing her for sure.

As the swirls of mist billowed, she turned her attention to what she could see of the garden. She took in each flower bed, making mental notes about what needed doing. Her eye was drawn to the far end of the property. The garden would need mulching pretty soon, she thought, and the roses would need pruning before the spring. All at once, something caught her attention, just beyond her property boundary. *It couldn't be, could it?* Standing up, she slammed the delicate teacup onto its saucer and dropped it unceremoniously onto the highly polished mahogany side table. Moving closer to the window to get a better view, she peered out through the white-veiled landscape before being sure. *Yes, it was.* Her breath caught in her throat. She placed a hand to her chest as she called urgently to her sister, whom she could hear making coffee in the kitchen.

"Lavinia!" Then, knowing once was never enough, automatically called again, "Lavinia! Lavinia!" Her usual Texas drawl was high-pitched, urgent, and repetitive.

In Betty Boop pajamas, an identical version of

herself shuffled into the room, a mug of coffee in her hand. Even though the cornflower-blue eyes and mop of thick brown hair, streaked with more than a few wisps of gray, were just like Lottie's own, once someone met the twins it didn't take long to know they were two very different people.

"What are you hollering about?"

"Look out there, Lavinia," she said in her older sister (be it only by two minutes) tone. "Look out there and tell me what you see."

Lavinia screwed up her eyes, which were a little sensitive due to the half a bottle of wine she had finished off the night before. She adjusted them to the bland morning light.

"Not much," she said, staring out into the swirling mist. "Oh yes, now I see something: the water. Somewhere in all that rice pudding, I see the water, as always." Her obvious irritation showed in her shortness of tone.

"Not there," answered Lottie, exasperated. "Over by the gate, coming up Marsh Road."

Lavinia squinted and looked toward the road that led up from the village. Her eyes strained to make out a looming figure in the distance. Then surprise registered on her face.

"A bear," Lottie vocalized her thoughts. "It's a big brown bear, isn't it? Marching up Marsh Road, bold as brass."

"Impossible," responded Lavinia incredulously.

"We don't have bears on the island. And why would it be walking on two feet like that?"

"Well, I don't know. Maybe it hurt its paw or something," said Lottie, the panic obvious in her tone. "But it's heading right toward our gate. Look. We have to stop it."

"Stop it?" retorted Lavinia. "What do you mean, stop it?" Lavinia placed her coffee down and started to hunt through the drawers in the front room. "What are you planning to do, have me wrestle it? Or do you want me to get Daddy's twelve-bore down from the attic?"

Lottie headed toward the phone in the hallway. "Of course we are not going to shoot it. What do you think I am? I'm going to call the sheriff. Surely the authorities have their own bear-trapping equipment."

Lavinia found what she was looking for and headed back to the window.

"Bear-trapping equipment? You think they have bear-trapping equipment hiding somewhere in that pokey little stationhouse in town?" Lavinia lifted a pair of her father's old binoculars to her eyes and trained them toward the distance. He'd always kept them in the drawer for whale watching and identifying his friends' boats on the water.

Her sister frantically dialed the telephone and asked for Sheriff Brown. As she did, she tucked in a curl that had worked itself loose from a curler.

"This is Lottie Labette over on Bay Road. Yes, tell him I have spotted a bear heading up from Marsh Road, and it's heading right toward our property. Tell him he needs to bring up his bear-trapping equipment right away. It's urgent. Yes, I can hold."

Still feeling hungover, Lavinia finally managed to focus the binoculars on the bear, and just for a fleeting second, the veiled mist cleared. A look of amusement crossed her face.

"I would wait on getting the sheriff to find that trap if I was you, Lottie," she said with a chuckle. She continued to observe the odd, lumbering sight moving toward them through her father's field glasses. "That's a bear, all right, sister dear, but not one you can easily entice into a trap."

"What do you mean?" said Lottie, covering the receiver with her hand and coming to her sister's side.

"Look for yourself," said Lavinia, passing the binoculars to her sister, who tried to juggle them and the phone before becoming exasperated and handing the receiver to Lavinia so she could place the binoculars to her eyes.

She stared in silence for a moment, then let out a long, slow, exasperated breath.

"Oh my. I don't believe what I'm seeing. Surely that can't be . . ."

In Lavinia's hand, an animated voice came on the line.

"Hello, this is Sheriff Brown. You have a bear sighting, is that correct?"

Lottie dropped the binoculars from her eyes and looked sheepishly at her sister.

Lavinia, an expert at getting herself out of her latest fixes, lifted the phone to her ear. "Hello, Sherriff Brown, this is Lavinia Labette. Yes, the other twin. Just a little false alarm, I'm afraid. It is a bear of sorts, but the human kind. It appears that Doris Newberry is heading from town wearing her papa's old beaver coat."

"Doris Newberry!" the voice spat out on the other end of the phone so loudly that Lottie heard it even though the telephone was right next to Lavinia's ear. "We don't have any trap strong enough to hold that Newberry woman."

Then, much to Lottie's relief, the sheriff dissolved into peals of laughter.

Lottie took the receiver back from her sister and added, "This is Lottie again, Sheriff. I'm so sorry to have taken up your time. It was my mistake."

"Taken up my time?" he echoed back enthusiastically. "You just made my morning. If that bulldozer is stomping around the town, it means she has some scheme up her sleeve, and I don't want any part of it. I was heading to the Crab for a sandwich, but I think I'll wait a while until some other unfortunate victim has been corralled. If she's heading your way, it looks like your

number's up. Good luck, ladies." He continued to laugh as he hung up the phone.

Lottie smiled sheepishly at her sister and replaced the receiver.

Then they both burst into uncontrollable laughter.

Chapter Four

BEAVER WITH KETCHUP & THE RETURN OF THE SNOW QUEEN

At five minutes to one, Doris led a march toward the Crabapple Diner. They were an odd sight as they paraded their way down Main Street. Doris was striding forward with determination as if all she was missing was a bandleader and a tuba. Beside Doris ran the tiny figure of her best friend, Ethel, her sticklike legs reminiscent of a preschooler's first family portrait. She clipped along in a scissored blur in order to keep up with her fearless leader in fur. Then, way behind them both, floating down the road in a world of her own, was Gracie. Looking a full ten years younger than her eighty-nine years, she traveled elegantly and wisp-like, humming to herself as she glided along on her tiptoes. With apparently no care for her daughter Doris's urgency, she stopped to wave to small children and admire the ice glistening in the library tree branches along the way.

Inside the Crabapple Diner, Gladys Binkley had slipped off her shoes and was huddled over the welcome desk, taking her own little private break while she sucked noisily on a stripy peppermint

sweet. As she readjusted her bra to accommodate the note pad she always kept neatly tucked down around her left breast, her face registered amusement as she saw the parade reach the diner.

They all strode in and up to her desk. Gladys stopped sucking on her mint to take in the full sight of them.

Doris bristled a little when she saw Gladys. There was history between them, but in small towns, you had to have a long fuse and a short memory in order to survive, and Doris was in business mode.

"Our usual booth, please!" she snapped as she strode forward.

"Your usual booth," said Gladys indignantly as she slipped her shoes back on. "Do you mean the one you and that crazy bunch sat in before? You mean that usual booth?"

Doris glowered at Gladys from beneath her molting fur peak and was matched eye-for-eye with a long, hard stare back. Ethel stood between them, looking helplessly from one to the other.

Finally Doris sneered, "Is it available?"

"Oh, it's available," said Gladys, eyeing Doris up and down, "but there's more chance of me getting discovered as a supermodel than you fitting in there wearing that front room carpet."

Doris sniffed indignantly, snatched a menu, and waddled her way back into the restaurant. Her faithful brood and Gladys followed in mild

amusement. As they reached the booth, Doris tried to slide in, but right from the start it was obvious that the Crab's oldest living waitress was right. They all watched helplessly, yet riveted, as Doris repeatedly tried to heave herself in as her coat continued to rise above her ears. It was like trying to squeeze Sasquatch into a matchbox.

Gladys folded her arms.

"Why don't you let me take that out to the kitchen and give it a bowl of food and some water?" she commented dryly.

Doris tried one last almighty shove, but the coat just rose above her nose. Reluctantly, she stood up, unbuttoned it, and handed it to Gladys.

Gladys shuffled off to the kitchen, making kissing noises at the coat, saying, "Come on, Fido, Auntie Gladys will find you a good home."

The ornate antique clock in Stems chimed an elegant one p.m. Flora was already wearing her coat, held her hat in her hand, and had a small pink flowery umbrella by her side in case the heavens opened. It had been a very slow morning in the florist shop, and that had not helped Flora's disappointed mood. Following Gladys's departure, the Doris Newberry encounter had forestalled her letter opening plans. Doris had stormed the florist, accosting Flora and appealing to her on behalf of a desperate community member.

"Flora," Doris had said, fixing her with a beady glare, "it will take all of us to sort out this mess of things. All of us working together for the betterment of good."

Flora had agreed to the lunchtime meeting at Doris's beseeching. Sitting selfishly to read a letter seemed to pale into insignificance compared to "working together for the betterment of good."

She would just have to wait till she got home to read Dan's note. She realized, with a sigh, how much she missed him. They had been dating for four months, one week, and three days, but she had hardly spent any time with him. He lived in Portland but had broken his leg not long after they had started dating, slipping on the ice just before Christmas, and that had totally incapacitated him. She was terrified to drive on the freeway, so Skype and the telephone had been their main way of connecting for months. She could have traveled down by train, but the only time he had off was on the weekends, and that was the busiest time at the florist. It had been exasperating for them both.

"I'm off, then," Flora said toward the office. Her boss was deeply engrossed in the paperwork that was spread in huge piles across her desk. She sat hunched over a calculator, adding up amounts, and didn't look up as she nodded her acknowledgment.

Flora looked out at the weather. Again, it echoed her mood perfectly—not unlike the rainy first day of a summer vacation. As she lamented, she caught sight of Janet running across the road to the diner. They had all been summoned, then, she thought to herself. All of the road-trip girls, as the rejection group had nicknamed them. Flora remembered, fondly, their road trip of a few months before. It already felt like a lifetime ago now. But if she hadn't agreed to go on that crazy road trip to convince a San Francisco publisher to reject Doris Newberry's book, she would never have met Dan.

She thought about their first encounter. The group had been having problems with their car in Oregon and had limped their way to a garage. The minute he slid out from under the car he had been working on and towered over her with his emerald-green eyes and thick black hair, she had been smitten. But never in a million years had she expected him to be interested in her. But through a lucky coincidence, he had joined them on the road trip, and a sweet romance had blossomed between them.

She sighed and wondered when she would see him again.

The florist owner appeared at the counter.

"Okay, I'm here. You can go now. Could you bring me back a tuna sandwich?" she inquired as she rummaged in her bag, pulled out a twenty-

dollar bill, and handed it to Flora. Flora nodded and put the money into her embroidered Victorian purse. "White bread with Swiss cheese." Then, as a second thought, she added, "If they have any of those slices of pumpkin spice tea bread, throw in one of those for me too. Keep me going through the afternoon."

Flora nodded and made her way to the door. As she opened it, thunder rumbled overhead. She automatically pulled her collar up closely around her ears and put up her umbrella as she ventured out into the street.

Inside the warm, cinnamon-fragrant ambience of the Crab, Doris, Ethel, and Gracie sat on the squeaky red-buttoned booth, huddled over their menus. I noticed them as I entered. I eyed their choice of table with concern. I had learned the hard way that you didn't want to be trapped in the center of Doris's favorite horseshoe-shaped booth. It just became nothing but a jumble of limbs once everyone arrived. As I sat down at the end of the table, I heard the strong "no" in my head again. I was ready this time to stop myself from any crazy entanglements. I would make all the right sympathetic noises but would be firm about not being involved. I probably shouldn't have come at all, I chided myself. But I had to admit my interest had been piqued.

Gladys pulled out her notebook from her bra

and huffed as she eyed the ever-growing number of bodies at the table.

"Is that knitter and the hippie and the rest of your brood joining you?" she sniffed as she folded her arms.

Doris responded curtly, "Yes, you should expect five more."

Gladys sucked herself in and girded herself before responding. "Well, I won't bother wasting my breath telling you about the lunch specials until all of the Addams family is here. Drinks?" she inquired, eyeing the rest of us pointedly.

Doris eventually slammed her menu shut. "A hot black tea," she said.

Ethel closed her menu firmly as well, saying decisively, "The same for me."

"Big surprise there, then," mumbled Gladys sarcastically, flashing a look of all-knowingness at Ethel over the half-rim of her spectacles.

"A Shirley Temple with two cherries," said Gracie buoyantly, enthusiastically clasping her hands together in anticipation.

I ordered a cup of tea. Gladys scribbled it all down and ambled off to fulfill the order.

Flora arrived. She was wearing her usual abundance of ruffles and velvet. A true romantic, an adamant Jane Austen fan, and a poet, she was an old Victorianesque soul even though she was

barely in her twenties. From a young age, she had rebelled against being a modern millennial and instead preferred wearing clothes and living a life that reflected a slower and more cordial time. Right behind her, Lavinia and Lottie arrived. They were dressed identically, as usual. Today they were in black pantsuits, white blouses, and little black felt hats. They greeted everyone at the table like long-lost family, even though the group had only just been together a couple of days before.

"Darrrlings," said Lavinia, throwing her hands into the air and drawing out the word in her overextended, Southern way. "So glad you all made it through this weather. First that horrible ice and fog this morning and now it's pouring down small animals out there. Lottie and I nearly had to run from the car. And we haven't done that since 1987."

Everybody took a minute to hug and settle as the twins slid into the booth, just as Ruby arrived. The radical hippie of the group was a very vibrant seventy-year-old woman who was mad into hot yoga and swimming in the chilly Puget Sound for exercise. She ran a little wool and hippie store next to Stems, a mixture of yarn, joss sticks, and goddesses. The store was named Ruby-Skye's Knitting Emporium. She was also renowned on the island for her very eclectic style of dress. She had once been photographed for a

fashion magazine, wearing one of her clothing creations as she pouted Twiggy-style over the counter of her shop.

As she grabbed a chair and joined me at the end of the booth, it was obvious from what she was wearing that she had just come from one of her yoga classes. Twice a week she taught classes on little pink rollout foam mats right there in her store. Everyone else in the village just knew that if you needed a ball of wool or a knitting pattern on those days, you would have to stretch around protruding arms and legs in warrior pose to reach things. Then leave cash on the counter next to a note signed "Namaste" with a hand-drawn daisy as punctuation.

Gladys shrunk back and took in what Ruby was wearing. She put down the drink order and clicked her tongue in disbelief.

It was mild for Ruby. She had opted for an ensemble she was calling "prism joy," if people asked, with inspiration from the rainbow colors that bounced around her shop from the crystals hanging in her windows.

As she unbuttoned her coat, I noted she had on green-and-yellow striped tights and red patent Mary Janes. Stretched over her slender figure was a yellow leotard from her eighties "Let's Get Physical" days. It was still in great shape, due mainly to the fact she had quickly become bored with "going for the burn," as she had told me

once. She had scoffed that it might have worked for Olivia Newton-John and Jane Fonda, but all that marching in place and bouncing around hadn't done a thing for her. Over her leotard, she wore a much-needed multicolored stripy cardigan, which was crossed at her waist and tied at the back.

Her neck was adorned with a handmade fabric daisy chain that a friend had made for her, daisies being her favorite flower. She loved to accessorize, but downward dog didn't work with the clunky chains, as she was fond of telling people.

She had pulled her white hair into a dozen tidy little bunches all over her head and secured each one with a colored elastic band. Each bunch had then been sprayed a different color: red, yellow, blue, and green. She also had an ostrich boa of luminous green plumes wrapped around her throat multiple times, the ends hanging down her sides in two long, feathery strands. Over her bright ensemble, she wore a thick hot-pink poodle-wool coat to keep her warm, and she now tossed it across the booth as she seated herself at the end of the table.

"I see the clowns are back in town," quipped Gladys, handing Ruby a menu. Before Ruby could respond, the last of the group, Annie, arrived at the table.

Annie's appearance instantly caught everyone's

attention; it was obvious to all of us that something was very wrong. Her usual clean, well-kempt appearance had an air of mismatch about it. Her curly white hair looked like it hadn't been combed, and her eyes were red and swollen from crying. Never without her latest knitting project to work on, her hands were empty and her face bereft of joy.

All a little taken aback, no one said anything—no one except Gladys, of course. She took one look at Annie and said, "I guess you won't be wanting tea. Something stronger, I think, judging by the looks of you."

Annie became flustered, took out a tissue that was tucked in her sleeve, and blew her nose. "Just a black coffee please, Gladys."

As Gladys walked away, an awkward silence fell across the table.

Finally, Doris stepped up. "Let's all order, then Annie and I can let you know what's going on." Then, taking Annie's hand firmly and squeezing it, she continued with determination. "And how we are going to fix it."

I was suddenly struck by Doris's kindness. Even though she had the sensitivity of an anvil and the tact of a typhoon, she was made of that pioneer spirit. You could imagine a whole horde of Dorises moving through the wild plains of Nebraska, leading the weak and infirm to higher ground.

Gladys shuffled back with Annie's coffee and went into waitress automatic pilot: "We have a happily apple-y tuna melt blue-plate special with anchovies, oriental pickles, and some sort of weird-smelling orange sauce, so I wouldn't recommend it. Our usual cook is out with his lumbago. The replacement cook has got this book on unusual cuisine, so she's been messing with the food all day. And even though I told her tuna's not supposed to be orange, she's still heaping that goop on top of it. So, I'm supposed to tell you about it. Also, the soup is black bean. The other chef made that, so you're safe. It hasn't been foofed with, if you know what I mean."

Gladys pulled her yellow pencil from behind her ear and stood poised.

"Ice cream," said Gracie, as if she were at a five-year-old's birthday party.

"She'll have the soup," stated Doris sternly.

Gracie frowned.

Doris added, "You can have ice cream after if you want, Momma, but you love the Crab's black bean soup."

Gracie sighed and nodded reluctantly. "I will have ice cream . . . after the soup."

Gladys scribbled it on her pad and took down the rest of our orders before fixing her gaze on Ruby, who was daydreaming and finally looked up.

"I'm on a detox," stated Ruby. "I'm not eating anything until five p.m. each day. I don't suppose you have some ironized water?"

"Ironed what?" spat out Gladys, breaking the nib of her pencil and giving Ruby the hairy eyeball at the same time. She added dryly, "We might have some iron filings out the back. Would that work?"

Ruby shook her head, which became a multicolored blur as she did. Gladys watched her, mesmerized.

"I'll just have warm water, then, and could you squeeze a lemon into it?"

Gladys adjusted her bosom.

"I can bring you a lemon, but you will have to squeeze it yourself. Squeezing lemons for people who don't have the strength because they are not eating is not in my job description."

They were waiting on Annie. She seemed unfocused and was just staring at the menu, as if waiting for it to come to life and tell her what she wanted. Finally she said, "I'm not sure I'm hungry."

"Nonsense," said Doris. "Get her a large bowl of the soup. That's exactly what she needs."

Annie nodded absently. Doris gathered up all our menus and handed them to Gladys, who sauntered off in her usual manner.

"Okay," said Doris. "Do you mind if I share what's going on with the group, Annie?"

Annie shook her head. "No. Everyone is going to know soon anyway."

Doris cleared her throat, then beckoned us all in closer. But before she could say anything, Gladys was back, making us jump.

"Before you all swap military codes," she said sarcastically, "I need to know what bread Janet wants her club sandwich on: white or wheat."

"Wheat," I said in response. Gladys left again, and we resumed the huddle.

Doris continued, "Our dear friend Annie is in trouble, and she needs our help. As you know, she runs a boarding kennel out on Fremont Road."

"The best on the island," added Lottie proudly as she tapped Annie's hand.

Annie allowed herself a tight smile as she pulled out another tissue.

Doris said, "And as we know, she also provides a great service to our community, as half of those dogs living over there are strays that she has taken in, and they live in the lap of luxury."

We all nodded, looking at Annie, whose head was down, staring at her hands locked in front of her on the table.

Doris continued, "Annie has fallen on hard times. With this recession, people have been having friends take in their dogs, or they are staying home. Things have become serious."

Suddenly, Annie burst out, "The bank is going to take the farm unless I come up with twenty

thousand dollars by the end of next month." She punctuated the end of her sentence by bursting into tears. Everyone took a minute to digest the news.

Flora, who was seated next to Annie, automatically took her hand as Doris picked up the conversation.

"So, we are going to raise the money. We have to. We can't have Annie lose her farm. It's been in her family for generations."

"My mother would be so disappointed in me," continued Annie despondently through her sobs.

"How long have you known about this?" I asked.

"A few months," said Annie as she squirmed in her seat and dabbed at her eyes, "but I kept hoping something would come up. I did the lottery every week, just in case. A few good boarding months, and I would have got caught up, but this recession has just dragged on and on, and I never thought the bank would do such a thing."

"You still have a mortgage on the place?" asked Ruby, handing Annie another tissue.

Annie blew her nose. "It was paid and cleared after my parents died, but with the modifications to get it up to code for the dogs, plus all the conversions I had to do, it just made sense to take out a loan. Up until a couple of years ago, things were doing fine. I knew I was never going to be

a millionaire, but I loved the dogs, and I'm so happy there. It was enough for my needs."

As she spoke, she rolled the tissue into knotted strings in her fingers and took in a deep breath before saying, "Now it looks like I'm going to lose everything, and I'm not only heartbroken about losing my childhood home, but also about the dogs. What will happen to them if I'm thrown off the farm? There's no one I know who has the space to take them in, so we would all be homeless."

She burst into tears again just as Gladys shuffled back to the table and placed down the food.

She muttered to herself, "I tend to cry *after* I've eaten the food here, not before. You haven't even tasted it yet."

She ambled away to get the rest of the lunch order.

I automatically went into problem-solving mode. "Is there no one you can ask for a loan?" I asked, my fork dangling in midair. I was unable to start eating. This news weighed heavy on me.

Annie answered by shaking her head. "I'm an only child. My mom wanted more but was unable to have any. I have an elderly spinster aunt on my mother's side, but my dad was an orphan, so there really is no one."

Doris picked up the thread. "It's up to us. Come on, let's eat and brainstorm. We have to figure a

way out for Annie. There is no way she is going to lose her farm and her home."

"The problem is . . . ," Flora said wistfully as she toyed with her salad. Not unlike most of the rest of them, she seemed to have lost her appetite. "It's such a short amount of time to come up with so much money. I mean, what can you do in eight weeks?"

The rest of the ladies nodded sadly in agreement, staring blankly at their plates.

Everyone except Doris, who heaped a pile of French fries into her mouth, her appetite apparently unaffected by the situation. Through a mouthful of fried potato, she boomed, "We are going to do it, so start thinking."

Very slowly, everyone started to eat as they thought.

"I will go door-to-door if I have to," said Ruby, her old hippie rallying spirit tweaked into life, "and I will put jars on all the counters of the stores here in town."

Doris shook her head. "Not enough time. Besides, those jars never collect more than a couple of hundred dollars when they go out for the displaced orphans."

"A bake sale," said Ethel out of nowhere. Doris's sidekick was always so quiet it was easy for the group to forget she was even there.

"Too much work for too little money," said Doris dismissively. "Besides, you'd have to bake

twenty thousand cookies just to raise that kind of money."

"What about a fashion show?" suggested Lavinia, her eyes blazing with excitement. "Lottie and I could be your runway models."

"Lavinia!" cried Lottie in her usual singsong way of admonishing her sister when she was most exasperated. "Whoever heard of such a thing? I couldn't go around parading like a peacock."

Doris dismissed that right away. "What would we show? The secondhand fashion at the secondhand shop?"

"I was actually thinking of Claudette's. Her stuff is swanky and a good, high price," added Lavinia.

Ruby shook her head. "Claudette would never let her clothes out of her shop. She keeps the door locked as it is. Besides, who could afford her prices?"

"What about a large garage sale?" I suggested hopefully.

Doris dismissed it again with a sweep of her hand. "Whoever heard of a garage sale raising more than three hundred dollars? It would never be enough, no matter how much we all pulled together."

"The doggies could come and live with me," whispered Gracie, gently stroking Annie's hand. Annie squeezed Gracie's hand, acknowledging her kind gesture.

We all fell silent to think, our communal attention focused on the condiment rack in the middle of the table.

Gladys came back to top off our water glasses. She observed us all apparently hypnotized by the ketchup bottle and snorted, "Did you find the answer to world peace in there yet?" Deep in thought, no one answered her, so she continued. "Will any of you be wanting dessert before you transcend to another plane?"

No one spoke.

"Anyone want pie?"

That broke the deadlock; there was a general nod around the table as eyes fell upon dessert menus with grateful sighs for a problem they could actually solve.

We all decided on our desserts, closed our menus, and looked up at Gladys in anticipation. Gladys put her hand behind her ear for her pencil. When she realized it wasn't there, she tutted and fished into her bra, first on the left side, then the right.

We all watched in amazement as she navigated all the tucks and folds of her brassiere, and I wondered if maybe she was going to pull out a rabbit or something. Finally, somewhere at the bottom of her left breast, Gladys located what she was looking for and pulled out her small yellow pencil. I just managed to stop myself from clapping and cheering.

Totally unruffled, Gladys stood, pencil in hand, waiting for the order, as if fishing through your underwear in company were the most natural thing in the world to do.

"Well, my," said Lavinia, placing a perfectly manicured pink fingernail to the center of her lips, "how entertaining. Dinner and a show."

"That's it," said Doris, slamming down her hand and bouncing condiments all over the table. Everyone, still lost in their own contemplations, jumped in the air too. "We will put on a show. Yes, our very own huge musical extravaganza. It will be like Broadway, but by the sea, or *Fame* with mature women. Maybe *Macbeth*, with a full female cast."

Doris prattled on, and in all her excitement, she neglected to notice that everyone else at the table was locked into shock like a modern art piece that could have been called *Statues Eating*. It was obvious by the horror on all our frozen faces that no one seemed excited about this proposition.

No one except Gracie, who just giggled, saying, "Can I be the fairy godmother?"

Gladys, pencil still in hand, surveyed the stone-faced tableau. All around the table, forks stopped on the way to mouths and glasses poised on frozen lips. She nodded slowly and knowingly.

She dispensed her pad to her breast cubby-hole and pronounced, "Well done, Your Majesty.

50

Looks like your magic worked again. I will start tearing up my Christmas list right away, and I'll be back when Aslan returns. In the meantime, it looks as if your news requires strong coffee."

It took a second, but Flora found her voice first.

"Doris, I think I misunderstood. Did you just say we were going to put on a . . . show? As in, on the stage, with people watching?"

Doris was on a roll now, her mind whirring in a million different directions, a crazed centipede on roller skates.

"Exactly," she said, her enthusiasm unmistakable. She rummaged in her gigantic purse, where she found a pen and a notepad, and started to scribble notes.

"Do you know anything about producing a show?" I asked meekly.

"No," said Doris, "but I was a Tupperware rep for a while, and I reckon it's about the same. Besides, those longhaired thespians that meet at the library put them on all the time, so how hard can it be? We should assign roles. I will start working on securing the theater, and Flora, you can be our female lead . . ."

Flora went ashen. "What?" she said in the tiniest voice possible.

Doris was writing. "I think we should do some sort of musical and, Flora, you will sing."

"Sing?" Flora squeaked. A thin, white, fluttering hand found its way to her throat. "I

don't sing!" she said, as if she had just been asked to eat worms.

But Doris was getting so excited that she was starting to foam at the mouth. I practiced my response in my head because I knew it was only a matter of time before I was next on the list.

Say no. I practiced. *Just say no.*

"Ruby, can you help with the costumes?" Doris asked. Ruby nodded enthusiastically. Doris continued, "I will produce and have Ethel help me. Momma, the twins and you could all be fantastic in the right stage role, and that just leaves Janet."

She eyed me like yesterday's kippers.

Just say no, I thought again. *No.*

An idea appeared to formulate in Doris's mind, and she pointed her pencil straight at me.

No. I said it to myself one more time.

"Janet," said Doris, obvious excitement in her tone, "would you have any objection to being our director?"

"No," I said with more vigor than I had expected. I was proud of myself. That was forceful, strong, and not confusing to interpret.

Doris slapped her pen down and shouted, "Good, that's all settled."

I was confused. Wait, what had just happened?

"I said no," I reiterated, even more forcefully, and Doris looked at me, a little annoyed.

"Yes, I know," she said with irritation in her voice, "and I have written you down."

I backtracked to what had just happened. Suddenly, I heard Doris's actual words play themselves back in my head.

But before I could say another word to clear up the mistake, Doris was talking. Uncharacteristically, she grabbed my hand and held it tightly, causing me to shut my mouth, which was still hanging open from the last exchange.

"Janet," said Doris, "I just want to really thank you for your support. You weren't one of our original rejected ladies, but without you, we would never have managed to secure all those rejection letters, keeping our rejection club going strong. We are so grateful that, even though you don't know us that well, you are still willing to help us."

As Doris finished her speech, Annie reached forward, her cold, pudgy hand taking hold of my other hand, and she squeezed it tightly, tears brimming in her eyes. "You are one of a kind, Janet," she finally managed to force out in a dry rasp as emotion overtook her one more time.

"You really don't mind being our director?" asked Flora, appearing to pick up some of my resistance.

"No," I said in a tiny, tight voice. What else could I say?

For the rest of lunch, Doris was positively

buoyant, planning what the show could look like and what sort of show it should be. She seemed blindly unaware that hardly anyone else was talking at the table. Only Annie seemed excited.

"I am going to look into scripts, and we can get together this week for a special Rejected Writers' Book Club meeting. We need to decide on a show."

At the end of the meal, Gladys arrived with the bill and, dangling on the end of her protruding finger, Doris's beaver coat. Ruby, who sat at the end, didn't see Gladys approaching, and she turned as Gladys started to speak.

"Here's your . . ."

That was as far as our waitress got because, on seeing the fur coat dangling in front of her, Ruby leapt to her feet and screamed.

"Oh my God, that's real fur!" she screeched, her voice piercing the restaurant clatter and bringing it to a deadly stop all around her. Then, without thinking, she picked up a pot of half-eaten salsa and emptied it straight down the front of the coat.

Everyone at the table froze for a second, and then, as if rehearsed, eight heads swiveled toward Doris, who sat white-faced and openmouthed.

Ruby started to rant as she picked up the ketchup and blasted the coat again. "How can anyone in this day and age condone such a thing? I am appalled!"

Totally amused, Gladys reached forward and

handed Ruby the mustard before Doris came to her senses and boomed, "Stop!"

Ruby turned, and as she looked at the faces around the table, the penny dropped.

"This belongs to one of you?"

No one dared say anything.

Gladys couldn't resist and chirped in, "Her Majesty, herself." She bobbed her head in Doris's direction, whose face had gone from white to red.

Plowing out of the booth and spraying bodies like matchsticks, Doris pushed her way to her feet and snatched the dripping coat from Gladys. She turned on her heels and stomped off toward the bathroom, spitting out over her shoulder, "This was my father's fur!"

Gladys couldn't resist getting in the last word as she shouted after Doris, "I always thought you were a son of a beaver. Now that confirms it."

Everyone jumped to their feet, no one wanting to be around when Doris returned.

Chapter Five

CAMELOT CROONERS & DONKEY TREKKING

As we left the restaurant, the storm was starting to pass and only a gentle drizzle remained on the tail end of it. The streets were wet, and the air smelled fresh and clean. We all stood outside with our own thoughts for a minute, looking out onto Main Street. The village itself sat like a bowl in the water that surrounded it on three sides and could be viewed to great advantage from the Crabapple doorway. Today, the tides of torrid waves were an angry steel gray as they reflected the aftermath of the passing storm.

Annie couldn't help but give each one of us a large, teary hug.

I walked back to the library and was still in shock. What had just happened? Had I imagined it or had I just agreed to direct a stage show? The words got stuck in my brain, like soap in a colander. I didn't know the first thing about directing a show. Sure, I had done a little acting in high school, but nothing that I could even vaguely remember.

Karen met me at the door.

"Well?" she said. "Don't tell me, you're going

trekking on a donkey across the Andes. Should I go and buy you a saddle?"

"It's worse," I said, shaking my head as I made my way to the back office.

Karen followed close behind, a smirk on her face.

"Much worse than that," I said as I sulked inside and took off my coat. "I'm going to be directing a musical."

Karen looked taken aback. "Have you done that before, then?"

I raised my eyebrows, confirming Karen's suspicions.

She couldn't help herself. She started laughing uncontrollably.

"Thank you for your sympathy," I said flatly as I straightened my clothes and moved past her into the library, hoping that the rest of my day would be calm.

But it had begun.

One hour later, Ethel and Doris marched into the library. I was under a fixture, retrieving books that had fallen behind the shelves, when I felt a tug on my leg.

"Great news," thundered Doris so loudly Homeland Security was probably alerted. "I think I can secure us a building. I want to go and see about it tomorrow afternoon."

I sat back on my heels, and from that position, Doris's towering bulk was even more formidable.

"Oh," I said, flustered, "I've been wondering if I'm the right person to do your show justice. I think you should be talking to someone with experience and—"

That was as far as I got, as Doris pulled me to my feet and took hold of me firmly by the shoulders.

"Nonsense! You are the perfect person. You're just lacking confidence, that's all. You can come over to my house, and we can watch musicals together, if you like," she burbled on excitedly. "I have tons of them. I have *My Fair Lady* and *West Side Story* and *Camelot*. I know all the words to the songs of *Camelot*."

"Oh, I don't think that's necessary," I said, frightening visions looming in my head of afternoons sandwiched between Ethel and Doris, a stack of videos and the far-from-dulcet tones of Doris crooning "How to Handle a Woman."

"Or . . . ," said Doris, who was getting her second wind, "we could, the three of us, go to Seattle together for a few days. We could bunk up together and take in all the shows."

"Oh no, I don't think so," I said, realizing every new objection was serving to draw me closer to a Doris encounter of the scary kind.

Doris's eyes narrowed as she loomed in closer to my face. "Maybe some books, then. You work in the right place."

"Perfect," I said quickly, hoping it would

mean that Doris would let go of the top of my arms. I was beginning to feel like a walnut in a nutcracker.

"Okay," said Doris, and I tried to wriggle free.

Doris finally obliged, and I breathed deeply as I watched her move toward the door.

Chapter Six

DEAD PLASTIC PLANTS & BEETHOVEN WITH CHICKEN

Flora pushed her narrow cottage door open, and Mr. Darcy, her cat, immediately warmed her legs as he weaved between them, purring his hello.

She picked him up and tucked him under her arm. She gently stroked his ears, cooing to him as she walked into her kitchen and placed her bag down on the counter.

She remembered the letter. After dinner, she decided; it would be a welcome hug at the end of a very difficult day.

As she moved around the house, plumping cushions and straightening lace doilies, she docked her iPod and put on some music. Beethoven sounded about right, she mused as she scanned to the right track, allowing exquisite piano music to fill the cottage. She noted the chill in the room and went to her tiny white enamel woodstove, which she always kept laid with a stack of wood, and struck a match. It erupted into warm, glowing firelight.

Humming along with "Moonlight Sonata," she went back into the kitchen and pulled out the bottle of white wine and the baked chicken

dinner she had just bought. The food smelled intoxicating and was still warm from when it had been handed to her at the deli counter. With its combination of vegetables and stuffing, it was the perfect comfort food for the end of such a day.

She took her wine and her dinner, sat on her cozy white sofa, and sighed. The day had continued to spiral downward after lunch.

If the thought of having to sing wasn't bad enough, she had also tried to reconstruct the window display and had retrieved the rest of the Easter decorations from the shop's tiny attic at her boss's bidding.

Late in the afternoon, Gladys had returned after her shift at the Crab. Flora had just finished laying out the rest of the Easter decorations all over the shop when Gladys arrived, demanding that Flora help her hunt through a stack of catalogs and books as Gladys scrutinized every conceivable potted plastic plant.

"The problem is," she pointed out to Flora, tapping a knobby finger on the stack of catalogs, "that these just don't look alive."

"That's because they're plastic," Flora answered shortly, her patience wearing thin.

Gladys sucked on her teeth and adjusted her bosom before answering.

"I know that, young lady, but I want them to at least look halfway lively. I mean, everything in these books is just a little too perky and perfect.

They need to have them lopping over on one side, or they should add a couple of shriveled-up brown leaves for effect."

Finally, after an hour, Gladys had ordered a string of ivy similar to the one she'd previously stolen from the window, and then she marched off to the library to do more research.

As her blue afghan had billowed in the door frame, she announced that there had to be something that was real and hardy, and she would go and rcad books about it and let Flora know.

Flora sighed, following Gladys to the door and shutting it behind her, watching the determined waitress march up the center of Main Street. Poor Janet would have her now, Flora thought.

It had been ten minutes till closing then, and Flora couldn't leave the shop in such disarray. She had clcarcd away all the decorations before she left, finally getting out by 6:20 p.m.

She poured the wine and took a large swig. She felt the warm tingling as it permeated her body and told herself, just as her grandma had, tomorrow was another day. She removed the food from its packaging and placed it on one of her blue china dinner plates. She would eat her dinner by the fire, and Dan's letter would be her dessert.

Chapter Seven

PAUL SIMON PRODUCTIONS & ALIEN WIVES

It had been a long day at the library by the time I arrived home, and I was pooped. It had only dragged after my lunch date with Doris.

As I opened the door, I heard Martin filling the kettle with water.

"Hey," I said despondently as I came in and took off my coat.

"I've put the kettle on," he shouted back over his shoulder. I heard the burner burst into flame.

"Great," I sighed.

I met him in our little blue Laura Ashley–decorated kitchen. I really loved this time of year, always had. Coming home when it was cold, frosty, or rainy into the warm little belly of my cottage usually warmed my heart.

"I had lunch with Doris Newberry and the posse," I confessed as I threw my bag down.

Martin raised his eyebrows. He was placing tea bags in a pot, his expression giving me the impression he had an idea where this conversation was going. "So, you will need this tea," he jested.

I gave him a look. "With brandy in it," I quipped back.

"Okay, what did she talk you into this time?" he inquired.

I shook my head and said, "This one you are not going to believe."

Martin was going to do his best to guess. "Drug smuggling in the Caribbean? Flamenco dancing on a cruise ship? Maybe a trip into space or . . . ?"

"Directing a musical show."

"Or directing a musical show. Which, unless you are an alien and possessing my wife's body, you know absolutely nothing about."

The kettle whistled, and he poured the water into the pot while I took off my shoes and threw myself facedown on the sofa.

"Exactly," I said.

"Which one?" he asked as he poured boiling water.

"Sorry?" I turned over.

"Are you an alien or my wife?"

I looked up, deadpan. I was not having quite as much fun with this as he was.

"It's not funny, Martin. I'm not sure I'm going to be able to get myself out of it."

"Well, marriage to you has always been entertaining," he said.

The phone started ringing. I absently picked it up. It was my very pregnant daughter, Stacy.

"The fridge is broken, again."

I sat down. I loved our daughter, but in her

64

twenty-four years, she still hadn't ever really mastered social graces. That didn't stop me trying.

"Good evening to you too."

My lesson was lost on her. "And I called someone, but they can't send anyone till tomorrow, and I have food in the top part of the freezer that's going to go bad so I have to cook all the chicken breasts in there, and chicken is totally turning my stomach right now."

Martin brought my tea over and mouthed the word, "Stacy?"

I nodded and curled my legs up under me on the sofa. I knew exactly how to handle this conversation.

"How are the babies today?" I asked the minute Stacy took a short breath.

All the air on the other end changed.

"Oh, they're doing great. I'm really starting to feel them move around now. It's so much fun."

I sipped my tea. Since we had been involved in a car accident in California a few months before and Stacy had nearly lost the babies, I had felt so much closer to my daughter. She had a challenging character—"the ice maiden," as Martin had nicknamed her when she wasn't around. But now we were closer.

Stacy cooed on for another five minutes or so about the nursery furniture she and her husband, Chris, had been looking at and the fact that

65

someone at work was knitting her something.

I continued to sip my tea, thinking this was a better conversation.

"Well, you know your father and I are planning on coming down in a couple of weeks or so to see you, so you take care of yourself and our grandbabies, do you hear?"

As I shifted on the sofa, our cat came to sit in my lap. We named him Raccoon after catching him in a raccoon trap that Martin had made. Raccoon was now a full member of the family, and he knew it. He pawed at my lap as I talked.

Stacy and I wound up the conversation and hung up. Martin sat on the sofa opposite me.

"Nice deflection," he said, smiling over his mug. "Now, Neil Simon, what were you saying about a Broadway show?"

I told him the whole story. He listened with concern to Annie's situation, then said something I hadn't expected.

"I think you should do it," he said, taking a sip of his coffee.

I looked at him like he had gone completely bonkers.

"I mean, how hard can it be?" he continued. "It's like building an airplane model. You have a blueprint—the script—and you put everything in its right place. Then make sure everyone gets on and off the stage at the right time, and voila, you have a show."

"Voila, you have a show?" I echoed back to him sarcastically. "If it sounds so easy, why don't you do it?"

"Oh no," he said. "You know I'm just here to observe all the tomfoolery you've gotten yourself into over the years, but you will not be dragging me into any of it. That's how we've stayed married so long. We have never needed TV because your life and lack of boundaries have been a constant source of entertainment for me."

I picked up a pillow from the sofa and threw it at him.

"Seriously," he said as he spun the pillow in his hand, "it sounds like Annie is pretty desperate. And you couldn't meet a more kindhearted lady. Look at all those dogs she takes care of."

As I finished my tea, I thought for a minute. "You don't happen to have a spare twenty thousand dollars you keep stashed away, do you? Something we could just use to pay her off and be done with it."

Martin beamed broadly. "Sorry, chickadee. I used it all up on fast cars and loose women."

Chapter Eight

OLD FLAMES & NEW BEAUS

Flora walked into town at 9:30 a.m. Plenty of time to drop off a letter at the post office, she thought. She couldn't wait to get another letter off to Dan. His letter had been filled with tales of his days in the garage, and at the end had been very cryptic. She still had the important words he'd written memorized:

> Flora, I have a big surprise for you, but I can't reveal it to you just yet. Be prepared for something amazing in the next week or two. All will be revealed soon, but until then, I want to keep it a secret. But I do have some very exciting news. All my love, Dan.

She had said the words at the end of his letter out loud to herself over and over again—"All my love, Dan"—because even though both of them had hinted at it over the last few months, neither of them had actually said the words to each other yet. Those words, those important shifting-the-relationship-to-the-next-level words that she had waited to hear with a mixture of excitement and

anticipation. She was glad he hadn't just said them over the phone as some glib, good-bye salutation, but maybe, not unlike her, he was waiting to say those words to her in person.

She hoped there wasn't a line at the post office. It was getting close to the Easter holiday, and she didn't want to be caught behind people with big packages of Easter goodies needing to be mailed off to the East Coast. She walked through the door and was relieved there was only one old man in front of her with a small parcel. However, that was where any post office sensibilities ended, as behind the counter, Mrs. Barber, the postmistress, was dressed as an Easter chicken.

Always a fan of celebrating all the holidays in style, Mrs. Barber, a perpetually round woman, was now a perfectly feathered tennis ball. Her enormous bosom only overemphasized the multitude of multicolored feathers on her chest. As she talked to the elderly gentleman in front of her, Flora was struck by the comical nature of the postmistress talking serious post office business with her face poking out through the bill of an orange beak. And on top, a plume of red spiky feathers bounced from side to side with every bob of her head as she discussed the finer points of sending a parcel internationally. As the older man shuffled out, Flora approached the counter.

"Cluck, cluck, cluck, what would you like,

duck?" squawked Mrs. Barber in a high-pitched, birdlike voice.

Flora wasn't quite sure how to respond to a tennis ball–shaped woman dressed as a chicken who looked like she was hiding two very large eggs under her chest feathers.

Mrs. Barber laughed at her own joke and then said, "What can I do for you, Flora, dear?"

"I have a letter to post, and I need a roll of stamps," Flora responded as she placed the letter on the counter.

Mrs. Barber picked it up and eyed it, forcing her beak wider with one hand to get a better view.

"Dan, eh?" she said with interest. "This is your new man, then? The one I've been hearing about all over town?"

Flora blushed and stuttered, trying to recover from such a forthright question, but Mrs. Barber didn't miss a beat.

"I will take that as a yes," she said, tapping Flora with a yellow-feathered hand attached to her wing.

It was well-known in town that Flora didn't date and had never had anything that remotely resembled a boyfriend. Flora was speechless, and Mrs. Barber gave her an all-knowing look.

"Good for you, Flora." The chicken picked up the letter and examined it carefully, as if doing so would give her some vital clue as to who the mysterious lover could be. After turning it over

70

and scrutinizing the address, she said, "Oregon, eh?"

Mrs. Barber was apparently enjoying herself. However, Flora was not. As she shifted from foot to foot nervously, she willed time to go faster. She was also aware that people had started to form a line behind her.

"Don't forget the stamps," added Flora, trying to change the subject, but Mrs. Barber was not having any of it.

As she stretched forward, her enormous feathered bosom slid across the counter. She placed the letter in front of her and ran her fingers in little circles over the top of it as she disappeared into her own reverie.

"I once had a young beau from Oregon," she said thoughtfully, her tone slow and winding. "A farm boy, all fresh-faced and freckled. He was lovely. Jimmy was his name. He was all burnished and bronzed from working on the land in the summer. We met while I was on vacation down there, and it was love at first sight for me. We spent all our time swimming and fishing. It was the time of my life, for a sixteen-year-old coming into full bloom. My father didn't like him, thought he wasn't for the likes of us. Wanted me to marry somebody educated, he said, and I did what my dad wanted. We all did back then, but oh, he was lovely . . ." She stared out of her beak toward the window, in her own reverie

as she looked for the right words. "Earthy," she eventually managed. "Is yours a farm boy?" she inquired, moving her beak in close to Flora and fixing her with an inquiring look over her reading glasses.

Someone coughed in the line behind Flora, and she felt even more awkward. Every local knew that going to the post office in town could take anywhere from five to twenty minutes, depending on the topic of conversation stirred up at the counter.

"No, he's a mechanic," she blurted out quickly, hoping that would be the end of it.

"Lovely," said Mrs. Barber, still in a deep trance. "Someone who works with their hands. You've got to admire that, Flora."

Flora reached for the letter. That seemed to jolt Mrs. Barber from her daydream adventure.

"Was that it, now, Flora?" she inquired. "Is it just a letter to your Oregon beau?"

"The stamps too," added Flora again.

"Ah, yes," Mrs. Barber said, pulling herself together and twitching her tail feathers as she fished into the file drawer for a new packet of rolled stamps. "Twenty or fifty?"

"Better make it a hundred," said Flora, secretly thinking that she didn't want to make it back here for a while.

"A hundred, eh?" said Mrs. Barber, opening her drawer and surveying her stamps. "This sounds

serious. I'd be careful, Flora. Oregon isn't close, and long-distance relationships can be difficult." She found the stamps she was looking for. "I would shop local, if I were you." She nudged her and motioned toward a young fresh-faced youth who had just joined the end of the growing line.

Flora was beside herself. The lad was a good five years younger than she, and Mrs. Barber was holding the stamps hostage in the air in her feathered hand.

"You know what you're getting locally," added Mrs. Barber with a giggle. "Homegrown is always best." She punctuated her statement by letting out a huge guffaw that made the whole bottom half of her shimmy like feathered jelly. She finally pushed the roll of little naked cupids toward Flora and said under her breath, "We don't normally give away the Valentines stamps after February, but I think we can make an exception, bearing in mind the occasion."

Flora flushed again, grabbed the stamps, shoved them in her purse, and, putting a fifty-dollar bill on the counter, hastily tried to leave the post office.

"Flora, love." Mrs. Barber flapped her wing at her. "Don't forget your change."

Flora was not going back in for the life of her and pointed at the charity jar.

"Oh," shouted Mrs. Barber, putting the change in the jar. "God bless you, love." As she closed

the post office door, Flora heard her shout, "I hope your young man knows what a gem he's got."

Doris had a lot of nervous energy. She'd already been to the stationery store and bought a couple of legal pads, different colored pens, and two clipboards, and Ethel had followed her around like a puppy.

"I have a friend," Doris stated with a sparkle, once they were both buckled up in the car. "I think he can help us with the building."

She put her car into reverse and backed out of the lot to the main road. In a few minutes, she was parked outside a white townhouse with a neat, well-kept garden. She took a minute to check her hair in the mirror as she continued to speak.

"A long time ago, when Jesus was a boy and before I met my husband, this fella was sweet on me," she informed Ethel as she bobbed at her appearance. Ethel looked horror-struck.

She pulled a comb through her hair, and she thought of a time gone by.

She remembered this string bean of a boy who had been no more than a lick of leather. As she had come down the stairs he was perched on one of her mother's pink parlor chairs, an awkward teenager in a tuxedo that seemed to be wearing him, holding a lovely boxed corsage in

his clammy, unsteady hand. They were going to the homecoming dance and were both terribly nervous.

She applied a liberal coating of lipstick to her plump lips. She would never forget the riot act her father had given him before they had even left the house. All about bringing her home on time and treating her like a lady.

They had gone off to the dance and sat there like two bumps on a log, neither of them having the courage to speak. About halfway through, he suddenly got up, like he'd been thinking about it for a while, and thrust out his hand, saying, "Do you wish to dance?" She'd blushed down to her toes for sure and, putting down her ginger ale, had taken his hand—a strong, warm hand—and walked with him toward the dance floor.

She giggled to herself as she remembered that night.

"Okay, I think I'm presentable," Doris then said as she shut her bag and opened the car door. They walked to the blue painted door, past the neat row of bushes and manicured plants.

Doris continued to recollect as she waited for the door to open. She realized that it had been more than four years since Catherine had passed away, four years in the fall. She knew it had been that time of year because at her funeral there had been leaves swirling around the graveyard as the minister had delivered his final eulogy.

She remembered the sadness in his eyes and the grief buried deep in the crevices of his face, the sort of pain there could only be after forty years of marriage. She took his strong, warm hand again and said how sorry she'd been, and something had passed between them: a knowingness, the familiarity of a time long ago when both their partners had been alive.

The door opened.

A tall, distinguished older man with gentle gray eyes stood in the doorway. He wore a light-blue shirt and smart beige pants, and his full head of hair was only just starting to gray at the temples.

"Doris," he said, appearing taken aback. He had obviously aged, but there was still that cute twinkle in his eyes, and the spindly youth had filled to a well-rounded, good-looking man.

"James, I hope I'm not interrupting anything."

"Not at all," he answered, eyeing them both with interest. Doris introduced Ethel, and he asked them to come in.

Pamela, who also worked at the cinema in the evening and did a little cleaning on the side to make ends meet, had told Doris that he had been one of her regular clients for the past few years. It seemed to pay off, for the front room was spotless, Doris observed, as he invited them inside. His house was bright, warm, and clean.

"Well, what can I do for you?" he asked encouragingly.

Doris, not wanting to beat around the bush, launched into the story of Annie's problem and the plans to put on the show.

James listened for a while and then said, "Why don't I get you ladies a drink? Then we can continue our discussion."

He flashed that warm smile again.

He served them tea and listened intently to Doris's story as he quietly stirred sugar into his coffee.

Then he said thoughtfully, "I'd love to be able to help, but the thing is, the theater needs a lot of work to be ready for anything that could resemble a show. I mean, it hasn't been used on a daily basis since the late eighties. The last show in there was, I believe, in eighty-nine. I've been working with the historical society, but we need elbow grease and willing volunteers to get it where it needs to be. We've had work done on the roof, and it's pretty much structurally sound now, and we have managed to keep the critters from moving in, but it's in a pretty poor state as the rest of it goes."

Then he continued, more wistfully, "I know I probably shouldn't have bought it, but there was talk about a gas station going in its place, and I couldn't bear the thought of seeing a beautiful old theater and a piece of our town heritage just disappearing like that." He sipped his coffee and chuckled, "I used to go there as a boy, you know,

when it doubled as a cinema. Spent many a happy afternoon on a wet Saturday morning watching a Buster Keaton or a Laurel and Hardy flick."

Doris joined in his reverie. "Do you remember that woman who used to work on the candy counter? Margie or Mary or something."

James chipped in. "May," he said with gusto. "May Barker."

They both laughed together.

"Horrible woman," continued James, "and she seemed to hate children. I remember her bending my ears once because she was convinced I had been the one to stick gum under one of the seats, when, in fact, it was Johnny Barton. And even though I pleaded my case, she never seemed to trust me again and always had her evil eye on me."

They both laughed freely, then Doris was straight back to business.

"Well, I'll put together a team," she decided in earnestness. "A group that could work together to get the place cleaned up. Would you consider having us work to get the theater in shape in exchange for the rent for three weeks of performances?"

James sipped his coffee slowly as he contemplated the idea. He looked unsure. "There's a lot to do," he said. "We have some money in the budget for a new stage, curtains, paint, and carpet in the main theater, but there's still more to be done to clean it up."

"Let me worry about that," said Doris. "But would you be willing to let us have the space for free?"

A broad smile spread across James's lips. "You're still hard to resist, Doris, when you're on a mission. There isn't anything that can stop you."

Doris colored slightly at the personal turn the conversation had taken but recovered quickly. "Would you?"

James didn't seem to be in any kind of rush, apparently enjoying the banter.

"Your husband always used to say, 'For heaven's sake, don't be giving my Doris bright ideas, because once she has one of those cooking, there's nothing that can stop her.'" He then stared at her for a long moment and said, "Okay, if you can get it cleaned up, I think I can foot the bill for getting everything up to code. And you'd be doing our community a huge favor in the meantime."

"Great," said Doris, putting her teacup in her saucer and slapping her thigh. "I'll get started on putting together a team right away. Maybe we could organize a weekend work party. 'Potluck and Paintbrushes,' we can call it."

Ethel immediately wrote that down on one of her yellow legal pads. James watched them and seemed charmed by the whole picture.

"Okay," said Doris, jumping up, "I don't want

to take up any more of your time. I'm sure you have more important things to do. We have to go. We have a lot to organize."

"Of course," James said, gathering the teacups and placing them on the tray he'd brought them in on.

Doris and Ethel walked toward the door, and James followed and opened it. As Doris left, he smiled and waved, and she waved back.

James Graham, she thought to herself. He still gave her a little sparkle, which, at her age, she thought, was no easy feat.

Chapter Nine

CRAZY BATS IN STRANGE NEW HATS

The next day, I made my way to Doris's house for a meeting.

The Rejected Writers' Book Club had been getting together for several years now. They were an assortment of women of different ages all brought together by a common purpose: reading their awful manuscripts to each other. All were rejected repeatedly by traditional publishers, and they now chose to celebrate their rejections in style with tea and cake and by collecting their rejection letters by the bucketload and putting them in a leather-bound album they called The Book. The Book was now stuffed full of well over five hundred letters that they had been collecting over the last few years, the last twenty-five obtained on a crazy road trip that we'd taken to California.

When I knocked, Ethel opened Doris's front door dressed as a gnome or something like that. She wore a red cotton hat, blue baggy culottes, stripy socks, and a blue-and-white T-shirt.

Wearing the costume of happiness and triviality and the face of foreboding, I had definitely made

some inroads with this vision of happiness and light over the year. At least she didn't click her tongue at me anymore, but it seemed she got up every morning and set her compass at gloom, doom, and despondency.

As I followed the dwarf of misery up the hall, it didn't get any saner in Doris's front room. It was always hard enough adjusting to Doris's décor: her green vinyl sofa was still covered in plastic, and the furry orange bucket chairs, all throwbacks to when the seventies were a child, were slammed right up against a splattering of country wicker that belonged to Gracie. But today, there was even more to pickle my brain.

In the center of the room was the regular circle of mismatched chairs, and, seated on them, the whole group of the Rejected Writers' Book Club. But all was not normal here in Crazy Town. Every one of them was wearing an outrageous outfit.

Same Bat day, same Bat channel, same crazy bats, I thought.

Ruby jumped up to greet me. She was wearing an extravagant Aladdin affair, with peach chiffon pantaloons and a cropped red sparkly top with white fringe and gold bells. Around her head, she'd wound a gold scarf into a turban, and as she clattered over, it appeared that her usual ensemble of bangles and beads offset the rest of her outfit nicely.

As I observed her more closely, I noted that even though she was a vision of *Arabian Nights*, she still proudly displayed her large peace pendant, and dangling from her ears were earrings with a picture of John Lennon. I also noted that, through her makeshift turban, her hair was sprayed in stripes of red, yellow, and blue.

Interesting costume combination, I thought. If Ziggy Stardust and Barbara Eden had a child, this would be her.

As I acknowledged the group, I guessed the character. Lavinia was a swashbuckling Robin Hood with long green pantaloons, high boots, and a feather cap. Next to her, Lottie was dressed as Maid Marian. On her favorite wicker lounger was Gracie in one of her fairy outfits. Next to her sat Flora, dressed up as a very uncomfortable pirate, a huge tricornered hat sliding around on her head with one dangling long white plume that she had to keep blowing away from her one good eye, as the other was covered with a patch.

Inside the circle, Doris stood to the side of a huge whiteboard. She appeared to be dressed as Captain Hook, complete with a hook arm and a fake parrot on her shoulder. The pirates apparently came as a matching set, I thought to myself. I took it all in with my usual filters of small-town tomfoolery. They looked like some manic recovery group for theater AA.

"Did I miss something?" I asked, looking

around me. "Aren't we just a little early for Halloween?"

Suddenly, Ethel strode up to me and pushed cat ears onto my head and thrust a cat nose at me. "Put these on," she said.

Not wanting to argue, and knowing it was only part of the ridiculousness that happened in this house, I did as I was told and sat down in my usual spot.

"Purrfect," I quipped back.

The humor seemed to be lost on all of them as they sat there, twitching and scratching in their costumes, looking very uncomfortable.

"What are we doing?" I whispered to Ruby, once we were seated.

She whispered back to me through a veil, which covered her nose and looped over her ears with elastic, "Doris thinks it would help with the process if we're all in costume. It will help us all think clearly and get into character."

Get into character? I thought to myself. Plenty of characters here.

"So glad you could join us, Janet," Doris said, tapping her hook on the board.

"Brainstorming" was written on that board in large black letters.

"Okay, this is what we're going to do," said our commander as she shifted from her peg leg to her good foot and adjusted the stuffed parrot on her shoulder. "We're all writers here, so we're all

going to write the story for the show together."

Everyone looked around the room at each other.

"I just hate to burst your bubble," said Lavinia, crossing one long leg over her thigh-high boots and adjusting her green corduroy pants, "but we are rejected writers. Not one of us has been accepted by a publisher. What on earth could we write that could be any good?"

"We are not bad writers," Annie piped up. "We are only rejected ones," she added, spouting one of Doris's favorite sayings. Annie was seated in the corner at the far end of the circle and, of course, was dressed as her favorite four-legged creature, a dog. She was wearing a brown nose and long, soft brown ears; she smiled up at us like a happy Deputy Dawg as she knitted.

"Of course we can do this," Doris said. "This is why we're all dressed like this. Look around and see what comes to you."

We all looked around the room. *One Flew over the Cuckoo's Nest* was the story that drifted into my mind.

Lavinia adjusted her breasts in her bustier. "Let's make it a love story," she said.

"Yes, with just a little bit of horror," said Ruby.

"I could add in a couple of psalms," said Lottie.

"With maybe one or two dogs," Annie added as she hooked a stitch, happily.

"I would love it if I could add a couple of my poems," said Flora quietly as she shifted

85

uncomfortably in the seat and moved her patch to her other eye.

"Perfect," said Doris. "I could add just a little Jane Austen or some time travel? What do we have with all of that?"

An old lady's LSD trip was my first thought.

I tried to be tactful. "I'm not sure you're going to be able to incorporate all those ideas into one story. Can you think of a story like that?"

Everybody stopped and stared at me, as if that thought hadn't entered into their minds.

"Of course there has to be something," said Doris. "Everybody, think. What story has a little bit of horror in it, and a little bit of romance, a whole bunch of dogs, people who say psalms, poetry, and maybe some Jane Austen and time travel?"

Everybody stopped and stared at the board. There was a long silence.

Suddenly, Ruby threw her bangled arms into the air and jumped to her gold pointy-toed feet, saying with theatrical flair, "We will be original, and I love it."

"True," said Doris, banging her hook again on the board. "Let's start pulling the main elements of the story together. Who could be the heroine?"

"Well, how about," said Ruby, "we make her a wholesome-looking girl, a fresh-faced girl-next-door type?"

"Who lives with her dogs?" added Annie,

smiling and making her doggy snout ride up on her nose.

"Yes," said Ruby, starting to parade around the circle, encouraging them all. "But deep down," she dropped to a whisper as she drew aside her yashmak, "she has this deep, dark secret that she murders people."

"Sounds a bit serious for a musical," snorted Lottie. "They're going to need my psalms in the intermission to recover."

"And my poems for the way home," said Flora as she grasped hold of her feather to stop it flailing about as she spoke.

"Yes, not too cheerful," I added. "Can't see us packing the house for the laughs with that one."

"But it could get cheerful," said Lavinia. "How about, she meets a big strapping handsome hunk that loves all the bad right out of her?"

"Then they travel in time and meet Jane Austen," added Doris, getting excited. Doris took her good hand and started writing ideas on the board. The ideas came thick and fast after that and became more ludicrous as she wrote.

I adjusted my cat ears and tried to imagine directing something like this. When someone had coined the phrase "herding cats," they had never met this particular group of writers, or the phrase would have been much different. I watched the ideas as they materialized in Doris's spidery scrawl. I didn't know much about the writing

process, but I was pretty sure that this wasn't it.

Then, suddenly, something came to me, and I blurted out, "Smee!"

Everyone stopped and looked in my direction.

"Did I say that out loud?" I said apologetically. "I just worked out who Ethel is dressed as. Smee from *Peter Pan*."

The Captain Hook in front of me didn't look impressed. She tapped the board again to bring our attention back to it. "Okay," she said, "that's enough for today. I'll divide the story up. Each one of you can write a part of it, and you can bring it to our next meeting. I will pull it roughly together and then give it to our director, who will make it perfect. Time for tea and cake," she announced. Smee strode off to do Hook's bidding.

I would what? My head was spinning. As much as I loved Annie, I was starting to realize I definitely wasn't the woman for this job. I wouldn't even know how to explain this story in a conversation, never mind direct it.

At the end of the evening, Doris thrust a pile of yellow notepaper at me, telling me she had made copies and to familiarize myself with the ideas.

"Do you think I'm a script writer?" I asked.

Doris sniffed. "I'm sure there's a book about it at your library that you can read. I will write a rough draft so we can sit down and read through it together, and then you can take it from there."

I sighed, folded the papers, and put them in my bag. This was going from bad to worse. I was going to have to feign some fatal disease or something to get out of this. I started scanning my mind for all the different diseases I could have to stop me being socially acceptable at rehearsal when Annie approached me and took my arm.

"Hey, Janet," she said. "I wanted to ask you about Stacy before you left. How is she doing?"

"Oh, wonderful," I said, and we fell into a very easy conversation about Stacy's pregnancy, the size of the twins, the movement she was feeling now, and all the food she wasn't eating.

"I'm just getting ready to send some baby clothes to her," I added.

Suddenly, Annie stopped me short.

"Oh, fiddlesticks," she said. "I just remembered. I had a gift for Stacy that I left at home. I thought I had put it in my bag." She shuffled through a massive purse brimming with wool, knitting needles, and patterns as she continued. "Any chance you could stop by the farm on your way home? I would love her to have it as soon as possible."

"Sure," I said despondently. I was already feeling pretty low and just wanted to get home and sulk. "Yeah, I can stop by. I'll follow you home."

As I got in the car, I looked on my passenger seat. On it, there was a pile of theater books I

had borrowed from the library and, underneath them, two books on how to be more assertive that Karen had left for me as a joke, with a Post-it note. I picked up the assertiveness books and looked at them. One had a bold orange-and-black cover with a strong, power-dressed woman on the front with her arms folded and the words, *Say What You Mean and Mean What You Say.* The other book had a picture of a woman with duct tape across her mouth, and the title looming above her head said, *Finding Your Voice.*

I placed the books on the top of the pile. I was not going to be dictated to this time. I was going to find a way out of this. I started to feel a twinge of guilt as I drove. But I continued to assure my sacrificial self that I was going to find just the right person to be the director that they needed.

Before long, we were at Annie's happy farm. A little red-and-white sign on the road read, "Doggy's Day Care and Spa, the Home of Happy Dogs." I followed Annie's car up the long, winding, tree-lined driveway to her house. About halfway up the drive, even with the windows closed, I heard them. The dogs were starting to bark. They obviously knew the sound of her car. When we arrived, I got out, and she was already calling out to them, cooing and chatting and greeting them. They sounded as if they were bouncing up and down in their cages to say hello back.

She opened a big barn door, where she housed the dogs. "I just have to let them know I'm home; otherwise, they'll pine."

I smiled, followed her to the door, and, to my surprise, found they weren't in cages at all. They were all kept in lovely, neat little wooden pens. They leapt up and down when they saw her.

I followed her around as she walked from one pen to another, opening their gates, rubbing their furry heads, and nuzzling their happy snouts. It was contagious. I couldn't help but join in and snuggle all the dogs as we went. There seemed to be hundreds of them, but I guessed there were about fifty. The noise in the barn was pretty deafening, but Annie didn't seem to even hear it. She addressed each of them by their name and introduced me to them. Each one had a story that she loved to tell in enthusiastic, high-pitched, loving tones, making the dogs yip and wag their tails madly. Some of them she had found as puppies, some of them had been dropped at the farm, and many of them were strays.

From the corner of the barn, an old collie wove its unsteady way toward us. He was obviously older and not in a kennel. It took him a while to get to Annie, but he seemed happy to greet his mistress, his tail high and bright, and his watery eyes could do nothing but display his love for her.

We leaned down and stroked his head gently.

"This is Bruiser," she said. "He's been with me a long time. I called him that because he used to throw himself so hard at me to greet me when he was a pup that he would often cause them. Not so much anymore, eh, old fella," she said, tickling his chin. A long, leathery pink tongue lopped out of his panting mouth as she continued to speak words of love to him. "He's like the guard dog here. He takes care of all the other dogs when I'm not here."

"That will be the collie in him," I added, smiling.

"Yes," she laughed. We walked around the rest of the stalls, and Bruiser stumbled behind us, slowly weaving his way the best he could. "He has arthritis now," she said, closing up the final pens and making her way toward the barn door. "But he's still as bright as a button." He followed us outside, and she locked up and shouted good night to her dogs.

I followed her into the farmhouse. I was amazed to see that there was more art featuring dogs and even statues of them. She had a whole wall of painted portraits of every dog she had ever owned. She showed me the pictures of all the dogs that she had lost, and with sadness in her eyes, she told me their stories, from people who had dropped them on her doorstep to heartbroken pet owners who had to give them up for medical reasons.

She took a picture off the wall and handed it to me. The happy little face that stared back at me had copper-colored fur with white flashes and a long, thin, slippery-looking tongue that drooped out of the side of his mouth. There appeared to be some whippet in his heritage. His mischievous eyes looked playful and adventurous.

"This was Dodger," Annie said with a knowing smile, and then she added, "He was a rascal. He turned up on my doorstep one morning as if he was here to pay a visit. It was really early, and I thought maybe someone had dropped him off. But I was soon to learn that no one really owned Dodger.

"He constantly came and went, no matter how hard I tried to secure him. The whole property is fenced, but somehow he found a way to escape. I would turn my back, and he would be gone, sometimes for days, then he would turn up on my doorstep again as if he hadn't been anywhere. He was like a wayward child."

She giggled as she continued to recount the little dog's story. "I named him Dodger after the Artful Dodger in *Oliver Twist*. Because I couldn't tie him down and because whenever he returned, he would bring me gifts—a scarf, a hat, or a shoe, and once a whole purse. He would just drop them on the doorstep and wait for me to open the door as if he was back to exchange them for his breakfast. I hate to think of the poor

woman's closet that was slowly being emptied.

"One day he brought me a surprising gift. He brought me Popeye the pug. I have no idea where he found him, but when I opened the front door that morning, there they both were, covered in mud, ready for their breakfast. Popeye was obviously well cared for, but even though I did a search, I never found the owners of either of them. I think they were just a pair of carefree bandits out roaming the countryside."

She placed Dodger's picture back on the wall as she continued to tell me story after story about her dogs. I was taken aback with her devotion.

"Let me get you a cup of tea, Janet," she finally said, "while I'm sorting out this parcel for Stacy." She led me into her sitting room. On a well-loved dark oak table, laid out in pink tissue paper were two matinee coats, several pairs of booties, and four little knitted hats.

"Oh, these are beautiful," I said.

"I knitted one for the girl and one for the boy," she said decisively.

"How do you know they're a girl and a boy?" I asked. Stacy had been very quiet about the sex of the twins, as she wanted it to be a surprise. It looked as if Annie already knew.

"I just have a feeling," she said confidently.

As she went to go and make the tea, I looked around the room. The whole room had the air of muddled love. There were piles and piles of

knitting patterns, books, women's magazines, and every conceivable kind of collectable plate. As I looked through her large picture windows, I saw a full moon had started to take center stage. A picture in a frame on the windowsill caught my attention. I picked it up and examined it closely. It was obvious from the resemblance that it must be one of Annie's relatives.

It was a black-and-white picture, shot in front of what appeared to be the farm a long time ago. Annie joined me with a mug in her hand and gave it to me. She noticed the picture I was holding.

"That's been on my sill for over forty years, and I don't think I've looked at it for ten. A piece of heaven," she said wistfully.

"Sorry?" I inquired.

She chuckled. "That's what my mother used to call it. The farm," she said, looking out across the rolling hills.

In the picture, her mother's hair was in the latest fashion for the time, an elegant cropped bob. She appeared to be in her farm clothes, her head tossed back. She was being held by a man, laughing, and I noticed that Annie had her smile.

"That's my father," said Annie, pointing to the man. "She had always wanted a farm and somehow she talked him into it. He loved her and would do anything that she wanted."

I looked at the man in dark pleated pants with the same shape face as Annie, his white shirt

turned to the elbow and his arms wrapped around his wife's waist.

"This was one of those official, move-into-the-property photographs," she laughed as she sipped her tea. "It was taken just outside here on the lawn. As the official photographer snapped it, Mom lost her balance on the uneven ground, and Dad had to catch her to stop her from falling. I love to look at it," she said. "It reminds me of my parents' laughter, and that they were young and alive . . . once." Annie fished out a tissue and blew her nose as slow tears ran down her cheeks, again. She brushed them away forcefully, saying, "There's no point in this. All this crying doesn't solve anything."

She took the picture lovingly from me and placed it back on the windowsill.

I looked around the room as I sipped my tea. And I thought she had a wonderful place, warm and friendly. Whereas my cottage had more of a modern, clean twist, everything in hers just felt loved to death. Old dark wood furniture and tapestry cushions and throws—everything frayed around the edges, but frayed with love.

Bruiser and four other dogs trotted into the front room to meet me. "This is my family," said Annie with a smile. She looked down at them as she introduced each one to me. One was obviously a Labrador; it was hard to figure out the breed for two of them. They had large,

96

buoyant bodies with wagging tails and kisses for both of us. However, the fourth one appeared to be the little pug from her story: a small black furry barrel. He nuzzled up to Annie and made strange sniffling noises as he rubbed his nose up and down her leg. She picked him up and introduced him.

"This is Popeye," she said as she carried him around.

She locked him under her arm as she expertly wrapped Stacy's gift with one hand and then handed it to me. I finished my tea, and she walked me out to my car. Outside, we were both drawn to the beauty of the moon and how it bathed the dark trees in its hypnotic, waning light. She rubbed her eyes.

"My mom would be so sad to know that I'm going to lose the farm."

A lump found its way to my throat, and I took her arm.

"No, Annie," I said. "You're not going to lose the farm."

She smiled and patted my hand. "I know that Doris means well, and you guys have been an amazing support. But somehow, I just have the feeling that this is not going to work out, and I'm going to lose all of this, and the thought of that crushes me like you wouldn't believe."

"It's not going to happen," I said, reassuring her. "We'll find a way. Don't you worry."

She smiled and nodded, but more to assure me than herself.

I gave her and Popeye a hug, saying, "I need to get home and see if Stacy called." I always carried my cell phone with me, but service was always sketchy on the island.

"Of course," she said.

I got into the car and noticed the assertiveness books still on top of the pile. I picked them up, gently slipped them to the bottom, and placed Annie's bundle on the top. I might not be the best director in the world, I thought, but I was going to help Annie in any way I could.

As I drove away, I looked in the rearview mirror. There was Bruiser and the three other dogs, silhouetted by her side in the moonlight. She still had Popeye in her arms. She was waving his little paw at me as she held him. I waved back behind me out the window and thought, Yes, we're going to fix this, Annie. I'm not going to let you lose your home.

Chapter Ten

OOLONG TEA &
JAPANESE SOYA BEANS

The next day, I was curled up on the sofa, sipping a cup of tea, when Martin came downstairs.

"Are you going to work at the library today?"

"I wish," I grunted. "I'm going to work for Doris."

Martin smirked. "Okay, what does she have you doing now?"

"Something apparently called Potluck and Paintbrushes, which, translated, means cleaning and renovating an old theater where, very soon I'm going to be directing a musical, which I am totally unequipped to do," I said.

Martin glanced down at the pile of theater books that had remained unopened on the coffee table in front of me. "How's that going?" he asked, smirking and sipping a cup of coffee.

"Fabulous," I responded sarcastically. "I'm absolutely the ideal person for the job."

"I think books work better if you open them," he said loftily.

I rolled my eyes. "Can you pass me a coaster?" I asked as I sipped my tea.

He picked up a book from the top of the pile and handed it to me.

"Okay, okay," I said, giving in.

I shook my head and reluctantly opened a book called *Theater Craft*.

Martin settled himself beside me.

I skimmed the first chapter, looking at all the pictures. The books were dated, maybe written in the seventies, early eighties, and the black-and-white pictures reflected that. In this first chapter were hippy, bearded men and leotard-clad women thrust into odd poses with "Warm-ups" typed underneath. Martin was highly amused as he pointed to a picture of a woman falling back and a partner catching her with the caption above it: "Trust exercises."

"This should be interesting," he commented, "especially if Doris partners with Ethel. In fact, I 'trust' that would be highly entertaining."

As I turned the page, there was a knock on the front door. My look of surprise indicated to Martin that I had no idea who it could be. Martin put down his coffee and walked toward the hallway while I listened with interest. Maybe Doris hadn't been able to wait another minute and had come by to pick me up on her way to the theater.

Martin opened the door, and I noted the sound of happy surprise in his voice. "What are you doing here?" he inquired.

"Surprise," came the voice in response. The word was a happy one, but the tone was of misery. I knew that voice of disappointment anywhere, and I moved to the door to confirm my suspicions. There was Stacy, a bundled-up pregnant woman who looked more than a little harrowed. The next words out of her mouth were, "What a nightmare getting here. Could you pay the taxi, Daddy?"

I sighed, glad to know that impending motherhood hadn't altered my daughter too much. I got to the door and hugged her.

"Darling, what are you doing here?"

She released herself quickly from my hug, saying, "It's a very long story. Could I come in and have a drink first?"

"Of course," I said, trying not to feel hurt as she pushed me away in her usual way.

While Martin went out to pay the taxi fare, I helped her with her coat and escorted her into the front room and to the sofa.

"Cup of tea?" I asked.

She responded automatically. "You know I don't do black. Do you have peppermint?"

I frowned. "Let me see. Maybe in the cupboard," I mused.

She continued, "I only want it if it's organically grown. Not spearmint. I don't like the taste of spearmint."

I frowned again, thinking she'd be lucky if I

could find any kind of mint. I didn't drink fruited teas. My grandmother, an import from Scotland, had been a staunch black tea drinker, as were my mother and I.

As I pulled out various tins from my tea cupboard—all those fancy Christmas gifts I had received over the years—Martin made his way into the cottage laden down like a packhorse, huffing and puffing all the way. He made it as far as the center of the kitchen and dropped the load.

Stacy's voice floated in from the front room. "I'm starving. While you're looking for a mint tea, Mom, any chance of a salad? Spinach would be great. Nothing with cheese. I'm not doing cheese, and onions turn my stomach, but I can stand a little grated carrot, tomato, cucumber, avocado, corn, beets, and either organic legume or edamame for protein."

Eda-what? I recalled that I had nothing but half a bag of leftover Caesar in the house.

It was as I was stumbling to the fridge, a crumpled packet of Earl Grey in one hand and an old bag of oolong in the other, that I caught my foot in a Gucci suitcase strap and tripped over the bags that Martin was still sweating over in the kitchen. Saving myself by snatching at the fridge door, I remembered once again why I was glad that my daughter had decided to live in California.

Later, Martin and I were sitting, glazed over,

on the sofa, a cold cup of coffee in his hand and a very strong black tea in mine, when I noticed the time. We had barely been able to get a word in edgewise for thirty minutes as Stacy started at the top of her day and complained about everything that had happened to her in the last six hours. Not that it mattered, but I found just saying "how terrible" every time she paused for breath seemed to be the correct punctuation to every sentence she uttered. From the tales of the sadistic taxi driver who had deliberately chosen to ride over every bump in the road to berating me for not knowing to refrigerate organic immature Japanese soya beans in the off chance that she might be popping in from California.

She informed us in the midst of it all that her husband, Chris, had gone to visit his mother in the hospital in New Jersey. They'd had a call late last night that his mother had taken a fall, and they had left early for the airport. Stacy, not wanting to be alone, decided to take the morning flight to Seattle at the same time.

Stacy screwed up her nose for the umpteenth time as she sipped her tea. It was tangerine, which was all I could find in a pinch. I gently approached the subject I knew was not going to make my daughter happy.

"I would love to talk to you all day," I lied as I got up and placed my empty cup in the sink, "but

the fact is, Doris has us all on a mission today."

Stacy ground her teacup into her saucer and pulled a face. "Who's going to look after me while you're gone?" she whined morosely. "I was hoping you would drive me to Seattle. There's an organic motherhood store that I read about, and I thought we could have lunch or dinner, spend some time down there."

I turned and noticed that Martin had mysteriously disappeared from the sofa, and I caught a glimpse of the tail end of him trying to sneak off down the hallway. I answered her in a loud enough voice so he could hear. "I'm sure Dad would love to catch up with you."

Out of the corner of my eye, I saw Martin stop dead in his tracks with one shoe on and the other in his hand. I grabbed my own shoes and breezed past the deer in the headlights who was rooted like a tree in the hall and tapped his face.

"Have fun," I whispered into his ear as Stacy's voice drifted down the hall, toward us. "Dad, could you get me a pillow? My back is still aching from the plane ride. Not feather. I'm not doing feather, unless it's duck. I can just about tolerate a little duck down."

"Duck?" he implored desperately as I opened the back door.

"Can't miss it," I responded dryly. "It's in plum sauce right next to the fish sticks in the freezer."

Through clenched teeth he whispered to me, "I

will give you five hundred dollars and will wash up for a week if you'll take this one."

I grinned broadly, shutting the door behind me, whispering back through the keyhole, "Not a chance in hell, mister."

Chapter Eleven

LIONS & TIGERS & BEARS, OH MY!

Ten minutes later, I swung my SUV into the parking lot behind the theater. Cars were lined up like a fleet of tanks waiting to go into battle, armed with their weapons of mass destruction: mops, buckets, and Pine-Sol.

I watched the show as various rejected writers performed a three-ring circus, attempting to juggle protruding implements without losing eyes or limbs.

We all gathered in a circle with our assorted accouterments. Lavinia blundered toward us, clinging to a rather bulky load of cleaning brushes in one hand while the other handled half of a cumbersome stepladder between her and her twin. The two of them looked adorable in their Rosie the Riveter–style headscarves, blue striped shirts, and overalls.

"So glad I joined this writing group," she complained sarcastically. She was out of breath as she threw down what appeared to be the entire contents of her broom closet. "It's so much fun sitting around discussing thought-provoking prose together."

The group's snigger was cut short by the appearance of Doris, who was wearing her don't-mess-with-me face. She walked around the group, checking off from a list the growing pile of paraphernalia. She stopped short in front of Annie and Flora, who both automatically stiffened to attention as she peered down at them.

"Toilet," she barked.

"I've been," said Annie, bewildered.

Doris shook her head. "No, you girls are in charge of the bathrooms."

"I'm sure there's nothing I can't handle after cleaning up after dogs all my life," commented Annie.

Flora just looked sheepish.

"You and Lavinia can start on the auditorium," Doris continued, pointing a pen at the twins. "Good, you brought the ladders I asked for. Janet," she said as she reached me, "I think I'll have you work backstage."

We all stumbled toward the door. Doris rustled in her purse to find the key. As I waited, I studied the architecture of the building. An enormous white brick building, it was faced with black-and-white mock Tudor paneling with ornately carved finials. The heavy oak door was painted white with comedy and tragedy theater masks stenciled on it in black. To the side of the door, a small, quaint bow window appeared to have served as the ticket office. Through the dirt-caked glass,

a yellowing poster, the faded victim of rain and sun, advertised a coming attraction, *A Murder Is Announced*, by Agatha Christie.

Doris produced a large brass key, placed it into the lock, and turned it. There was the unmistakable scurrying sound of animal movement and a blast of bleak, ice-cold air as the door creaked open. Inside, the lobby was pitch-black, and a faint smell of mildew crept up from the carpet to meet us.

Doris stepped boldly into the foyer and, reaching into her purse again, pulled out a flashlight. Mumbling something about the main switch that the theater owner had told her about, she stumbled off into the darkness. We all watched as her pinprick of light bounced away from us, till eventually we were just staring into the bleak abyss once more.

Sweet Gracie communicated the feeling of foreboding that we were all experiencing. "Come out, come out, wherever you are," she sang.

Ruby arrived, and her face joined the bouquet of heads surrounding the door. "This would make a great setting for one of my horror stories," she mused, her voice barely above a whisper. "Couldn't you imagine a darkened dressing room full of the heaviness of broken dreams and a drunken puppet master controlling a weak-minded woman?"

"Sounds like my second marriage," quipped

Lavinia, who had been married three times before her twenty-fifth birthday.

"Lavinia," spat out Lottie in a heightened whisper, "no one needs you to air all your dirty linen."

"Air it? I could have kept the Sheraton chain in bedding with all my dirty linen."

Ethel stared up and blinked at her in disbelief.

"Do you think Doris is okay?" I asked nervously. "She's been gone a long time. Maybe one of us should check on her?"

"I'm armed," said Lavinia, holding up her broom. "Or do you think this would be better?" She held up a toilet plunger, Lady Liberty–style.

I took one step into the foyer and held up my phone in front of me, using the soft glow to illuminate the blackness ahead. All the girls followed, stepping gingerly just inside the door.

From a corner, there was another scurrying noise. I swung my phone in that direction but couldn't see anything.

"Doris?" I shouted into the darkness.

Behind me, a heavy hand landed on my shoulder. I jumped and screamed, setting off a chain reaction of screams throughout the group.

As if on cue, the whole foyer burst into light, and I turned.

Behind me, a good-looking middle-aged man with graying hair beamed at me. "I'm sorry. I didn't mean to make you jump," he said. "I just

came by to check on you. I'm James Graham, the theater owner."

"The puppet master," growled Ethel as her eyes narrowed.

Doris rejoined us as we took a tour of the building. The reality was that the theater really needed a lot of work. Years of nonuse had created all kinds of problems: mildew, rotting wood, peeling paint. Doris made extensive notes. James informed us at the end of the tour that he was leaving right away to meet with a group of volunteer workers who had agreed to tackle the major repairs. Our job would be to start cleaning and getting it shipshape.

"Leave it to us," Doris shouted after James as he left for his meeting.

Doris escorted me behind the stage. I couldn't believe the mess it was in. It was as if whoever had finished their last show had just pulled everything offstage and piled it up behind the curtains.

"What do you want me to do with all this?" I asked Doris.

"There's a little room back behind the stage for the bigger pieces," Doris said. "And up there"— she pointed to a rickety set of stairs and a flimsy makeshift stepladder painted purple—"and through that door, there is an attic to store all the smaller props."

Doris handed me a basket that contained a

110

bunch of copper pots from what I assumed was a pioneer show.

"Like these," she continued.

I looked at the steep steps that stretched to the top landing above the theater and thought I would definitely be keeping the journey to a minimum. And I rolled up my sleeves and got started.

Chapter Twelve

HITCHCOCK MOVIES & REINCARNATED RELATIVES

Flora put on her dust mask, picked up her bucket and rubber gloves, and followed Annie down the long corridor. The last place she wanted to be was in an old theater, cleaning its toilets. She wanted to write Dan a letter or go into town and buy him a card. He had called her just before she'd left that morning, and he had been very cryptic on the phone, saying the surprise he had for her would be arriving in the next day or two and that he couldn't wait to see her reaction to it. He had something to tell her too, but she would have to wait until the surprise arrived.

As Annie reached the bathroom door, she stopped short. "Oh, I've forgotten my mop," she said. "I've left it in the foyer. I'll be back in a minute."

Annie exited the bathroom and left Flora alone.

Flora took a deep breath and reached for the light switch. She flicked the switch up and down several times, but nothing happened. She was about to leave to inform Doris when she heard something from across the room. She stopped to listen, but it stopped too. She turned to leave,

then heard it again. She couldn't quite place what it was.

Even though she wasn't feeling very brave, her curiosity was piqued. Her eyes were starting to get used to the dark as well, aided by a little light from a cracked window that ran above the stalls. Feeling her way across the room, she headed toward the stall where the sound was coming from.

Flora stood in front of the door. It was an odd sound, gentle and rhythmic. She could hear it clearly now, like a curtain flapping in the breeze. She gently pushed the door open.

Annie managed to find her bucket and mop and was just heading back to the bathrooms when there was a piercing scream.

Suddenly the bathroom door flew open, and a blur of petticoats, layered clothing, and flowing hair sprinted out as Flora came running out at top speed, nearly knocking Annie clean off her feet. She seemed to be oblivious to the fact that Annie was even there.

Doris managed to stop her by planting her feet in front of Flora and tackling her, football-style. Flora bounced right off Doris's voluminous chest and was knocked to the floor. If Doris hadn't stopped her, she looked as if she might have run all the way to Canada.

"Flora, get a hold of yourself!" Doris blasted her, taking her firmly by the shoulders.

Flora's screams turned to sobs as she buried her face in Doris's shoulder. Finally, she caught her breath enough to say, "There's something very alive in the bathroom."

Lavinia, Lottie, Gracie, Ethel, and Ruby all appeared in the foyer in response to the commotion. Gracie placed an arm around Flora, and Lottie quickly went to fetch her a glass of water. Doris took charge. She marched down the hallway, grabbing a broom as she went. Lavinia, Ruby, and Annie all followed behind.

Tentatively, Doris pushed on the door to the ladies' room. The room was dark and still. She crept in, and they all followed, quietly moving toward the stalls. All at once, there was noise that sounded like someone flicking through the pages of a book. They all froze. It appeared to be coming from the left stall.

They reached the stall door. The group filed off to one side, and Doris pushed it open sharply.

It was like a fox had gotten into the chicken coop. There was a frantic flapping of wings, and it rained down feathers as dozens of pigeons started to circle the bathroom ceiling. Some flew straight out the cracked window. Everyone automatically covered their heads as the birds continued to circle.

"Good grief," shrieked Lavinia. "It's like something out of an Alfred Hitchcock movie."

Annie shouted over the din, "Looks like they've

114

been getting in through that window. We should get it boarded up."

"We should trap them or poison them," hollered Doris back over the mayhem.

"Over my dead body!" shouted back Ruby. "One of these marvelous creatures may be one of your ancestors."

The birds stopped flapping, quieted, and started to settle.

"See," said Ruby. "They heard me."

From the corner of the room, Lavinia shrieked, "Ooow!"

They all turned to see that a wayward pigeon had well and truly marked her.

She swore loudly, adding, "Yep, you're right, Ruby. I'm guessing this one is my Great-Uncle Lionel. He did that to me a lot."

"Let's see if we can encourage them to fly out the window," responded Annie hopefully, one arm still wrapped firmly around her head.

Doris nodded and made her way gingerly toward the window, not wanting to ruffle nervous feathers. She managed to reach up and flip the catch. It arched open and creaked loudly from the ancient hinges, sending the birds into a blind panic again. Lavinia screamed as one dive-bombed toward her.

"What did I do in my past life that you all hate me so much?" she screamed up at them.

She took off running out of the bathroom door,

causing a small flock of them to fly after her into the foyer. All that could be heard was frantic flapping and Lavinia swearing like a sailor as she ran, waving her arms above her head.

Flora started screaming again, and, above it all, they heard the unmistakably exasperated sound of Lottie Labette admonishing her twin. "Lavinia!"

Chapter Thirteen

CHARLES DICKENS'S GHOST & FLYING HANDKERCHIEFS

After her frightening pigeon ordeal, Flora was more than glad to join me working backstage.

"I find it kind of magical," Flora giggled as she placed things in piles. "Not unlike an adult's dress-up session. Queen crowns here, fairy wings over there, Egyptian costumes added to the box marked 'Joseph.' "

To finish, Flora mopped the stage beautifully, and we just had to move the boxes upstairs to the prop room. We both made our first precarious trip up the stairs and weaved our way through the flies.

The prop room was located at the end of a little planked galley, through hanging ropes and chains and a door painted emerald green with the word "Doctor" on it. This door had apparently been used in a show or two.

Inside, it was like an Aladdin's cave: from lamps to rugs and Japanese boxes to telephones from every era to pots, pans, daggers, doorbells, and wigs. It smelled of stage powder and paint.

By our third trip, we had a huge pile in the middle of the floor. I looked at my watch: 4:45.

Good. That gave us fifteen minutes to find places for all the props.

The room was musty. To let in some fresh air, I opened a small, high window at the end of the attic just as Flora opened the door with her last armful of props. A strong wind from the window whipped through the attic, moving rigging in the rafters and rattling the chains in the flies. It sounded like something out of a Charles Dickens novel.

Flora dropped the props, and a second, stronger blast rushed through the passages of the attic, almost knocking us off our feet. Without realizing it, we had created some sort of wind tunnel.

Pans and kettles hanging on ceiling hooks clashed together in a symphony of grinding metal, and a pink ostrich-feathered fan ruffled and floated to the floor. From behind us, I heard the door slam shut.

Flora picked up the feathers and pretended to fan herself romantically. We both laughed and started to tuck items away on shelves.

As I placed the last turban on a high shelf, I looked at my watch.

"Perfect. Two minutes to five," I commented out loud.

"I'm finished too," replied Flora.

Flora and I moved toward the door. She reached for the handle. As she turned it sharply to the right, something clicked but nothing happened.

Flora looked over her shoulder, saying, "It's really stiff."

We swapped places, and I turned it back and forth, then shook it gently. Nothing. So then I turned it hard to the left and jiggled it. All at once, something came loose.

"I've got it," I said.

Then, we heard something clatter to the floor on the other side of the door. The handle suddenly became limp in my hand. The doorknob moved back and forward freely, but the door didn't budge.

Flora looked anxiously over my shoulder and bit her lip.

"I think that might have been the handle on the other side of the door," I surmised.

"Is that bad?" asked Flora.

I tried to remain calm. "It may mean we can't get the door open."

"Oh no."

I turned the door handle once more. It just slid around in a circle. Trying a new approach, I slammed my shoulder against the door and pushed as hard as I could. Nothing budged.

After several more attempts, we made our way back, deeper into the attic, and I climbed up to the window to look out.

"We need to see if we can get someone's attention to let them know we're here," I stated.

The one window was high on the wall and very

small, so it was impossible to make a lot of noise. As I stood on a bench, I saw the twins and Ruby chatting in the parking lot as they piled mops and brushes into the back of their cars. I rapped on the window.

"Here, try this," Flora said. She had tied a large white handkerchief onto a gray play sword. I took it from her and pushed it through the window.

I started to wave it furiously. We were very high up, and I knew it would be difficult to see unless someone looked straight at us. Flora started to bang on the window at the same time I continued to fly the flag.

Suddenly, the handkerchief blew right off the sword and fluttered down to the parking lot. It landed in front of one of the cars, but no one noticed. They appeared to be saying their good-byes to each other, then they got into their cars and drove off.

My shoulders went limp.

We were heading back to the door to bang on it and hopefully get someone's attention when all at once we were plunged into darkness.

If James had just shut off the lights, that meant he, Doris, and Ethel were on their way out of the theater, and they would be heading to the parking lot.

I felt my way along the wall, back toward the window. Flora followed. In the new darkness, the attic felt very different. I reached the window. I

climbed up and knocked as loud as I could, and then I watched, in despair, as James and Doris had a short conversation and drove away.

Flora sat down heavily on a bench.

I searched my pockets for my cell phone. I could call Doris and tell her we were both trapped. Then I remembered. I'd put it down on a Greek pillar backstage after I had last spoken to Martin.

"We won't stay trapped for long," I said, trying to bolster Flora's spirits. "Someone will notice that we're gone."

"Tomorrow is my day off, and no one's going to miss me. And if we don't get out of here, Mr. Darcy is going to be all alone."

"That's not going to happen, Flora. My family will notice . . ."

I stopped midsentence as I recalled the last conversation I'd had with my husband in which he told me he was taking Stacy shopping in Seattle and then maybe to see a show. Stacy liked to stay overnight; she loved the city. The thought of it made me sit down hard next to Flora. I don't know if it was psychological, but I suddenly felt cold, and I shivered.

"Let's see if we can find a flashlight or something while we still have a little light from the window."

We both started to feel our way around the room. I heard Flora trip and catch herself as she landed on a box.

"Ooh!" she screamed. "There's some sort of animal in here!" Flora scrambled toward the window seat and pulled her legs up to her chest.

I moved toward her and felt down, tentatively, toward the box she'd talked about and located what was inside. I pulled the object out and looked at it against the silhouette of the window. It was a gorilla suit.

Tapping Flora on the leg, I handed it to her and realized she was freezing.

"It's only a gorilla suit," I stated. "You should put it on. It'll keep you warm. We may only have about thirty minutes of light from this window, so we should keep looking."

Flora nodded and climbed into the costume. It was odd how cold it had suddenly become.

I continued to search, first through a pile of Japanese masks, then a bag of flat feather boas. Suddenly, I felt something metallic. It felt like a huge copper gravy boat with a lid. I lifted it to the window so I could get a better look at it. As I did, the silhouette was unmistakable: an Aladdin's lamp. I shook it gently. There was definitely some sort of liquid inside. *Dare I hope that it might be something I can light?* I sniffed at the spout. There was the unmistakable smell of lamp oil.

"I found something," I called to Flora. "It's a lamp. If we can find matches, we'll be able to light it."

My spirits were buoyant, but Flora just seemed more disheartened.

"Where are we going to find matches?" she asked.

"Keep looking," I encouraged.

Feeling around, I started to get bolder. A hammer, a box of screws, a paint pot, and an unwashed paintbrush. It was like some sort of parlor game: blind man's bluff with objects. The next thing I felt, I was sure, was a tape measure.

As I continued to feel along the breadth of the shelf, I shouted out loud the names of each object as I did. Then I came across a round object and a sharp, jagged stone. I held it up toward the window as I tried to figure out what it was. Flora gasped as she saw the silhouette of what I was holding up.

"Can I see that?" she asked, excitedly.

I handed it to her. She rolled it around in her hand and felt all the corners.

"I know what this is," she said with excitement. "My grandfather had one of these. It's a stone and an old-fashioned tinderbox."

"Do you know how to work it?" I asked, getting excited.

"It's been a very long time since he showed me, but sometimes he let me use it carefully. I was always mesmerized by the little white sparks that would fly up from the stone whenever he would strike it."

"Great!" I said, hugging Flora. "Let's get this lamp lit."

With the tinderbox in hand, we made our way back to the window seat. As we crept along, I thought about how odd it was that only twenty minutes before, we'd walked boldly up and down this room with piles of clothes and how I had been worrying about how I was going to deal with Stacy and direct a show, and now I was just overjoyed to find an old tinderbox and a prop Aladdin's lamp.

I reached the window bench and the lamp.

"We need to try and find something we can light—a piece of paper or cloth. You know, I remember seeing a box of old programs and playbills over on the other side of the room."

I carefully walked across the room, getting myself jumbled up in something on the way and scaring myself to death.

"Are you okay?" Flora called out when she heard me yell.

"Just found myself inadvertently directing a puppet show."

I managed to locate the box. The pile of paper programs and playbills smelled a little musty and a little damp, but they were dry enough, I hoped, to be able to light.

As I reached in, I screamed and withdrew my hand quickly.

"What is it?" asked Flora. "Another puppet?"

"No," I said, lifting my hand in the air. "A spider."

"Ooh!" yelled Flora with distaste.

I put my hand carefully back into the box and pulled out a few programs.

"Now," said Flora, "if this is right, this should work."

Flora picked up a piece of flint that was attached to the side on a little chain and struck the box. It made a grinding sound, but nothing happened.

"You have to hit it at an angle," she said.

She struck it again, this time at a steeper angle. Little white sparks jumped up from the box. We both whooped in delight. That moment of illumination lifted our spirits.

I quickly found a copper pot and was surprised at how accustomed I was becoming to feeling my way around in the darkness.

Putting it next to the tinderbox, I started to tear the programs into tiny, thin threads and then placed them in the bowl. Flora started to fill the pot with bright, white sparks of magical light. It was beautiful. I blew on them gently, with a renewed sense of determination.

Flora struck furiously again and again. A sliver of paper caught light, and I gently blew on it. It started to glow. Suddenly, the bowl erupted into flames.

Both Flora and I cheered.

"Now we're getting somewhere," I stated as I lit the wick on the Aladdin's lamp.

As it illuminated the room, I could see all the corners clearly now. It was almost cozy.

"We need to find more light and supplies just in case we're here for a while."

I didn't want to say the words "all night," because I didn't want to frighten Flora, but that was going through my mind. I headed out to the end of the attic where all the bigger boxes were stored. One was labeled "Anne of Green Gables."

"Help me get this down, would you, Flora?"

Flora, swaddled in the gorilla suit, waddled over and helped me pull the heavy box from the top shelf. We pushed it toward the window seat. Flora held the lamp aloft while I began to unpack the box. Inside, there were more copper pots and jugs, old-fashioned hair adornments, and a silver-plated comb and mirror set. At the bottom was a large patchwork quilt that was just beautiful.

Flora oohed and aahed at this; it was handmade.

"This will come in handy."

Flora nodded reluctantly. We pulled out the quilt and set it aside. Right in the bottom, I located something that made me whoop with joy: three brass candlesticks with white candles in them. We both clapped our hands and pulled them out.

I placed them on the table in front of the

window seat, and we decided to burn them one at a time. With this new light, we could both move freely around the room and find everything that we needed. Somehow, nothing seemed quite as intimidating as before.

I looked at my watch; it was 6:45 p.m. We'd been trapped in the attic for nearly two hours, but already it felt like days.

As I watched Flora and her candlelight disappear to the end of the attic, I turned my attention to another big box with the word "Pocahontas" scribbled on its side. I was intrigued. Maybe more candles. As I unwrapped it, it was magical. All the tribal Indian colors were illuminated brilliantly in the lamplight. It was funny that, in this intense quiet and darkness, everything just seemed so much more vibrant and alive. As I thought about the Native Americans and the hard winters they had to survive, I felt a kinship with them on my own little quest of survival here.

I pulled out a musket, an Indian doll, pictures, and, at the bottom, a beautiful Indian outfit, embroidered and warm. I couldn't resist it; I had to slip it on. I placed the whole thing over my head and laced it up. I thought about the actress who had worn this costume. I wondered if she felt as regal in it as I was feeling just then.

I walked over to the mirror propped in the corner, feather headdresses and fishnet stockings

dangling from its corners. I turned the mirror to myself just as Flora came back.

She let out a little cry. "Oh, you surprised me! You look so different, like a Native American princess."

I surveyed myself in the mirror. Yes, Flora was right. I did look different as a princess.

"I am the Hiawatha of the attic," I said, holding the lamp.

We stood next to each other, looking in the mirror, me with my Pocahontas costume and Flora in her gorilla suit. We looked ridiculous and started laughing.

"Come on," I said. "Let's see if we can find anything else useful."

We continued our search.

I uncovered a bottle of brandy and whooped again.

"What have you found?" asked Flora.

"Hmm. Something of interest," I said.

"I bet it's not as exciting as what I found," she said mysteriously. I wandered over to where Flora was.

She lifted a lid.

"It's a gramophone player with a whole collection of records inside!" she said triumphantly.

"Let's have a party," I continued. "After all, we're already dressed up. Why not enjoy our captivity?"

I pulled out a teapot and teacups from the Anne of Green Gables box and inspected them; they seemed pretty clean. I put them on a silver tray and set the tray on the window seat. I poured the brandy into the teapot.

"Milk and sugar?" I mocked.

"Of course," said Flora. "Slice of cake, Janet?" she added.

"I wish."

Flora sat there with her little finger out, pretending we were at the palace. She sniffed at the cup. "Oh, I don't really drink."

"A small cup will keep you warm," I reminded her.

We drank the brandy, and without any food in our stomachs, it went straight to our heads.

I pulled out a record titled *Al Bowlly's Greatest Hits*. I placed it on the turntable and wound up the player. The sound was crisp and clear. It permeated the whole room, and with the candlelight, it was a magical moment—a little brandy tea party. We sat listening, lost in our own thoughts, swaying to the music.

"Love is the greatest thing," crooned out the singer, and I guess both of us felt a little tearful. There was a crazy beauty to this moment, and the experience made me appreciate the loves in my life. I wanted to see Stacy more than anything, my wild child.

"I'm in love with Dan," blurted out Flora.

"Wonderful," I answered, toasting her with my cup of brandy.

Flora wiped away a stray tear from her eye.

Al Bowlly continued to croon. "Love is the greatest thing, the oldest yet the latest thing. I only hope that fate may bring love's story to you."

She sipped her drink. "When we don't see each other for a long time, I wonder if it's real or if it's just a dream. I haven't been out to see him since he broke his leg. It's been really difficult for us both. I can never imagine leaving the island or my friends, but if he had to move here, he would have to leave his family and find a new job. So it all just seems so impossible. But I want to be with him."

As Al Bowlly finished his rendition, I reached forward and grabbed Flora's hand. "Give it some time. It will work itself out, you'll see. Is he coming to see you soon?"

"I think so," said Flora coyly. "He left me a cryptic message in the last letter he wrote to me about a surprise. He has family up here—his Aunt Karen works with you."

I nodded. "Try to just enjoy one another and this incredible experience you're having."

"I just can't believe that someone as wonderful as Dan could be interested in me," she said thoughtfully. "There are so many more interesting girls, and I'm sure there are plenty where he

lives. The longer we don't see each other, the more I wonder if he'll meet one and fall in love."

"You are a lovely girl," I reassured her, "and I'm sure if Dan wasn't interested, he wouldn't be writing to you. Try not to overthink it too much," I added.

We continued to play records until Flora yawned. I looked at my watch: 10:30 p.m. I poured us both another brandy, and it made us feel sleepy.

"I think I'm going to try and get a couple of hours' sleep."

"Me too," Flora responded as we grabbed the beautiful handmade quilt from the Anne of Green Gables box and curled up like a pair of cats on the bench seat.

Flora leaned forward and pulled out a little green stocking cap from a box marked "Seven Dwarves" and put it over her head.

"My ears are cold. Make sure we have the tinderbox and a playbill ready," said Flora, yawning for a third time. She pulled out a fancy pillow from a box marked "French Bedroom Scene" and tucked it under her head.

As the gramophone music wound down and stopped, Flora blew out the candle. We both put our heads down for a minute when, suddenly, a noise made us sit upright. From nowhere, an odd sound rang out in the darkness, like phantom piano music. In the complete silence of the

theater, it was eerie and haunting. Flora screamed and buried her head into my shoulder. I listened carefully. Somewhere out there, someone was playing "The Entertainer." I realized with relief that it was my cell phone ringing out on the side stage.

Lying back down, I listened to the twangy tones. Its perky melody seemed appropriate, with us both lying there, locked in a theater attic, wearing crazy costumes, surrounded by past show memorabilia.

"It's only my phone. Martin thought it was funny to change my ring tone to something artsy," I reassured Flora. "It's probably him ringing to tell me the show is finished in Seattle," I said drowsily.

Flora's stomach grumbled loudly. We both giggled again.

"By the time they find us, we might be just two skinny stickwomen under this quilt," I said.

We laughed again, but exhaustion had over-taken us both, and we were soon asleep.

Chapter Fourteen

POCAHONTAS & THE GORILLA

Doris arrived in the parking lot at practically the same time as Martin and Stacy, who had decided to return home after the show. They jumped out of their cars. Doris was dressed in her flannel nightie, beaver coat, and fur boots. Martin was dressed in a suit, and a very pregnant Stacy was dressed in a lovely evening gown.

"Her car is still here in the back parking lot, as you thought it might be," said Martin.

"Yes," said Doris. "I definitely checked the whole theater before I left, though. Maybe she was somewhere I didn't think to check. I tried to call Flora, too, and there's no answer, and that's unusual for her. She's always in bed by nine, so wherever they are, they're together."

They all stood in the parking lot. Martin looked nervously at his watch. It read 1:30 a.m.

"Did you manage to get hold of James Graham?" he asked.

"Yes," said Doris. "He's on his way here too."

Just then, the familiar blue sports car zoomed into the parking lot, and James jumped out, dressed in a burgundy paisley dressing gown and slippers.

"This seems to have turned into quite an adventure," he said, in good spirits. "Let's get inside, shall we?" He headed toward the door, and the group followed him.

Inside, James threw the main switch, and the whole foyer burst into light. They ambled inside like refugees looking for a place for the night.

"The last place we saw them was over on the stage," said Doris, leading the way. They all moved into the main theater. It was dark and cold. "They were both on the stage, sorting costumes," Doris said. They looked around the space.

"Were they working just in this area?" asked Martin.

"Yes, mainly," said Doris. "They were tidying this side of the stage, moving and putting props away."

"Away where?" Martin asked.

"Up in the stage attic . . . ," Doris said, her voice trailing off.

"Could they be up there?" asked Martin, pointing toward the rickety purple stairs.

James appeared from around the curtain. In his hand was a mobile phone. "Is this Janet's?" he asked, handing it to Martin.

Martin nodded. "She wouldn't have gone anywhere without it, so she has to be here somewhere."

Martin headed up the stairs. They all followed.

At the top, the group walked carefully along

the corridor. They arrived at the green door, and right away, James noticed the door handle was missing.

"If this happened while they were on the other side, then they could have found themselves locked in."

"How do we get in there without a door handle?" asked Doris.

"It was here before. I was up here a month ago," responded James, "so I'm guessing it fell out while they were up here. It has to still be around here somewhere."

The group spread out and looked around for the doorknob. Doris located it down in the corner of the floor. She picked it up and handed it to James, who placed it in the lock, and, after several adjustments, he managed to fit it in and snap it into place. They opened the door, and they all filed through. They saw Flora and Janet sleeping soundly.

"Looks like we found them," said Doris.

"Shame to wake them," remarked Martin as he gently shook his wife. "Come on, Pocahontas, bring your gorilla, and let's get out of here."

Chapter Fifteen

A FRIGHTFUL SCRIPT IN SHERWOOD FOREST

Doris called me that morning to inform me that the scripts were ready for us to read. I entered the Crab a little after eleven. Gladys was ringing up a customer. She nodded at me, saying, "Give me two ticks, and I'll be with you."

I looked around the restaurant and couldn't see Doris anywhere. She wasn't in her usual booth. Instead of her stoic frame, a picture-perfect family was laughing together, eating pancakes and eggs. Surely Doris wasn't late; that was unheard of.

Gladys shuffled back to the front reception area, grabbed a couple of menus, and sniffed. "I suppose you'll want to be with the rest of the merry men," she said flatly.

"If that's Doris's group you're referring to, then yes," I said hesitantly. "Are they here?"

"Are they here?" echoed Gladys. She pretended to tic, contorting her face and blinking one eye while she jerked up her shoulder. "Can't you see my twitching starting? They're not in their usual spot. Robin Hood has taken to the woods. She Who Must Be Obeyed finally realized that the

booth was too small, so she decided she wanted a new place. I hope you brought your hiking boots. You better follow me."

I was a little intrigued by her comments as she weaved me through the restaurant, which was packed with the buzz of happy people eating and enjoying Saturday morning brunch. Finally, Gladys arrived at the back of the restaurant. Still, I couldn't see Doris or the group. Gladys nodded her head toward the bathroom. It was then I understood the Sherwood Forest comments. The group was seated at a table that had been dragged into a darkened corner next to the bathrooms, three huge potted plants concealing them.

"I never knew you had a table back here."

Gladys looked at me sharply, saying, "We didn't until ten minutes ago. I'll leave you to guess how they and the plants all got there. I'm sure it will come to you. You need to make your way through the woods just like Little Red Riding Hood. The Big Bad Wolf is already waiting for you."

Gladys fought her way through the foliage, adding a story time lilt to her commentary. "Here we go through the *Hevea brasiliensis* and the *Ficus benjamina* to Grandma's house." I looked at Gladys, impressed that she knew the Latin names for the plants. She caught my expression. "I've been swatting up on my plants with those plant books you gave me. You wouldn't believe

how many innocent plants in my garden could kill you stone dead."

I nodded nervously as she winked at me but decided to skip ordering the loose tea just in case.

When we got to the table, Doris seemed a little annoyed. "Here you are at last, Janet," she said, puffing out her cheeks. "As our director, I thought you'd be here early."

I glanced at my watch. It was only seven minutes past eleven. I wasn't going to bite. "Well, I didn't think to bring my machete," I joked lightly.

"Isn't it exciting?" said Gracie, clapping her hands together. "We are having a picnic in the woods!"

Doris stared at me and blinked as if she hadn't the slightest idea of what I was talking about.

The twins arrived, a vision in blue skirts and pink blouses, all breathless and excited.

"Hi, y'all," Lavinia said, pulling the bushes apart dramatically and posing diva-style. "Isn't this fabulous, reading in the forest? I loved writing my part. I can't wait to hear the whole story."

Lottie was juggling a pile of library books that I'd stacked on the hold shelf for them the day before. She piled them up in the middle of the table, and they both slid into chairs. Three spicy romances were on top, and a book on the Lord's Prayer was at the bottom. No need to guess which was for whom.

Doris started to hand out the scripts to all of us. Typed on the front of the cover were the words, "*The Merlin of Ooze* by Doris Newberry."

"*The Merlin of Ooze?*" Lottie said, wrinkling up her nose. "That doesn't sound very nice."

"It's just a working title," Doris said hotly.

"Well, I would work that in right under the roses if I was you. It stinks worse than manure," added Lavinia.

"It will all make perfect sense," said Doris dismissively as she opened her script.

Gladys arrived back at the table and also noticed the title.

"*The Merlin of Ooze?*" she commented, unimpressed. "It sounds like the guy who used to work in our kitchen years ago before we fired him." She slammed down the water glasses, looked around the table, pulled out her pencil, and observed us all. "Meatloaf's off, fish is on, soup is minestrone. How can I happily apple-y serve you today?" she said in her brusque way.

"What kind of fish?" asked Doris.

Gladys peered at her through her glasses. "The sort that swims in the sea," she said sarcastically.

"Does it have a name?" Doris inquired, crisply.

"John," responded Gladys, as quick as a whip. Then she cackled at her own joke.

Doris gave her the hairy eyeball, and Gladys huffed and muttered that she would find out as she shuffled away. Two minutes later, she

139

parted the branches and hollered in, "Blackened salmon! It's his specialty, apparently, though why anybody wants something all black and burnt, I don't know."

"I will have it," said Doris, slamming her menu shut.

"Just a peppermint tea for me," said Flora, sliding her menu across the table.

"You're looking awfully skinny," commented Lavinia, taking hold of Flora's hand. "You sure you wouldn't like something else?"

"No," Flora said decisively. "Just tea."

The rest of us put in our orders, and then we went back to the scripts in front of us.

"The point of today," said Doris, "is to read through the script together before Janet edits it and figures out the auditions."

"Auditions?" I asked, nearly choking on my water. "We're doing auditions?"

"Of course we're doing auditions," Doris replied. "How are we going to find the rest of the cast?"

"Okay," I said, "but I've never done anything like that before."

"I'll be there to help you," Doris said.

"Of course," I said, a little more sarcasm in my tone than I had intended.

Ruby breezed in. She was wearing a languid, wafting sari affair in gold, purple, and pink, and her hair was pulled up into a lilac knotted

kerchief. Her outfit seemed to trail forever as she wove her way through the plants.

Gladys, who was approaching the table, nearly tripped on her train. "I think you're missing some bridesmaids."

As we all opened our scripts, the excitement around the table was palpable. Lavinia couldn't help but introduce us all to the story. "The first part of the script is the part I was asked to write," she said excitedly. "I think you're going to like it a lot." She read out loud, "A young woman moved through the . . . plains of Nebraska. What? I set this in Italy," she said in confusion.

"I cut that," responded Doris shortly. "Too difficult to create an Italian set, and there's nothing to see in Nebraska, so that will be much cheaper to build a set for."

"Okay," Lavinia said, obviously disappointed. "Won't be quite the backdrop I had envisioned for this torrid love affair, but I guess we are on a budget." She sighed and continued to read. "When she came across a . . . Goddess of the Corn?"

Ruby got excited. "That's one of my characters."

Lavinia's voice was high-pitched and unparalleled. "But I had her having a chance romantic meeting with a wonderful young man who was going to steal her heart away."

"Had to cut that too," Doris said sternly. "We don't have much choice for Flora to kiss."

Flora gulped. "I'm going to kiss somebody?"

Doris continued sharply, "If you become our ingénue, that is standard stuff, but the rest of the cast is probably sitting right here, and we are just a bunch of middle-aged women. I had to scrap all that stuff."

Lavinia pulled off her reading glasses and looked sternly at Doris. "I suppose that means the love scene of them rolling around naked next to the waterfall is cut as well."

Flora interjected again, "I'm rolling around naked?!"

"Not anymore," stated Doris. "You're meeting the Goddess of the Corn."

Flora looked visibly relieved.

"Why did you bother to ask me to write if you just planned to cut everything I wrote?" snapped Lavinia in a high, exaggerated pitch.

"I didn't," responded Doris tartly.

"What exactly is left in here that I actually wrote?" inquired Lavinia.

"You did a beautiful job with the opening," Doris said.

"So, you are telling me that for all the hours I put into writing this, the only words of mine you have not cut are 'a girl moved through the'?"

Doris scanned the script and then nodded. "I liked it. I thought it worked."

Lottie started to chuckle as she studied her fuming twin. "Stop ya carrying on Lavinia. After all, your writing can be a little racy for the likes of the wider Southlea Bay community. Doris has to think about all of that."

"Exactly," said Doris. "Now, we really must move on. Here is a piece I added in." Doris continued to read the part about the meeting between the goddess and the young girl, finishing by saying, "So, Dorothea walked away to the fields with her little dog, Tito, and looking up into the sky as if addressing her maker, she said, 'Oh God . . .' "

Lottie squealed. "Here comes my psalm. I took it from a compilation of my favorite psalms in my book, *Listening to God with Lottie*. You know, I have read excerpts from it many times at our book club."

The group nodded, and we all turned the page to read Lottie's psalms as Doris continued reading out loud.

"Oh God . . . it looks like rain."

Interesting start to a psalm, I ruminated. Though not really a scholar on the finer points of the Bible, I couldn't help thinking that King David was having an off day when he wrote this one.

"What?" Lottie shrieked. "Where is the psalm I wrote?"

"It was too long," stated Doris plainly. "I thought this was better."

"Just the words 'Oh God'? It sounds like she is saying a profanity."

"Well, wouldn't you if a storm was brewing?" Doris snapped back.

Lavinia cackled by her sister's side. "Oh, sister dear, you got left with less than me."

"May I remind you all," Doris said, slamming her script down on the table, "that we are under pressure here to get this show out quickly, and I had to do the best I could."

Everyone around the table became silent.

"I like it," said Annie as she hooked a twist of blue wool. "It's short, sharp, and has a dog in it."

"Let's keep going." Doris picked up her script again. "Suddenly, from nowhere, a green witch appeared."

"That's one of my characters too," stated Ruby excitedly.

Doris added, "And then, floating in a bubble of pink happiness, her sister, another witch, arrived. From the trees and bushes, out popped Minchkins, a group of little people that lived in the far reaches of Nebraska, and they told Dorothea to follow the blue sparkly road."

"Hold everything," I chided, as I suddenly put all the pieces together. "This is *The Wizard of Oz*, without a tornado."

"No, it's not," snapped back Doris. "It's *The Merlin of Ooze*, and besides, we couldn't afford a tornado."

"But it's a rip-off of *The Wizard of Oz*," I stated.

Doris looked down at her script and sniffed, "Well, maybe it's a little like it."

A little? I thought to myself. It could have been the MGM version, except all the names had been changed, and odd parts from the Rejected Writers' Book Club had been shoved in different places.

"That's all well and good," I said, wearing my librarian hat. "I'm sure the book is old enough to be in public domain, which means you can use the story, but I'm not sure that the film is, and this is looking an awful lot like that."

Doris squared up to me. "Those people at MGM had some good ideas. I just improved on what they started."

I shook my head. There was no reasoning with this woman.

As we continued to read, we met the Scaredy Lemur, the Man in the Can, and the Merlin of Ooze himself. I shook my head. I was going to have to do a lot of "editing" to make this different enough from the movie version.

Doris continued to read through the script until she came to the final scene, where she had the Green Witch doing battle with the lead character.

"This is a great scene," Ruby said. "I wrote this too." Ruby jumped to her feet, moving around the table to reenact it for us. "I saw it going something like this," she said. "Suddenly,

Dorothea and the Green Witch circle each other nervously, ready to do battle as the blood-curdling cries of every demon from hell circle overhead."

We all watched Ruby, mesmerized as she moved around us.

"Suddenly, the Green Witch strikes a blow with her broom."

Ruby picked up her bread knife and thrust it toward the bushes just as Gladys appeared carrying the food order.

"Hey, back up!" shrieked Gladys, stepping through the bushes. "The salmon is already dead!"

Then Gladys started plonking plates down in front of us as she continued to rant. "Most people just come here to quietly eat food. What is it with you lot? You can never just sit still."

"I was acting," Ruby stated calmly as she gathered up her sari and readjusted her turban.

"Acting up, more like," Gladys replied. "Now, I have another load I'm coming back with, so be warned. I don't want to have to fight you off with my dinner tray, 'cause I don't get paid enough for all your tomfoolery!"

"Nice acting," stated Doris curtly, "but I've cut the fight scene. Dorothea just throws a bucket of water over the Green Witch instead. I thought that would be cheaper."

We finished reading the script, and Flora shook her head.

"Did I miss my poems?" she inquired.

"There wasn't a place for them," Doris said, slapping the script shut. "I thought we could print them out and hand them to people on the way out of the building."

Flora looked disappointed but also preoccupied. "Okay," she said. "I suppose you know best. Anyway, I have to go. I have a lot to do." And she stood up.

I noticed she had barely touched her peppermint tea, and she was wearing makeup.

The penny dropped, and I realized what was going on. "It's Dan, isn't it? Dan is coming to visit you from Oregon."

Every eye at the table turned to her as she blushed scarlet.

"So that's why you're all tarted up," said Ethel curtly.

"How wonderful," Annie said, smiling and grabbing Flora's hand.

Flora just looked down, saying quickly, "I'm not sure he's coming. He just said I was getting a surprise this afternoon."

"And that's why you aren't eating," said Lottie. "Take it from me. Men don't like their women too skinny, so if I was you, I'd take a piece of pumpkin pie to go."

Flora brushed her off and threw down three dollars on the table. "That should be enough for my tea, and now I really do need to go."

After Flora left, Doris continued, "We have to figure out how to find the rest of the cast." The table nodded in agreement as she continued. "The biggest problem as I see it is men." She said the word as if it were dirty. "We are definitely low in the men department, and I definitely want the Man in the Can to be male, so we need to brainstorm to see if we can come up with a few."

As if on cue, a young, blond busboy arrived through the bushes with a jug of water and started refilling our glasses. Doris wasn't about to waste any time, and she didn't hide the fact that she was checking him out. As she did, she started nodding. The rest of the table couldn't help but be drawn in. I found myself looking at this fresh-faced boy and imagining him in a princely costume on the stage. The boy appeared to sense the attention he was getting and stuttered at Doris, "Is there anything else you need?"

Doris broke into a broad smile that always looked out of place on her stern face as she noted his nametag. "Kyle? Do you sing?"

"Sing?" he said, flushing red and nearly dropping his jug. "No, all I do is waiter."

Doris narrowed her eyes, as if she, too, were imagining him in a costume on the stage. "But would you be open to doing it?" she asked him.

"I don't think so," he stammered again, clasping his jug to his chest and leaping right back through the ficus, apparently scared half

to death by a table of middle-aged women who appeared to be asking him to perform for his minimum hourly wage.

Gladys appeared, the same water jug in her hand, and plopped it down, saying, "I don't know what you said to our busboy, but he's hiding in the kitchen saying he doesn't want to come near you all, so you'll have to serve yourself your own water." She shook her head, mumbling under her breath, "Cougars."

Ten minutes later, there was a rustle in the trees and Gladys returned.

"I hope you enjoyed your stay at the Amazon Cafe, here in ficus corner," she said sarcastically. "Anyone for dessert? Unfortunately, the splits are off. The monkey stole the bananas."

We ordered drinks, and Gracie ordered an ice cream sundae.

Later, as we paid our bill, Gladys couldn't resist one final joke at our expense. When she brought our credit card receipts back to the table, instead of stripy peppermints on the little receipt tray, there was a pile of peanuts.

Chapter Sixteen

AN OXYGEN MASK &
A PRAYING MANTIS

Flora hurried out the door and crossed the street. Her stomach was twisting like a pretzel. She was excited and scared and frightened all at the same time. She had been unable to sleep, and eating was out of the question. She had tried to sleep, of course. She had even gone to bed extra early with a cup of hot milk, but her mind had been reeling all through the night, and then she'd been back up at midnight with only one thought: What if he didn't like her? What if all the romance of the road trip was just that, a holiday romance? He had seen her in an environment that wasn't real, on the road with a group of other women. Other people who could help fill in the conversation, making jokes with him when Flora got tongue-tied. Flora didn't know any jokes. How would she be everything he'd expect her to be? Like, interesting?

A car horn blared, shaking her from her reverie. She'd walked out into the road without even looking, and the car that had slammed on its brakes was about a foot away from her. The man who ran the local supermarket stuck his head out

the window, saying, "Watch what you're doing, Flora! I nearly had you that time!"

She waved to him apologetically as she walked to the shop. Safely inside, she realized her whole body was actually shaking.

Mrs. Bickerstaff looked up at her as she entered. "It's been crazy since you left. I'm glad you're back," she said curtly. Then she softened as Flora drew closer. "Gracious me, Flora, dear, you look as white as a sheet. You should . . ."

Those were the last words Flora heard as she crumpled to the floor and passed out cold.

Somewhere in the distance, Flora could hear Santa, and there were these little sleigh bells. She felt something cold on her skin. She must be at the North Pole. The snow on her face was cold. She wanted to see Santa, and she wanted a talking doll for Christmas.

Slowly, she opened her eyes. There seemed to be a large polar bear in front of her. No, it wasn't a polar bear. It was a rabbit. A huge, white, fluffy rabbit. What was that doing at the North Pole? Something wasn't quite right. Rabbits were supposed to be small, and this one was big, and it leaned in, saying her name over and over again. And it seemed to be wearing cheap perfume and peach-colored lipstick.

"She's awake," the rabbit said. "Flora, love," it continued, bending close to her, giving her another whiff of the perfume. "Are you okay?"

151

Flora realized all at once that she was lying on the floor of the flower shop, and the rabbit was none other than Mrs. Barber from the post office dressed in yet another holiday costume. Flora tried to open her mouth to speak, but nothing came out.

Mrs. Bickerstaff hovered above her. "I've called 911," she informed them both. "They should be on their way."

Flora realized she must have fainted. She tried to get up and make a sound, but her heart was pounding in her ears, and her mind was swimming. She closed her eyes, licked her lips, and tried to gather herself. She heard the bell over the shop door tinkle and then Mrs. Bickerstaff saying, "I think we should get her some water."

She opened her eyes again to agree, and for a minute she thought she saw Dan. She blinked a couple of times. He was never far from her thoughts, but it really looked like him this time. Since her mind was now mush, she wasn't quite sure what was real.

All at once, he was down on his knees beside her. "Flora," he said, the concern obvious in his voice. "What happened?"

Mrs. Barber found her I-work-for-the-government tone. "Please stand back, young man, and let this poor woman breathe. You won't help her leaning over her, sucking up all her oxygen, now, will you?"

Flora still couldn't speak. All she could do was look at him. He was even more handsome than she'd remembered. His dark wavy hair framed his face, and the deep-green eyes showed such concern. She couldn't help herself. She felt tears well up in her eyes. Then, suddenly, next to him, there was another face glaring at her, a young woman. Someone she knew but couldn't quite place. The woman moved toward Flora, ignoring all of Mrs. Barber's directions, and said brusquely, "Hello, Florence. Do you remember me from the ball in Oregon? You know, I'm Dan's friend?"

There was something about the way she said "Dan's friend" that set alarm bells off in Flora's mind, even though it was cotton candy. Of course she remembered her. This was the girl who had openly flirted with Dan at the ball he had taken Flora to when they had met on the road trip. It had been obvious then—and was now, as she rested her hand comfortably on Dan's arm—that a friend was the last thing she intended to be to him.

Before Flora could respond, Mrs. Barber nodded her rabbit head, her interest apparently piqued. "Oh, you're the Dan from Oregon, are you?" And then, to make things worse, she added, "We've heard all sorts of things about you, but I must say, you don't look much like I expected, and it's a shame you don't work on a farm, but

153

I'm pleased to meet you." She held out a rabbit paw.

Flora was mortified. "Please stop; please stop," was all she wanted to say. Instead, she coughed as Mrs. Barber eyed the woman with Dan distrustfully.

"And who might you be, young lady?"

She didn't miss a beat. Thrusting out a cashmere-gloved hand, she said, "I'm Marcy. I'm here with Danny."

"Praying mantis" were the first words that entered into Flora's mind, and this glossy, fur-clad floozy was preying for sure—preying on her guy!

Flora was about to try to say something again when the shop bell rang and in came a line of EMTs. They automatically started to clear the way and attend to Flora. Flora looked longingly at Dan as the EMTs asked her questions and took her temperature and blood pressure. This definitely wasn't the reunion she'd hoped for. Dan just stood there, looking concerned and helpless.

One of the EMTs stood up and said to Mrs. Bickerstaff, "I wonder if we could clear the room."

Marcy tugged at Dan's arm, responding in a firm voice, "Of course. Dan and I will go." Then to Dan, "Let's go and get some lunch, shall we?" Dan looked helplessly from Marcy to Flora, who was now wearing an oxygen mask.

Before he could even try to object, Mrs. Barber started pushing him toward the door. "Yes, you'd better let her get her breath back. I think going over to the Crab would be the best thing till Flora gets herself together."

He was halfway to the door, sandwiched between the rotund Easter Bunny and the fur-clad preying mantis, when he found his voice. "I'll call you, Flora," he said, almost desperately. That was all he could say before the newly massed members of the animal kingdom hustled him out of the shop.

Chapter Seventeen

A WALKING VEGAS
SLOT MACHINE

As we left the table, my mind was whirring with all I would need to do to edit this script for Doris and the crew. And I really needed to get home to Stacy. We were on the way out the door when Annie suddenly tugged at my sleeve excitedly, pointing toward a table in the corner. Dan was sitting there, alone.

"Look who's here!" she exclaimed, her excitement difficult to hide.

Dan's head was bent down as he looked at his menu, and she walked right over to him. We all followed her.

"Dan," shrieked Annie. He looked up and was quickly on his feet, hugging all of us.

Doris looked at him over the brim of her spectacles. "I didn't think I would see you in here today. I thought you'd go straight over to see Flora at the shop." Her expression reflected her disapproval.

Before he could answer, Marcy slipped into the seat next to Dan and responded to Doris, "He did go over and see her, but she has some sort of problem going on, so we came here for lunch instead."

The whole group was stunned into silence by Marcy's arrival. We watched, mesmerized, as her glossy blonde hair, blown into a slick bob, swished from side to side as she talked. Dressed from head to foot in money, the jewelry adorning her body shimmered like a slot machine in Vegas. She seemed oblivious to our shocked silence as she talked about her trip up to the island from Medford with Dan.

Lavinia whispered to no one in particular, "Looks like she's here for more than lunch."

Marcy finished her rendition of their trip and smiled insincerely. With total poise, she carefully unfolded her napkin, placed it on her lap, and sipped demurely at a glass of water.

Aware of the awkward silence, Annie spoke. "Your face is familiar. You are . . . ?"

Marcy's fake smile disappeared, and she appeared irritated that Annie had forgotten her name.

"Marcy," she said slowly, as if reminding a small child. "We were introduced back in Medford."

Doris couldn't help herself. She folded her arms and blurted out, "Where is Flora, and why is she not having lunch with you, Dan?"

Dan opened his mouth to answer, but Marcy was first to speak. "I told you already, she's not well," Marcy said offhandedly. "We had to leave the flower shop. The EMTs insisted."

"EMTs," echoed Annie, alarmed. "What EMTs?"

"The ones that came out to see why she collapsed," said Marcy, as she ran a hand slowly through her hair.

"Collapsed," I responded, startled.

Dan finally spoke. "It seems she passed out in the shop, and we arrived just afterward so I was unable to stay with her. The EMTs insisted we leave."

"We'll see about that," said Doris, rearing her old bulldog self.

She started to the door, the whole group of us in tow. When we got to the shop, only Mrs. Bickerstaff was there. Doris walked right up to the counter.

"Where's Flora?" she demanded.

"God bless her, Doris, someone has taken her home," she responded. "The EMTs didn't think it was serious, but they wanted her to go home and rest for the rest of the day. Apparently, she hasn't eaten today, and it caused her blood sugar to plummet. Then, poof, she was on the floor."

"How awful," said Annie.

"I'm not surprised," sniffed Ethel. "She eats about as much as a sparrow."

"Who dropped her off?" I asked.

"Mrs. Barber from the post office. She had her car in town, and it's her afternoon off, so she said she would stay with her for the rest of the day," she answered.

Good grief. She'll probably talk her to death, I thought.

"I'll pop in on her later," said Annie decisively.

"I wish I could stop by," I added. "I need to get started working on this script, and my daughter's in town, and I've hardly seen her."

"I'm going to go home and cook her something for her freezer," Doris chimed in. "Maybe that way, she'll eat."

She bustled out with Gracie and Ethel padding along behind her. Then she stopped short.

"I think I'll send Ethel back inside the restaurant to keep an eye on all this Marcy malarkey," Doris added shrewdly. Ethel nodded and made her way back into the Crab to stand guard. She pulled up a chair at the table next to Dan and Marcy's and sat there, glaring at them both as she sipped the glass of water the busboy handed to her. When she saw who her new customer was, Gladys just put her hands on her hips, shook her head, and rolled her eyes.

Chapter Eighteen

MUMMIFIED FLORISTS & BUNNIES IN BELLS

Flora lay very still, wishing more than anything that Mrs. Barber would leave. She had talked nonstop since they'd left Stems. She had insisted that Flora go right to bed, and Flora was now cocooned in her bedclothes like a baby swaddled for a trip to the Arctic.

Mrs. Barber had insisted on tucking Flora in and making her a hot water bottle and some toast, even though the EMTs had already given her an energy bar. She had also spent the last twenty minutes enlightening Flora about all of the town's latest gossip as she continued to nervously tuck and retuck Flora tighter and tighter into the bed. Only the whistling of the kettle in the kitchen had saved Flora from complete mummification.

Once Mrs. Barber had left Flora's bedroom to make tea, Flora couldn't help herself. The tears just below the surface rolled down her cheeks in a steady, warm stream. She kept seeing Marcy's perfect white teeth and cashmere-gloved hand resting on Dan's arm. All the fears she'd imagined before he got here came back to haunt her. Marcy

was everything she was not, and it was obvious Dan liked her, or why would he have brought her into town? Why was she here, anyway? Was that the surprise he had talked about? Were Dan and Marcy an item? After all, he had never actually told Flora he loved her. He had written it, yes, but he never told her in person. Maybe he just saw her as a good friend. Now she regretted never telling him how she really felt. Her tears flowed freely, and she managed to liberate an arm to reach for a tissue.

As she sobbed quietly into her pillow, she could hear Mrs. Barber moving around in the kitchen, putting together a tea tray, and she could smell newly toasted bread. Mr. Darcy jumped up onto her bed and, seeming to sense her sadness, curled his body in a coil in front of her, reaching out one ginger-striped paw toward her face. She stroked him lovingly.

Minutes later, Mrs. Barber placed a tea tray on Flora's lap. "I threw a couple of boiled eggs on there for you too. You'll be needing the strength."

Flora's house phone started ringing, and she tried to de-sandwich herself from the bed. A bow fixed around Mrs. Barber's bunny neck jingled as she bobbed her head from side to side, saying, "No, you don't, young lady. It's probably just Carol Bickerstaff checking in on you. You lay there and be a good girl and eat your eggs."

Mrs. Barber left the room, her fluffy pom-pom butt waddling off down the stairs toward the phone. Flora listened intently as she nibbled on the edge of her toast.

She heard Mrs. Barber pick up the receiver, listen, and then say in her official post office tone, "No, this is not Flora. She is detained at the moment. This is the postmistress. To whom am I speaking, please?" There was a pause again, and she added, "She is resting now and having some lunch, and then I'm going to make sure she has some sleep. Call back later this evening or, better still, tomorrow morning." There was another pause, then, "Absolutely," Mrs. Barber said in her official tone. Then she hung up.

When she arrived back in Flora's bedroom, Flora looked up expectantly.

"Is the shop very busy?" she inquired. "I feel terrible leaving her on her own right before Easter."

"It wasn't her," answered Mrs. Barber, starting to tuck her in again. "I think it was that boy from Oregon. Don or John or something."

"Dan," Flora said, throwing the toast back down on the plate.

She tried to make her way out of bed again when Mrs. Barber put a paw up to protest. "I must insist you stay in bed, young lady. You've hardly eaten a thing, and all this excitement could

have you swooning again. Don't even think about getting up."

Flora sat back down despondently and dutifully finished the rest of her food and drank her tea while Mrs. Barber hovered above her, telling her stories of how dangerous low blood sugar could be.

Once she finished, Mrs. Barber took her tray, saying, "Now, get your head down for an hour, and we'll see how you are after that. I'm not leaving the room till I see you sleeping soundly."

Flora laid her head on the pillow and decided to sneak downstairs and call Dan the minute Mrs. Barber was back in the kitchen. Intending to fake sleep for a while to send her jailer on her way, she closed her eyes and settled down. But overwhelming tiredness overtook her completely, and within minutes she had fallen fast asleep.

Annie knocked at 6:30 p.m., and a middle-aged bunny in orange lipstick opened the door to Flora's quaint, Victorian-style cottage.

"Good, the second shift," said Mrs. Barber, who had removed her paws and was wiping her hands on one of Flora's pretty, flowery dish towels.

"I'm happy to help," Annie said, pulling out her latest knitting project from her bag as she entered the cottage. "I have someone sitting with the dogs this evening so I can come and keep Flora company, if she needs it. How is she doing?"

"Been sleeping like a baby all this afternoon," nodded Mrs. Barber. "God love her. There isn't a lot of stamina in that chicken, I'm afraid. I better get off to my husband, Norm. He'll be expecting his dinner." She put on her fur gloves again, walked to the door, and, with a wave of her paw, was gone. Annie closed the door behind her.

Annie looked around at Flora's lovely little cottage. It was totally charming, and it reminded her of a Victorian children's storybook brought to life. Annie crept up the winding stairs. Mr. Darcy met her halfway up and threaded himself through her legs, saying his own feline hello. She got to the narrow wooden doorway at the top of the stairs and quietly opened the door. Flora stirred and, seeing it was Annie, whispered with hopeful anticipation, "Has she gone?"

"Yes," answered Annie with a chuckle. "Was she trouble?"

Flora sat up in bed and yawned. "She wouldn't let me get out of bed. I felt like an invalid."

Flora reached out to her bedside table and switched on an ornate brass lamp covered with a starched cream lace shade. The whole room erupted in magical yellow light.

"How are you feeling, Flora?" Annie asked. "What happened?"

Flora explained the lack of sleep and her inability to eat. Then she said, "While I was being treated by the EMT, Dan arrived."

"I know," Annie interjected. "We saw him at the coffee shop. He was really concerned."

"He came with Marcy," Flora spat out. "Don't you remember her from the ball in Oregon? The girl he knew from school?" She added in a quieter tone, "He acted as if they were a couple."

"Impossible," sniffed Annie. "Dan wouldn't date a girl like that. Besides, he's head over heels in love with you. Anyone could see that."

"I'm not sure," said Flora reluctantly. "It's been weeks since we last saw each other. What if it was just a road trip fling or something?"

Annie sat in a little white wicker bedroom chair and started hooking a stitch while she thought for a second. "I've never heard of one of those before, but I don't think for a minute you were one. He's genuinely a nice young man. And if Marcy is here too, I'm sure there is a very good reason for it, so I think you can stop worrying about that. Have you tried calling him?"

"Not yet," answered Flora. "Mrs. Barber banned me from leaving the bed except to go to the bathroom, and my phone is downstairs. He did call earlier, though."

"There, you see, why don't you try calling him? Maybe if you are feeling well enough, he can take you out to see the new romantic comedy that is opening at the movie theater tonight."

Flora cheered up a little and put on her cotton

and lace nightgown and trotted down to the phone.

"I'll see about feeding Mr. Darcy," Annie shouted after her, dropping her knitting on a side table and picking him up from where he had entwined himself around her legs.

Flora picked up the phone and dialed

Chapter Nineteen

A CIRCUS PONY IN
RUBY-RED PUMPS

Dan sat at the dining table in his Auntie Karen's kitchen, finishing up the last of the lovely dinner she'd prepared for him.

"That was amazing," he said, clearing the plate with his fork.

She waved her hand dismissively, saying, "Just leftovers put to good use, that's all. But you're welcome."

Dan's phone rang. Picking it up quickly, he hoped it would be Flora. Barely able to hear the person on the other end, he walked out the porch screen door and onto his aunt's wooden deck overlooking the water, where he knew there was a better chance of hearing. Outside it was crisp and cold, and the moon was a luminous globe hanging low in the gray sky, reflecting its brilliance in the rolling waves.

"Hello?" he said again urgently.

A female voice answered.

"Flora!" he said, relieved. "I'm so glad to hear your voice."

"No, guess again," said the voice, icily.

"Marcy," he said with disappointment, berating

himself for not looking at the number on the phone before he'd picked it up.

"So, there's a movie playing in town at seven thirty, and I thought you might like to pick me up at seven so we can go," she said brightly.

"I'm waiting for a call," Dan replied, unable to keep the annoyance from his tone.

"From that girl, Florence?" retorted Marcy, like she was talking about yesterday's mashed potatoes.

"Yes. I haven't managed to speak to *Flora* yet"—he made a point of emphasizing her name—"and after all, it's her I've come to see."

"I think you're being awfully optimistic thinking she will call tonight. She looked very sick when we saw her last. I'm sure she's probably sleeping soundly. You'll have plenty of time to see her tomorrow."

"I still want to check in with her," he said firmly.

"Surely she would have called by now if she wanted to see you," Marcy responded tartly. "What's the point of moping around your aunt's house tonight? We might as well go and see a movie, and you can introduce me to a few people. I really don't know a soul."

"I don't know a lot of people myself," responded Dan. "I just came on vacation here as a boy growing up. Most of the people I know are from the summer crowd."

"That's still more than I know," whined Marcy. Then she added, taking on a pitiful note, "You're not going to have me go out into town alone, are you?"

Dan sighed and let out a long, slow breath. He didn't want to leave Marcy hanging, but he didn't want to miss the chance to see Flora either. Maybe Marcy was right. Surely Flora would have called if she was well enough. What was he going to do all evening anyway? Sit in his aunt's house, watching TV?

"Okay," he said reluctantly. "I'll be over soon."

Fifteen minutes later, Dan arrived at the home where Marcy was staying, and she came trotting out like a little circus pony the minute she saw him draw up. He noted once again that she was way too overdressed for the island, and he felt a little awkward in his jeans and T-shirt. She hopped into the car, glowing. She was a pretty girl, that was for sure, but Dan had never really been attracted to her. He knew many guys from school who were, but she just wasn't his type. She was too materialistic. It made him think once again about Flora and how he missed her, especially knowing she was so close by. He couldn't wait to see her again.

He pulled out of the driveway as Marcy prattled on about the movie they were going to see.

Dan arrived at the town center and drove slowly toward the movie theater. There wasn't

any parking close by. He circled the block, not really wanting to drive to the large parking lot at the end of the street because it looked like it was going to rain, and he had only pulled on a thin leather jacket as he was leaving. One look at Marcy and he knew whatever she was wearing would not make it through streets of puddles and driving rain. Her hair alone looked like it would not survive a harsh blast of wind. It was all fluffed up.

He peered through the windshield despondently as a light rain started to fall, pattering rhythmically against the pane. He squinted through the raindrops, turning on his wipers as he scoured the street for a place to park. Suddenly, he got lucky. As he crawled alongside a line of cars parked right in front of the theater, he saw reverse lights. He stopped his car and backed up to wait.

After parking, they jumped out of the car and made a short run for it, Marcy clicking along beside him atop her high-heeled, shiny red pumps. Once inside, she hung on to Dan's arm, deliberately making her way to the front of the darkened movie theater that was pretty packed already. Dragging him by the arm, she roughhoused her way along a row so she could tuck them into a dark corner close to the wall.

Back at Flora's cottage, Annie had just finished adding Mr. Darcy's food to his elegant blue china

plate when Flora slunk into the cottage kitchen and sat down despondently at her scrubbed farmhouse table.

"What did he say?" Annie inquired.

"The phone went straight to voicemail," she answered dejectedly.

"You didn't leave a message?"

"I get tongue-tied with message machines. I was going to speak, then I thought that maybe he was in the middle of something or with . . . someone," she added, crestfallen.

Annie sat at the table too. "Maybe Karen's house is in a cell phone dead spot. You know how it is on the island. I'm sure we could get Karen's home number. You could call him that way."

"No, it's okay," said Flora. "He would have called me if he wanted to. Maybe he has plans." Her voice trailed off sadly.

"I have an idea," said Annie buoyantly. "Come on. Let's go see that movie in town. It's supposed to be really funny, and it will make the night go quicker. I'm sure you'll get to see him tomorrow when you're feeling better. Someone is with the dogs tonight, so I can drive us in. We can have our very own girl's night out."

Flora's response was half-hearted. "I don't think so. Maybe I should wait to see if he calls later."

"You can keep your phone on silent in your lap in the movie theater and watch for it to light up.

171

Better than sitting here waiting all night. It might cheer you up to get out and do something."

Flora reluctantly agreed. "Maybe you're right. I'll go and get dressed." She sighed again, unable to keep the disappointment from her voice.

"It's already ten past seven," Annie shouted up the stairs after her. "Try not to be too long, and we should make it."

Flora was back downstairs and ready in her coat by 7:22, and as Annie opened the door, there was a low, gentle rumble, and a light rain started to fall.

"You should probably take an umbrella," Annie suggested as she noticed Flora's attire: a burgundy crushed-velvet hat and Victorian lace-trimmed jacket.

Flora ducked back inside and grabbed her umbrella from her coat stand.

Annie pulled the car out of the drive and drove the short way into town. On arriving, she looked at the clock on her dashboard. It read 7:25. She was pretty sure that they would be parking at the end of the town in the big parking lot, but maybe they would get lucky. As they arrived outside the theater, Annie saw someone just pulling into the last available parking space. She drove to the end of the road and parked at the end of town.

When Flora and Annie finally got inside the movie theater, it was already packed. In the small

172

town, there wasn't much to do at night in early spring, so when a new movie came out, it was normally pretty popular.

As they walked into the movie theater, the lights were just going down, and they had to stumble around to find a seat. From nowhere, a hand came out and grabbed Flora. It was Doris. She was seated next to Ethel on the back row.

"Here," she said. "There's a couple of seats right here." She pulled them down into a pair of seats just as the coming attraction started.

The movie was very funny, and as much as Flora had not wanted to, she really enjoyed it, except there was a twinge of sadness. She wished Dan had been next to her, holding her hand. She had kept her phone on silent in her lap the whole time, but there had been no incoming calls.

The lights came on, and everybody started to move. Flora darted out into the aisle. "I'm just going to pop to the bathroom before I go."

"I'll come with you," Annie responded. They said their good-byes to Doris and Ethel, who seemed comfortable to sit and watch the credits as they finished a huge bag of popcorn.

Chapter Twenty

THE KISS OF DEATH &
AN ISLAND TYPHOON

Farther down the rows of seats, Marcy jumped to her feet and motioned to Dan. "Come on, let's go." She stepped out into the aisle and, hooking her arm into his, fluffed up her hair. He felt very uncomfortable but just wasn't sure how to deal with the situation. As they got to the top of the aisle, he heard someone call his name.

It was Doris. She was standing in the center of the aisle with her arms crossed, looking very severe. Dan was acutely embarrassed about Marcy hanging on his arm again. "Hello," he said, trying to sound buoyant.

But before he could say any more, Marcy pulled him in closer and giggled. "It's us again."

Doris looked at them coldly, saying with obvious distaste, "Yes, it is."

Marcy was all teeth and sunshine as she burbled on. "Nice to see you, but Dan and I should really be going." Then she tugged at Dan's arm, and they were swept away by the heaving throng.

As Dan and Marcy exited the theater, they both stopped short. Rain was bucketing down like a waterfall, pouring off the theater roof in a heavy

stream and bouncing up off the pavement in an angry torrent. Dan was glad he'd managed to park so close.

"Come on," he said. "Let's run for it."

"No way," Marcy said, wrinkling up her nose. "I'm not going out in that. My hair would be a mop before I even reached the car."

She looked around and pointed down the street. Under the protection of a line of awnings, light streamed out into the night from a window. Above the window, a jaunty, creatively painted sign with the words "The Wine Nook" swung back and forth in the storm.

"Let's go," she said, enthused. "We can get a glass of wine or something until the rain stops."

Dan was disinclined. "I'm really tired, and I would like to get home."

Secretly, he wanted to call Flora one more time. He really wanted to speak to her.

"Oh, come on," she said, pouting. "One drink won't kill you, and by then it should have passed."

Dan looked down at his clothes and realized that even parked so close he was still going to get soaked, so he reluctantly followed the crowd of people running under the shelter of the awning. All of them seemed to have the same idea.

Careful to avoid the puddles, they made their way toward the wine bar. Once they got inside, they saw it was packed. Marcy pushed her way

through and found a little table close to the window, overlooking the street with a view of the bay opposite. She pushed Dan down into a chair, then pulled assertively on the arm of a server who was taking an order behind them. He took their order too, then squeezed his way through the crowd back to the bar. Marcy drew up a wooden stool close to Dan and giggled.

"Now, this is more like it," she said, looking at the heaving throng. "Finally, some life on this dead-end island. Let me know if you see anyone you could introduce me to."

Dan checked his phone. He was discouraged to see that his battery was dead. He put his phone away and tried to concentrate on what Marcy was saying. She was babbling on about some school play they'd been in together.

There was a long line in the bathroom. Flora and Annie waited patiently, talking about their favorite moments in the movie.

When they eventually walked outside, the onslaught of rain was overwhelming. Annie pulled up her coat collar and opened the umbrella she had brought with her. "I'll run for it," she shouted to Flora over the deluge. "Be ready to jump in when you see my car."

"Okay," Flora shouted back, just about being heard above the sound of the cascading rain.

Annie dashed to the road and headed for the car.

Flora put up her own umbrella and decided to walk down to meet Annie halfway. Walking up to just underneath the last awning before the parking lot, she decided she could keep fairly dry underneath it.

As she waited, she noticed she was standing outside the Wine Nook, and she turned to see if she there were any familiar faces inside. The windows were pretty steamed up, the rain mixing with the hot air created by the usual busy weekend crowd. As she peered in, it seemed even more packed than usual, with hordes of people apparently taking shelter from the weather.

All at once, for a fleeting moment, she thought she saw Dan through the misted window—or maybe someone who looked just like him. Her heart skipped a beat. She stepped closer. Yes, it was definitely Dan, and he was talking to someone.

Oh, she felt overjoyed. Maybe she could just pop in and give him a hug or at least say hello quickly before Annie made it back up the busy street, maybe even invite him back to her cottage.

She turned to walk toward the door when the person Dan was talking to leaned forward and kissed him on the lips. Flora stopped and drew in her breath. Her heart felt as if it had been squeezed in an ice-cold vise. Her mind just wouldn't believe what she was seeing. Distraught, she struggled to see the girl, who was

sitting with her back to her. The girl tossed her hair back over her shoulder, and the move was unmistakable. It was Marcy.

Traumatized, Flora stood rooted to the spot, unable to move or breathe as her blood felt as if it had just run right out of her body. Suddenly, from behind her, a horn honked. Flora couldn't move. She was frozen, replaying what she had just seen over and over again in her mind. She just peered at them both through the window. Dan seemed totally serious and engaged in the conversation. The horn blasted again, and when she finally turned, she saw Annie motioning her through her windshield.

Blankly, she stepped out into the rain, not even bothering to put up her umbrella, allowing the rain to mingle with fresh tears as it soaked her to the skin. She was truly gutted, and now she understood why people said that. It actually felt as if someone had kicked her in the stomach.

So, this is heartache, she thought as she got into Annie's car. This was how it felt to have your heart broken by someone, and it was about the worst thing she'd ever experienced in her life.

She felt as if she held her breath the whole way home. She kept replaying the picture in her mind. As she did, her chest seemed to tighten and tighten until she couldn't wait to leave Annie's car and get out into the cold damp air. It was hard

to digest. She couldn't even bring herself to tell Annie about it, didn't want to admit it outside of her head, didn't want the words to leave her lips. Flora kept thinking if she didn't say it out loud, then maybe somehow it wouldn't be real. She was smashed to pieces. She felt everything she had hoped for, everything she had trusted and loved, had been taken from her in one fleeting moment, and she felt that her life would never be the same again.

Flora got out of the car, walked quietly into her cottage, closed the door, and crumpled into a heap behind it, sobbing.

Dan didn't know what to say at first. He was completely taken aback. Marcy had just kissed him, and he had no idea why.

"What are you doing?" he demanded with a mixture of anger and confusion.

"The play I was telling you about."

"What?" Dan said, not wanting to admit that he had not really been listening. It was just too hard for him to focus on her over the clamor in the bar.

"The play we were in, remember? *Seven Brides for Seven Brothers*, and you were one of the brothers."

"Yes," he said, vaguely remembering an awkward costume and dance moves he had hated. He looked at her again, intently, trying to make sense of what she was saying.

"Don't you remember, you had to kiss me at the end?"

Dan was not sure. He remembered the play, but he'd forgotten that it was Marcy he had kissed. He'd been more concerned with the tight shoes he had to wear, a whole size too small. "What about it?" he asked, none the wiser.

"Weren't you listening to me?" Marcy asked, more than a little put out.

Dan didn't know what to say.

Marcy huffed and said with much irritation, "I just said to you, 'Do you remember the kiss,' and you said, 'Yes,' and I said, 'Do you remember how awkward we both were?' and you said, 'Yes,' and I said, 'We could always try it again now that we're older. I bet that would feel better,' and you said, 'Yes,' so I kissed you."

"I didn't hear that with all the noise in here," he said, slighted. Then he added, more seriously, "Don't do that again. It could give people the wrong idea about us."

Marcy pouted and was about to respond when their drinks arrived, and someone who recognized Dan came up to say hello. Marcy came alive and started to flirt openly with her new audience.

By the time the rain stopped and he had managed to talk Marcy into leaving the wine bar, it was almost 10:45, and by the time he'd dropped her off, it was after eleven. Too late to try phoning Flora again, he thought.

Marcy had recovered from his rejection pretty well and had been her usual happy, narcissistic self. The friends Dan had introduced her to had apparently liked her. She was an island novelty; new people often were. They had buzzed around her like bees around a honeypot. They had also invited her into town for a coffee the next day.

As she got out of the car, she asked if Dan minded picking her up. He had first said no, as he wanted to get to Flora's early, and then she had whined, not letting go of the open door. She had reasoned that if he was going to town to see "that girl," then he was going to drive right past her house, and surely it wouldn't be much just to swing by and drop her off on his way. She made it sound so simple that he had reluctantly agreed, stressing that she would need to find her own way home.

He drove back to his aunt's house a little sad. He hated the fact he had been unable to see Flora. For a wild minute, he thought of turning the car around and driving to her house, then he thought of how ill she had looked earlier that day. She probably needed to sleep. He could see her in just a few hours.

Chapter Twenty-One

A VISIT FROM STEVE MCQUEEN

Annie was up early, exercising all the dogs. She'd had a wonderful fenced-in play area built just for them, and she'd nicknamed it Dog Disneyland. Filled with toys, tunnels, and tires, it was a dog's haven of fun and discovery. She took them all there to play every morning and evening, and it was the highlight of her day. She had never married or had children of her own, so these dogs were the closest thing she had to family. The fact that these bundles of fur and fun would greet her every day with such unconditional love meant the world to her.

After playtime, she sometimes liked to take the dogs for a run in her woods. It was such a lovely day that she decided to go exploring. Spring had arrived, and the higher ground on her property was now firmer and accessible. Her merry band leapt and barked around her feet as she threw the occasional stick for them and ruffled their damp, shaggy coats. With her happy group surrounding her, she made her way to the top of her property, which afforded her the best view. As she looked out across her farm, she felt the now-familiar knot return to her stomach.

Suddenly, one of the dogs spotted a wayward squirrel, and the pack careened off, bouncing and barking deeper into the forest, with Annie chasing and shouting at them to heel. She finally caught up with them, and after admonishing the ringleader, a spritely liver-and-white-spotted terrier, she sat down on a log to catch her breath. As she sat in the sunlit coppice, she noticed spring flowers were starting to raise their heads, and new green shoots were thrusting forth from the soil through carpets of soggy fallen leaves scattered on the forest floor. She had the most beautiful woodland flowers in the deepest parts of her property and decided to gather a bunch to cheer up her kitchen windowsill.

She led her tired little band back to the barn, and after closing up the last kennel, she stepped out into the morning sunlight. As she did, she took a moment to look out over the farm once again. She had so many warm memories of this place. She'd had a golden childhood, one that had seemed to go on forever. The happiest days for her had been working in the kitchen with her mother, baking banana bread and chocolate chip cookies made with fresh eggs she had gathered from the henhouse and helping her dad in the fall when many crops needed to be brought in. Back then, they had hundreds of fruit trees, and she had loved being a part of her father's work, gathering fruit side by side with him and

the people he employed to pick. The memories of her childhood were full of wonderment, and she knew losing the farm would be like losing her parents all over again. She was suddenly so grateful for the Rejected Writers' Book Club and the community she lived in. They were going to make this plan work. They had to.

She had just entered the farmhouse when she heard a car in the driveway, heralded by the chorus of dogs in the barn. She picked up Popcyc so he wouldn't run away when the door opened, and the rest of her family of five gathered in the hallway, barking and wagging their tails, ready to greet a new visitor.

Annie opened the door, regarding the young man who stood on her doorstep, and the first thought that entered her mind was a young Steve McQueen dressed in a smart, light-gray suit and blue shirt. His eyes flashed as he thrust out his hand, saying, "Annie Thompson?"

Annie took his hand and thought that maybe he had been just a little too eager with the aftershave, but it wasn't unpleasant. He didn't look local, she thought as she released his grip. There was the air of the city about him.

"Yes," said Annie cautiously.

"Beautiful day, isn't it?" he said, turning and looking out across her vast pasture.

She thought maybe he was from the church or looking for a charitable donation, but didn't those

people always come in packs? He seemed a little too friendly, as if he wanted something more from her.

"John Meyers," he said, as he spun back around to greet her. "Nice to meet you." Before he even explained who he was, he looked across the farm again, saying, "Yes, it's some place you've got here."

Annie waited patiently as he continued to take in the view. Realizing she had boarders arriving with two dogs within the hour, she asked, "Can I help you?"

"Oh, I'm sorry," he said, turning back toward her and laughing to himself as his blue eyes twinkled. "I just was so struck by this beautiful view." He slipped his hand into his pocket and pulled out a card with the polished speed of someone who had done it a hundred times before. "I'm the guy the bank sends in to talk through the details of your farm. We find it friendlier to meet the homeowners in person as we aim to work through any issues."

Issues? A lump found its way to Annie's throat. This good-looking, sweet-smelling man was the person who was going to try to take her property from her. She wanted to shut the door and run away, but instead she just swallowed hard and said, "Oh, okay. But you should know that I'm actually going to be paying back the past mortgage payments and get myself back on track.

I have a plan in place to raise the money, so there won't be much for us to talk about."

John nodded. "Of course," he said, appearing to shrug off any serious intent to his visit. "I just have to check in with you and see what help we can offer, take a look around the place, that sort of thing."

"You're here to assess it," stated Annie plainly, the penny finally dropping.

"Among other things," he responded quietly, and for the first time, he raised his intent gaze to a spot just over her right shoulder. Then he rapidly changed the subject. "I see you have dogs. I love dogs. I've got two myself. Irish wolfhounds. Lovely animals. Sure is a beautiful home for dogs here," he said once again. Then, as if he were rehearsed in getting into people's homes, added, "Can I come in?"

Annie wanted to say no, but instead she nodded and opened the door wider.

That was the signal for Annie's entourage of wagging tails to come forward to greet the young man. As they gathered at his feet, he bent down and took a minute to ruffle all their ears. They were eager to respond with happy noises, except Bruiser. He ambled toward the young man, and as John stretched forward to stroke him, he backed up and started to growl in a low, threatening way.

Annie was surprised. She admonished her dog and apologized for him. "I'm so sorry," she said.

"He's normally very friendly, but he's getting old. I guess we all get a bit crotchety as we age."

John stood swiftly to his feet, apparently not even willing to try to win Bruiser over as he followed Annie into the sitting room. He placed his briefcase on her table.

"What do you need from me?" asked Annie suspiciously.

"This is just a friendly chat," he said matter-of-factly. "I just want to talk about the house and the different things that you've done here and on the land. Maybe even get a little tour," he added, raising his eyebrows in expectation.

The last thing Annie wanted to do was give him a tour, but she remembered her manners. "Would you like something to drink?" she asked.

"I'd love a cup of coffee, two sugars, and creamer if you've got it," he said, placing out his paperwork on her table.

Annie stood up and sighed heavily as she made her way into the kitchen. He was apparently planning to settle in, and this was not going to be fun, she thought, disconcerted.

An hour later, he left, and as much as Annie had wanted to dislike him, he had won her over with his charm and apparent kindness. He listened intently to her story of the dragging recession and made all the right sympathetic noises in all the right places. He even talked about his parents having a similar experience

with their small business. Then he had practically gushed as she had shown him around the farm. They had parted ways amicably and only once had she felt a twinge of apprehension: while she had been signing paperwork that he had insisted was standard procedure. He had assured her that these papers were "just in case" they needed an agreement to find alternative arrangements to the repayment plan that Annie had said she would be putting into place.

She had sensed a change in his demeanor then, as he had whipped one document after another in front of her. Gone was all the laid-back charm. It had felt orchestrated, with carefully rehearsed statements as he gave her an overview of everything she was signing.

As she waved good-bye to her visitor from her doorway with her fur family gathered at her feet, her feelings were mixed. Even though she was glad he had been so friendly, she still couldn't seem to shake the feeling of impending doom that decided to lodge itself in the pit of her stomach.

Chapter Twenty-Two

A RED, BLOTCHY FACE &
THE RETURN OF THE ICY CLAW

Flora had been up since six, and now her thoughts were clearer than ever. She'd had a very sleepless night, and at about three o'clock, she'd made a decision. She wasn't going to let this one man destroy her. Yes, she'd loved him, but she was also not naïve. She had her own strong moral code about what was right, but she knew that not everybody was the same. Dan obviously had no problem showing attention to more than one woman at a time, but that was not how she was built. She would be polite to Dan, but at some point, she would let him know that she believed that she was worth more than that, that she was worth being the only one in someone's life. She sipped her peppermint tea by the fire. Even though her heart was shattered, her mind was clear. She wasn't going to let anyone determine her self-worth.

Her house phone started ringing, and it gave her a start. She'd been so deep in reverie, it jolted her back to the present. She walked quickly to the phone, and her hand hovered over the top of it before she picked it up. If it was Dan, she wanted

to be ready to be strong. She took a deep breath and picked up the receiver.

"Hello," she said.

"Flora."

It was Dan, and even though she'd made a decision to be strong, she couldn't help it. Her heart leapt into her throat at the sound of his voice. She locked her jaw for a second to stop from losing it and managed to squeeze out, "Yes?"

"It's me," laughed Dan. "I'm so glad to hear your voice."

The picture of him kissing Marcy swam into her thoughts yet another time, but she still managed to control herself. Her heart was beating like a drum in her ears. She didn't answer him; she just wasn't sure she believed him.

"I was hoping to come over and see you this morning," he said, unable to contain his excitement. Then, when she didn't automatically respond to that, he added softly, "If you're feeling well enough today, of course."

"I'm fine," said Flora curtly. Then her next words had an edge of bitterness, which she knew was out of character for her, but they were out of her mouth before she could stop them. "What about Marcy? Won't you be seeing her?"

On the other end of the phone, Dan paused, as if he were taken aback. The ice in her tone was having its effect. She knew she didn't sound

like herself, and he appeared to be completely stunned by her comment.

"Marcy?" he replied. "What about Marcy?"

Flora drew in breath, knowing she was committed to a path. "Won't she want to see you today?"

"I'm sure she has plans, and I want to see you," he stated imploringly.

Flora didn't know what to say. He was so brazen about it. Marcy had plans, so instead he would see her?

Before she had time to respond, Dan continued, "So, if you're feeling better, I'm going to pick you up. I thought we could take a walk on the beach. So dress warmly, and, Flora, I can't wait to see you."

Then, without another word, he hung up.

Flora was flabbergasted. He was coming to her house right now? She flew up the stairs to try to make herself presentable. She was still in her white cotton nightie, and her face was a red, blotchy mess.

She was still in the bedroom, trying to patch together her face, when she heard the bell ring. He must have jumped into his car the minute he'd put the phone down. Karen lived clear across town, and he'd made it in record time. She gave her nose one final blow and looked at herself in the mirror. This would have to do.

She walked slowly down the stairs and

unlatched her front door. He took her in his arms before she had fully opened it, and as much as she tried to resist him, it felt so good to be this close to him. His arms were powerful around her, and she was greeted by the clean scent of fresh air and his light aftershave.

After what seemed like forever, he finally released her and looked at her. She fought back tears as she looked deep into his eyes.

"So good to see you," he said.

She'd waited for this moment for over four months, and now all she could think about was Marcy.

She suddenly realized that they were still standing on the doorstep.

"Will you come in?" she said politely.

Dan seemed tickled by her sweetness and responded, "I would be delighted." They stepped inside, and she closed the door.

A moment of awkward shyness followed, where he just looked at her, and she reciprocated by looking at the ground.

"Would you like a drink?" she asked politely.

"Okay," he said enthusiastically, appearing not to care what they did.

She rushed past him into the kitchen as he took off his coat and threw it across one of her chairs. Mr. Darcy was instantly around his ankles, saying his very own feline hello.

Dan picked him up and started to whisper to him,

sweetly, "Hey there, little fellow, how are you?"

Even as hurt as she was, Flora couldn't help but feel her heart stretch toward him. She put on the kettle and prepared him coffee. Her heart ached. She wanted this to work with Dan, but if she couldn't trust him, then how could that be possible?

"I love your house, Flora," Dan shouted from the living room.

She could see him wandering around the room, looking at her photographs. Mr. Darcy sat purring in his arms as Dan tickled his ears. The kettle boiled, and she made up a tea tray and walked into the living room. When he saw her, he beamed.

"You look lovely," he said.

Flora blushed, saying, "I poured you coffee."

As she put the tray down on the table, he reached for her hand, covering it with his own. It was a tender moment that sent a shiver up her arm. He looked at her then, his gaze intent on connecting with her on a deeper level.

"I've really missed you, Flora."

She wanted to say the same. Instead she found herself asking coldly, "Would you like some cream with your coffee?"

He pulled away slightly, apparently aware of her spurning. "Yes, thank you," he said, taking his hand gently from hers and wrapping it around the mug.

They made small talk, and she could tell he was being careful, as if he were not sure of his footing. She watched him, trying to separate all the feelings that were whirring around her mind regarding how she felt about him. He finished his coffee, got up, and walked to the window.

"Fancy a walk, Flora? It's cold, but it's a lovely day."

She was relieved at the chance of a distraction and got her coat, boots, and hat.

As they exited the cottage, Dan took hold of her hand before she got a chance to object. As much as she wanted to be strong, it felt warm and comfortable to be holding it.

"Want to go to the beach?" he inquired.

She nodded. They walked toward the water. Flora's closest beach was just a five-minute walk and was one of the prettiest on the island. With a beachfront that stretched for a mile in either direction, it was awash with a multitude of stones, shells, and wayward sun-bleached branches that collected in droves upon the shore. With a 180-degree vista of the water and surrounding islands, the backdrop was a spectacular view of the snowcapped Cascade Mountains, dominated in the foreground by the majestic presence of Mount Baker.

As soon as they got to the beach, Flora realized she should have put a sweater on under her coat. It was sunny but biting cold, and the wind was

whipping around her. As they stepped on the sand, she shivered. Dan pulled her close and gently put his arms around her, and she felt herself relax into him a little.

As they looked at the calm rolling water, a heron took off into the sky. Dan's arms around her felt good. As much as she wanted to be upset with him, this felt so right. She thawed toward him a little.

Gently, he turned her chin toward him until she was inches from his face. She could feel his breath on her cheek, his eyes searching hers. Then, in a moment, his lips were upon hers. They were dry from the wind but warm. He gently held her face in his hands, and the back of his fingers brushed gently down across her cheek. They then moved to stroke her hair, tenderly. She had been so surprised by his kiss that she hadn't closed her eyes, and now she was drinking in every inch of his face, from his soft, black lashes to his wavy black hair as it ruffled gently across his forehead in the breeze.

She closed her eyes and felt herself giving in to his kiss, and his urgent need to be close to her became apparent. Pulling her body deeper into his, his hands continued to caress her hair and then her back. And though it was demanding, his kiss continued to be soft, gentle, and loving.

But all she could think about was Marcy.

Finally he pulled away, and she was breathless.

"I've wanted to do that since I saw you yesterday. It is so good to be here with you, Flora."

Flora couldn't help herself; all her ideas of being strong were melting away. She felt tears sting her eyes with her wave of mixed emotions.

"I've missed you too," she finally said.

Maybe she had imagined it yesterday. Maybe he hadn't kissed Marcy at all. Maybe what she had seen had been distorted by the rain. Surely someone couldn't kiss her like that while having feelings for another woman. Maybe she should give Dan a chance to explain what had happened the day before, she thought to herself.

She was just about to ask him about it when his cell phone started ringing. At first he didn't answer it, but it just continued to buzz until it became obvious he felt resentful that it was holding them hostage. He reached into his pocket and took the call.

Flora drew in breath as Dan said, "Hello, Marcy." Then Flora watched as he stiffened. He released Flora and turned toward the sea, gazing out at the view as he said, "I completely forgot."

Flora could tell he was going to say something else, but she could also hear Marcy talking ten to the dozen on the line, although she couldn't make out what she was saying.

Dan interrupted Marcy, saying, "It's not really convenient right—"

Then she must have cut him off. He responded with, "Yes, I know that, but—" Apparently not listening, Marcy spoke over him again.

Dan reached out to play with Flora's hair as a concerned look clouded his face.

"Hold on," he said into the phone.

He laid the phone against his chest and looked at Flora.

"Would you mind if I went and picked up Marcy?"

Flora was so horrified that she couldn't speak. Dan appeared to take her silence as a yes and continued, "She's meeting people for coffee at the Coffee Spot, and I forgot she'd asked me to give her a lift into town. Now she's stuck out at her uncle's farmhouse, and they've all gone out for the morning."

Flora felt the icy claw from the night before take hold of her heart once more. She stared at Dan for a long, hard moment, then shrugged her shoulders dismissively, saying, "I need to get back anyway."

Dan looked desperate. "No, please, you have to come with me. It will only take us twenty minutes. I don't want to ruin our time together. Please say you'll come, Flora."

Flora was distraught. Her mind was a blur, though she knew clearly that the last person in the world she wanted to see was Marcy. Before Flora could say anything in response, she heard

Marcy's voice on the end of the phone asking if he was still there.

Dan put the phone to his ear, saying, "Okay, okay, we'll be over in about ten minutes." Then he hung up and reached out to Flora. "I'm so sorry," he said. "She doesn't really know anyone but me. I forgot her family was over on the mainland, and she can't pick up a car until after the holidays. I forgot I told her I would do this for her today."

He pulled Flora in for a hug, but the moment had passed, and now it felt awkward. Already Flora's thoughts had moved back to the kiss she'd seen the night before.

Chapter Twenty-Three

FROZEN HUSBANDS & FLYERS OF FANCY

I trotted downstairs to make myself a cup of tea and noticed Stacy was already up. She wasn't drinking anything with caffeine and was treating coffee like a poison from hell. Just the smell of it made her gag. So poor Martin had to brew and drink his coffee in his garden shed. As I reached the kitchen, he stepped back in from outside, sending a blast of frigid air throughout the house. His stiff, ice-cold body shuffled through the door, wearing his dark-blue bathrobe and brown leather slippers. Folded under his arm, in frigid sheets, was the morning paper, and clutched in a frozen, white clawlike hand was his empty coffee cup. He looked positively blue.

Fortunately, my drink of choice, tea, was less ominous to Stacy, so I turned on the kettle. As I looked out the window, I noted it was still dark. Now, once again, I questioned my decision to direct this show. The auditions were the next day, and I had never felt less qualified. Martin handed me an advertisement he had circled in the newspaper. It read:

Do you want to be in a show? Doris Newberry could use YOU. The Rejected Writers' Book Club is organizing a fundraiser for a friend in need: a musical extravaganza produced, written, and directed by talented local writers. We heartily welcome you. Here is our criterion:

No late arrivals.
No loiterers.
No time wasters.
No kids.
No food or drink.
No bad singers.
No bad dancers.
No bad actors.
Come on down. It will be fun.

I threw the paper down on the kitchen table. I knew that Doris had also made flyers and put them up all over town. I was guessing they would be just as "inviting." Maybe I was worrying for no reason. God knows who was going to be brave enough to turn up.

Stacy sat at the kitchen table, tossed her toast down on the plate, and complained that she needed different bread. Once again, for the hundredth time since she'd arrived, she complained about how backward the island was

and how she could get anything she wanted where she lived in San Francisco, including hot French bread straight from the oven right down the street.

She was feeling extra grumpy this morning because she had received a call from her husband, Chris, the night before. He said that though his mother was much better, he had to go on one last overseas business trip in order to be able to take some time off to help her in the last month of her pregnancy.

I tried to distract myself from biting back by asking her about her job. That was the wrong thing to ask though, because Stacy then went into an emotional rampage about how she didn't like her replacement and wasn't even sure she would have a job to go back to once the babies were born. But the company had encouraged her to take some time off and start her maternity leave early, as her job in advertising could be so demanding.

"That seems reasonable," Martin said, folding the newspaper he'd been finishing over his breakfast. "You do work very hard."

"I know," Stacy said, irritated. "Everyone is right, but I just don't know if I want to do this with my time. I hate sitting around at home. I need to be busy."

"I'm sure you can find something of interest to do with your time off," I added.

I finished my breakfast and cleared away the dishes while Stacy waddled to the sofa and sat down, sighing. She picked up a fashion magazine and started flicking through it.

I sat down too. I knew I needed to start thinking about the show I was directing. I pulled out the script and started making notes about the edits I would need to do to make it less like *The Wizard of Oz*. Stacy glanced over and noticed me working.

"What are you reading?" she inquired.

I told her the whole story, and she balked.

"You're directing a show? How would you know how to do that?"

"It's for a good cause," I said, a little irritated at my daughter's lack of confidence in me. Even though my thoughts were along the same lines, I wasn't going to let her see that. "It's for Annie," I continued, "and she has no one but us to help her, so I'll figure it out somehow."

Stacy sniffed her disapproval and went back to the magazine she was reading. I could tell she was thinking about something. She turned a couple of pages, then threw the magazine down on the table. I could sense she was about to announce something profound.

"I could help," she said.

"What?" I asked, unfamiliar with these particular words coming from my daughter's lips. At the table, Martin seemed to choke on his toast.

"Direct. I could help direct. I did a lot in college. I'm good at directing."

"I wouldn't want to bother you," I said.

"It would be no bother. I could just stay a little longer now that Chris is going to be gone, and help you get started. At least help you through the auditions. I know what to look for and how to get people to audition so you can get the best out of them."

I had mixed feelings. I loved the idea of a chance to work with my daughter on something, but up to now, I had never managed to find anything that we didn't end up fighting about. On the other hand, Stacy was a hard worker, but working with people really wasn't her strength.

"I think I could manage. You have the babies to think about."

Stacy raised her eyebrows. "Manage an audition? Let me tell you something. Half the work of getting a good show going is in the casting. You cast it right, and the job's a dream. Cast it wrong, and you create an utter unholy nightmare for yourself."

I started to feel apprehensive. I hadn't really thought that much about the casting. I just planned to see who turned up and make the people fit. If there was more than one person interested in a particular role, I'd planned to maybe toss a coin.

It was as if Stacy read my mind. "You can't

203

just cast the first person that walks in and wants the part. There's a lot to consider, not only their willingness, but also their ability to play the part, who they are, and if they fit with the other actors on the stage. Also, if they're believable in that role, whether they have what it takes to pull it off."

I started to have a minor panic attack. I hadn't thought about any of these things, and I thought, for a minute, that maybe having Stacy by my side for the auditions wasn't such a bad thing after all.

Chapter Twenty-Four

CONFESSIONS OVER FROTHY COFFEE

Flora was alone with her thoughts as they drove in silence to pick up Marcy. She tried to excuse herself one more time, but Dan had looked so crestfallen at her attempts to go home that, in the end, reluctantly, she'd agreed to go.

They reached Marcy's house, and she came bounding out. Flora felt instantly underdressed. Marcy was decked out as if she were on her way to a swanky New York restaurant, not to have coffee with a bunch of locals. Marcy's hair was gathered in two sparkly clips, pinned up on both sides, and her abundance of curls shone in the sun as she bounded toward the car.

Marcy saw Flora sitting in the front seat and looked perturbed. Flora looked over at Dan to see if he caught it, but he was too busy parking the car to notice Marcy's expression. Ignoring Flora, Marcy marched all the way around to the other side of the car to the driver's window and rapped on the glass.

Dan looked shocked as she loomed large, and he rolled down the window. A cloud of frozen air crept in as Marcy spoke. "Dan," she shrieked as

if they were long-lost friends, "so glad you could come. This coffee place sounds so intriguing. I can't wait to get to know your friends."

It was obvious to Flora that he didn't know how to respond. He just said, "Marcy, you remember Flora, of course."

Marcy pretended she didn't hear him. Instead, she jumped into the backseat behind him. "Such a lovely day," she said, staring out the window. "All crisp and winterish."

Dan repeated himself as he started to pull away. "Marcy, you remember Flora, don't you?"

"Of course," said Marcy, rubbing her highly glossed lips together and looking out the window. "I remember the girl in the oxygen mask."

Flora didn't know how to respond, and by the look on his face, neither did Dan. Not that it mattered, as Marcy knew how to suck up all the air and make it her own. She talked about how cold the weather was and how she hadn't known what to wear and her excitement about the fact they were going out today. In fact, Flora was pretty sure she didn't draw breath the whole way into town.

As Marcy continued to speak, Flora felt herself becoming smaller and smaller by the second. All she wanted to do was go home. She certainly didn't feel sophisticated at all. In fact, she felt like a country bumpkin next to this girl. Dan looked over at her at one point, and the apology

was obvious in his eyes. They pulled up outside the coffee shop.

"Here you are, Marcy," he said, sounding like he wanted her to get out.

Marcy looked at him in the rearview mirror, then blinked a couple of times. "Surely you're not expecting me to go in that strange coffee shop all alone, are you?" she whined like a four-year-old.

Flora couldn't believe this girl's gall. *Miss Overconfident, could steal your boyfriend before breakfast but can't walk into anywhere alone?*

"It's just a coffee shop. How strange can it be?" said Dan flatly.

Flora felt annoyed. "People go in there all the time alone," she said, feeling the need to defend her community. "We're a very kind and accepting town."

Marcy answered her coldly, avoiding Flora's gaze and instead looking intently at Dan. "Well, locals, I'm sure, have no problem doing that," she said offhandedly. The way that she spat out the word "locals" made Flora bristle, something that didn't appear to go unnoticed by Dan as Marcy continued. "But I'm not a local, am I? I can't just walk into some odd coffee bar like that. Please, Dan," she implored, "could you just walk me in so I'm not alone?" She swished her hair back over her shoulder, and Flora got a whiff of what smelled like Chanel perfume.

Before either of them could answer her, Marcy was out of the car and waiting by the door. Dan looked over at Flora, who was trying not to lose her cool. This girl was really working it, she could tell.

Dan rolled down the window and started to protest, but Marcy cut him short. "Oh, come on, Dan," she said, hopping from foot to foot. "It's cold out here, and it will just be for a minute."

He sighed, then looked at Flora, gave a shrug, and climbed out of the car.

Marcy finally looked at Flora for the first time, saying bluntly, "You can just wait here in the car. We shouldn't be too long."

That was all it took. Flora had the door open and was out before Marcy could finish her sentence.

"I'd like to come," said Flora, firmly, "and see if there's anyone there I know."

But before Flora could protest, Marcy linked arms with Dan and pulled him toward the coffee shop, leaving Flora to drag behind.

Inside the Coffee Spot, it was warm and cozy. It was a small cabin-type building that had started out as a family home but over the years had been converted to various shops due to its close proximity to town. It had once been a toy shop, then a pharmacy for many years, and for a short time, a gift shop. Then, about three years ago, someone had broached the idea that the

town needed a coffee shop, a modern one that created drinks out of espresso and steamed milk and flavoring and served them alongside slabs of lemon or gingerbread cake. So the Coffee Spot was born. Painted in cheerful colors of burnished reds and mellow yellows, the main wall contained a bookshelf of well-worn books, and the other walls were adorned with posters of modern art. It had a warm wood fire and a lively clientele of mainly students.

Marcy bound in on Dan's arm and looked around expectantly. The people she was meeting did not appear to be there yet, and her disappointment showed. Flora couldn't help thinking that Marcy's plan might have been to give the impression to her new friends that she and Dan were intimate. Flora thought of the kiss again, and her stomach knotted. How could Dan not be interested in someone so glamorous and poised?

"Okay," Dan said, taking action and detangling himself from Marcy. "You're in now, so have fun."

Marcy looked at him sharply. "Sorry?" she said. "You're going to leave me here on my own with all these stranger people?"

Flora looked around the room. Most of them were a gathering of the local community she knew by sight. Some had jobs in the town as shopkeepers or at the local plant center. There

were also some students from the local college, and other visitors here for spring break. Most she only knew by sight, but dressed in colorful woolens and blue jeans, these were not the kind of people one would describe as "strange."

Dan responded firmly, "I want to spend more time with Flora. I didn't get to spend any real time with her yet, and if you remember, that's why I came this weekend. I think you're going to be fine until your friends get here."

Marcy pouted, but Flora's heart soared. It was the first time he admitted why he was here— and to Marcy! She suddenly started to see a glimmer of hope. Surely if he were also dating Marcy, he wouldn't have been so dismissive toward her.

Flora felt more and more embarrassed that she'd suspected anything from that kiss, if it had been a kiss at all. Now she was pretty sure it was all in her imagination. After all, it had been raining. With this new generosity of spirit and the fact the coffee shop was so warm and cozy, Flora found herself saying, "We could stay for just one cup of coffee, if you'd like, Dan, until Marcy's friends get here."

Dan looked at Flora, bewildered. "Are you sure?"

Flora nodded, taking off her coat and placing it on the back of her chair at a nearby table.

"There," said Marcy, her tone betraying that

she wasn't totally happy with the fact that Flora was staying too.

Dan shrugged and asked them what they'd like to drink. Marcy ordered a complicated coffee drink that took Dan a couple of tries to remember, and Flora ordered a peppermint tea. Dan left for the counter.

Marcy arranged herself in the best chair, obviously wanting to look her most stunning and have a good view of the door of the coffee shop. She straightened her blouse, adjusted a cream silk scarf that lay in folds around her neck, and tightened her hair clips. Eventually, she cast an ungracious gaze over Flora as she continued to peel off her layers.

"How long have you lived in this town?" she asked, only appearing mildly interested as she looked over Flora's shoulder.

"Most of my life," answered Flora. She was beginning to think that Marcy was the one who was instigating everything with Dan, and she was ready to deal with whatever that meant.

"I'm thinking of moving here," Marcy said without much conviction.

"Really," said Flora with distaste. "Why?"

Marcy looked surprised at Flora's directness. So was Flora, but she was suddenly feeling bolder.

"Danny's talking about maybe doing that, and I have some family here. I thought with Danny

being here, and the fact that I could come and stay with them, it might be interesting for a while."

Flora shook off the familiarity of "Danny" and allowed this new piece of information to sink in. Dan had been thinking about moving to Southlea Bay? He hadn't mentioned that to her. Maybe he hadn't wanted to get her hopes up. But the thought of having him right here with her made her heart soar.

"What would you do here?" she asked.

Marcy started to inspect her beautifully manicured pink nails. "I'm not sure yet. I usually find something to keep me busy. I saw an advertisement for a show coming up. Danny and I used to act in shows together all the time in high school."

"I know about the play in town," answered Flora. "I'm considering playing the lead in it." Flora cringed inwardly. Why had she said that? She didn't want to compete, but she knew it would score points.

Marcy actually looked a little impressed, but then the shutters came down, and she quickly continued, "Yes, I suppose there's not a large pool of talent to choose from here."

Flora could feel the red creeping up slowly from her neck to her cheeks. She looked over at Dan. He was still in line.

"I'm auditioning tomorrow," added Marcy.

"Good," said Flora. "I'll be there."

"Good," responded Marcy. They faced off as Marcy added, "There's obviously not much else to do here."

"There's a lot to do here," Flora said defensively. "There's the art gallery and restaurants and the movie theater."

"Yes," said Marcy, then she paused and seemed to enjoy this next statement. "Danny and I were at the theater yesterday and also the local wine bar."

Flora wished she could confront Marcy. She wanted to say, "I saw you. I saw you in the window kissing my boyfriend. Yes, *my* boyfriend. What do you think you were doing, kissing him like that?" But Flora didn't feel brave enough to say those words, so instead she just said, "I know. I saw you there."

Instantly, it appeared Marcy seemed to know what Flora was thinking, and she looked amused, so she continued. "The Nook is a great place. Lots of nice people and a great atmosphere. Danny and I really enjoyed it."

"You seemed to," said Flora, pushing again. She wanted Marcy to acknowledge it.

Marcy responded, "We have known each other a long time. We feel very comfortable with each other," she added, adjusting her skirt.

Flora felt something rise up inside her and totter just under the surface of her feelings, something

akin to rage. She heard herself speak, and it wasn't quiet, and it wasn't weak. It was forceful and challenging, and she couldn't believe herself.

"When I looked in the window, you were very close. In fact, you appeared to be kissing him."

There, it was out on the table, the elephant, the huge matzo ball, and the weight hanging in the air between them.

Marcy laughed a gentle laugh. "Of course," she said. Then, seeming to relish this next statement intently, she stated, "That wasn't the first time we've kissed, you know."

Flora opened her mouth to respond, but she couldn't say anything. Her mouth just flapped about like a distressed seagull.

Dan arrived at the table, juggling their drinks. "Here we are," he said merrily, placing the cups on the table. He noted Flora's discomfort. "I hope Marcy's been behaving herself."

"Of course," said Marcy, answering for Flora, who just continued to sit there with her mouth open. "Flora and I were just getting to know each other. We know where we stand, don't we, Flora?"

Dan looked nervous. He responded defensively by taking Flora's hand. She felt the warmth of it pressed against hers and noted her own felt like a block of ice. He appeared to be about to ask her if she was okay when the people Marcy had been waiting for came in, and Marcy leapt to her

feet. The moment was lost in the flurry of all the introductions.

Flora looked at the group that had pulled up chairs and stools to join them. She knew some of them by sight, but that was all. The island attracted two types of people: the bohemian artist set and the very rich. The artistic community was attracted to the beauty and peacefulness of the island to create their art year-round. They lived on a shoestring budget and did myriad part-time jobs just to survive. The other set arrived during summer vacation, and they spent their days fishing out on their yachts on Puget Sound to provide for their extensive cookouts on the beach in front of grand waterfront holiday homes. Flora knew a lot more of the first group than the second. This group was very obviously city folk who liked to play summer islander.

A dashing young man who had introduced himself as Jeremy thrust a hand into Flora's and then Dan's. Once it was established that Dan worked with cars, Jeremy slid into an easy conversation along those lines about his new sports car and then on to his latest handheld gadget.

Marcy fit in perfectly, whereas Flora didn't actually follow a lot of what they were saying. She found it hard to be up on all the latest trends. It was like they were speaking a different language. She just quietly sipped her tea, trying

to digest the words Marcy had said that were now echoing over and over in her mind. "That wasn't the first time we've kissed, you know." Flora was sure that's what she had said—so brazen, so self-assured, it just must be true. And now Flora knew for sure that what she'd seen had been real, and it was like she'd been kicked in the gut all over again. In fact, it was actually giving her a real stomachache.

Dan looked at her with concern. He continued to make small talk with Marcy's friends but constantly looked Flora's way as if he were trying to read her. He sipped quickly at his hot coffee, making the right conversational noises at the right times, but even Dan seemed unable to keep up with the group after a while as they chatted on about their electronic toys.

Flora watched Marcy with envy as she dominated the conversation, and the three guys that had joined them didn't seem to mind that at all. Marcy was a novelty, she decided, something shiny, a new thing to add to their collection. What was making her angry was the way that she kept referring to Dan and herself as "we."

Dan finished his coffee quickly and said, "Flora, are you ready?"

Flora had hardly touched her drink and had just sat there in silence while the group had talked around her. Flora nodded absently, and

Dan grabbed Flora's coat and helped her into it before she even realized what was happening.

Marcy stopped talking and started to protest. "You're not leaving already, are you, Danny?" she said, pouting again. "We've only just got here."

Dan didn't take the bait. He hurriedly said his good-byes. Flora just turned and was already heading for the door. She hadn't even bothered with good-byes. She noticed that the group, full of its own importance, hadn't even noticed.

It appeared that Marcy was not going to miss her chance, though. She jumped to her feet and threw her arms around Dan before he reached the door. "Good-bye, Danny!" she said and hugged and kissed him dramatically on the cheek.

As she opened the door, Flora turned just in time to see the display, and her stomach added another knot to the tension that was already there. She walked quickly to the car, breathing deeply. Her head was swimming. She really did not want to pass out again.

Dan wasn't far behind her. He was at her car door before she got there and opened it quickly. Flora jumped inside and breathed a sigh of relief, so glad to finally be away from Marcy.

Dan jumped into the driver side, saying quickly, "I'm so sorry about that, Flora. This is absolutely the last way I wanted to spend our first day together."

Flora nodded. She couldn't manage words, not yet. All she wanted to do was go home.

He started the car, saying, "Where would you like to go now?"

Flora found her voice. "I'm not feeling so well. I would actually like to go home."

Dan looked concerned and dispirited. "You seemed quiet earlier, but I didn't realize you were still feeling ill."

They drove back to Flora's house in silence. She needed to get away, needed to be alone, needed time to process all this. She felt as if she were suffocating next to him and didn't want to hear anything else today that would make her heart hurt. "That wasn't the first time we've kissed," was all she could hear over and over again in her thoughts.

As they reached her house, Dan asked her if there was anything he could do.

"No," Flora said as she pulled open the door forcefully. "But maybe you want to wipe that lipstick mark off your face." Flora's face was flushed as she leaned back in the car and handed him a Kleenex from her bag.

Dan looked in the mirror. There was indeed a large pink lipstick mark on his cheek where Marcy had kissed him. He scrubbed at it furiously.

"Flora," he said desperately. "What can I do to make this right?"

"Stop kissing other girls in bars," was what she wanted to say, but instead she said, "Nothing. I'm fine." And she slammed the car door.

But she was far from fine, and she knew by the expression on his face that he could tell. She hastened to her door, and Dan shut off the engine and followed her, still rubbing at his cheek.

She opened her front door and walked quickly in before he had a chance to follow. Her emotions had switched from hurt to livid, and she didn't want him to see her angry.

"I'm going to lie down," she shouted over her shoulder as Dan hovered at her gate. The last thing she saw were those beautiful green eyes flash with sadness as she closed her front door practically in his face.

"I'll call you later," he shouted after her.

But she was already inside.

Chapter Twenty-Five

CRAZY TWIRLERS & FUNERAL SINGERS

I had decided to bring Stacy with me that morning, and we arrived at the theater for the audition. Doris was already there. By her side, Ethel was holding a stack of clipboards. The heat was on in the theater, and it was positively balmy.

"Wow!" I said. "What time were you here to get it so warm?"

"I got here thirty minutes ago," Doris said. "James apparently came here at eight a.m. to warm the place up. Very nice of him."

James appeared from the office with a cup of coffee in his hand. "Hello," he said in his lighthearted, breezy way. "How are we all doing today? All ready for the big push?"

He made it sound like we were going into battle, and it didn't feel far from the truth.

"Anyone for coffee?" he inquired, lifting his cup and waving it under our noses.

"No, thank you," I said as Stacy scowled, and her face paled.

"Where's the bathroom?" she growled in one long, disgruntled monotone. I pointed in the right direction, and Stacy dashed away.

Annie sat at a table in the foyer, encouraging people to fill out forms Doris had typed up for the potential cast. She looked pretty flustered. I could see why. The foyer was already full of a slew of people, apparently of the artistic persuasion. They were all milling around in an array of jaunty outfits. The whole span of our island's population was represented in that one room, from serious contenders wearing expensive tight spandex, full bodysuits, and shiny dance shoes to happy hippies in organic cotton T-shirts and vegetable-dyed llama-wool hats. One man was wearing a whole clown costume and was juggling Beanie Babies. A large woman was wearing a huge flowery hat and singing scales in a booming voice. Along one wall was a whole gaggle of girls from a local dance school. They stood in professional-looking lines, kicking up their legs and stretching.

I asked Annie how it was going. She pulled me in close and answered in a hushed tone, "I've been raising dogs most of my life, and I can't believe what a din this lot can make."

I noted that it was pretty loud as James came out and gave Annie another cup of coffee. He seemed to be enjoying the hubbub.

"Marvelous, isn't it?" he said. "I love that you're beginning to fill the place with life again."

Annie nodded hesitantly.

I moved into the main theater. Doris had placed

herself in the middle of the auditorium, with her clipboard and its attached light placed on her lap. She motioned to me. "Here's our criteria," she said, handing me a board. "I have added to my original list so we can get the perfect cast. We don't want to drop our standards now, do we?"

I looked down a long list of things Doris had written. She had extended it from the flyer, adding more attributes that she deemed unacceptable. It included:

Flat feet
Too quiet
Too loud
Too happy
Not happy enough
Swearing
Drinking
Drugs

Just looking at the now-long list, I was thinking of hitting the last three myself. I wondered if this list counted for directors too.

Just as I finished wondering where I could get hard drugs, the Labette twins arrived with Dan hooked on Lavinia's arm and Gracie on Lottie's. The twins looked very avant-garde in black pantsuits, silk blouses, and chic little black French berets. Lavinia did an impression of Marlene Dietrich.

"We thought we would go all Hitchcock on you, as we hadn't a snowball in hell's chance of knowing what to wear for an audition." Then she pulled Dan forward. "Look who we found loitering over at the coffee shop. Thought we might bring him along to keep us all company."

Dan smiled half-heartedly, as he appeared to urgently search the auditorium for Flora.

Gracie, who had apparently had a sleepover at the twins' house, was already kitted out head to foot in a full-blown fairy costume. She waved her wand above us all and said in a mystical voice, "I'm ready to be the fairy, and I'm using all my secret fairy powers to make you all pick me for the role."

"Very nice," Doris said, looking up briefly from her clipboard. "But there are no fairies in this script, only a good and a bad witch."

"Oh dear," said Gracie, pondering for a minute. Then she started waving her wand again, saying, "I'm using my magic powers to have you put a fairy into the story."

It was as she was sprinkling fairy dust from a little pouch held around her neck that Stacy finally returned from the bathroom, sat down hard next to me, and scowled.

I sighed. I had a feeling this was going to be a long day.

Flora arrived, looking flustered. She froze when she saw Dan, and his face lit up.

"Hi, Flora," he said carefully. "I called you, but it just rang."

We all looked over at Flora, who was squirming around in her skin as if she had fleas in her pants. This is interesting, I thought. It looked like a lovers' tiff. The whole group sensed it, and there was a polite hush as we watched with interest this dramatic moment play out.

Flora spoke in an icy whisper. "Yes, thank you."

The cold shoulder, I thought to myself.

But Dan wasn't giving up that easy. He moved toward her as if to hug her. I cringed inwardly. This can only end badly. Even Ethel seemed riveted. As Dan leaned in to embrace Flora, she jumped back, saying, "What do you need me to do, Doris?"

Dan stepped back, surprised.

Doris looked from Dan to Flora with a hard stare before saying, "In a minute you'll be singing. Did you forget?"

She has forgotten, I thought, watching the color drain from her cheeks.

Dan moved closer to her again. "I can't wait to hear you," he said gently, then added, "You never told me you could sing, Flora."

Flora nodded absently and became intently interested in staring at the footwear she had chosen that day. What followed was a very long, awkward silence before I tapped gently on the frost with an ice pick.

"Dan, I was wondering, as Flora will be preparing for her audition, would you mind helping backstage, organizing the people coming on?"

"I could do that," he said quietly.

Doris stared at him over the top of a pair of half-moon glasses she had perched on her nose. "You can tell people when to come onstage. Make sure they're ready and not goofing off."

"Okay," Dan said reluctantly, and he slouched up the little stairs to wait backstage.

Annie arrived. "The first ten people are ready," she said breathlessly. "I have them lined up in the hallway, like you asked me to."

"Great," Doris said. "Fetch them around to the backstage and have them check in with Dan."

As the odd carnival of talent paraded to the back of the stage, Doris leaned across to us all and commented, "We are looking for main cast. But we are also looking for the chorus. They need to be able to sing, dance, and look good, so keep your eyes peeled for some talent."

Slumped down low in her seat, Stacy noticed the group as they exited backstage and muttered, "Good luck," in a sarcastic tone.

Doris stared at Stacy. "What, exactly, is that tone supposed to mean, young lady?"

"Well, come on," said Stacy. "Be realistic. This is a small town. You'll be lucky if you get more than three people who can sing in tune."

225

Doris was about to answer her when Dan walked onstage saying, "Your first person is ready."

"Okay, great!" I shouted back, cutting off the pair of them before they locked horns.

A spunky blonde, no bigger than a jackrabbit, with swishy braids and a huge boom box in her hand, bounded onstage. "Hi, my name is Tanya," she called out, as upbeat and perky as a kindergartener on her first day of school. As she spoke, she seemed unable to keep her body still. She twitched and bounced from foot to foot.

Doris shouted back at her, "What are you going to do for us, Tanya?"

Tanya giggled as she continued to gallop on the spot. "I would like to sing," she said. She was more spritely than anyone should be this early in the morning, I thought to myself.

"I'm going to sing 'Defying Gravity' from *Wicked*," she added, clapping her hands excitedly.

"Oh no," Stacy said by my side. "That used to be one of my favorite musicals. I see it's going to be butchered today."

Fortunately, Tanya, who was busy fiddling with her boom box, didn't appear to hear her.

A karaoke-type version of a musical number burst out of her machine and filled the auditorium with an impressive canned orchestra.

Tanya came alive and started to sing at the top of her lungs. I sat with my pen poised over the

clipboard of a thousand reasons to say no and listened. She's wasn't too bad, I thought. After all, this was a community event.

Tanya continued through the melody of the song until there was a key change in the music, and she seemed to be oblivious to it. In response, she clashed painfully with the melody as the music went in a completely different direction. She seemed to realize something was wrong and started to screech at the top of her voice to compensate.

"Oh God," Stacy balked beside me. "I hope they're not all going to be this bad." For once I actually agreed with her. Somewhere outside, dogs were howling for sure.

"Thank you," Doris shouted, abruptly stopping Tanya halfway through a very painful crescendo that was climbing to a place that threatened to make our ears bleed.

Tanya, taken by surprise, stopped singing but quickly returned to her bright, breezy self. "I dance too," she said, enthusiastically.

Doris looked at her doubtfully.

Tanya continued, "I've been practicing all morning." Then, sensing we needed more convincing, added, "I would love to show you."

I could tell Doris was about to give her the don't-call-us-we'll-call-you speech, when I got ahead of her. "We'd love to see you dance. Please go ahead and do something for us."

"Great!" said Tanya, appearing jubilant to get her chance. "Hold on a minute." She held a cute little finger in the air. "First I need to go and get my prop."

As Tanya exited the stage, the whole production team glared at me.

Stacy was the first to find the words they all appeared to be thinking. "Mom, what are you doing? She's awful. Why are you even considering her?"

"Because," I said, defensively, "the girl has spunk. I like her upbeat, go-get-'em personality. It would be good to have that kind of positive energy in the cast."

Lavinia looked over at me. "We had a pig that could squeal that bad when we were growing up in Texas, and it couldn't wait for us to slaughter it and put it out of its misery. I think we should be kind and do the same."

As I looked around the group for support, I noted Ethel was etching a huge red X next to Tanya's name on her clipboard.

Ruby came clattering down the aisle, late as usual. She seemed to be wearing some bohemian affair and had doubled up on her usual amount of baubles and bracelets and was jangling like a gypsy.

"Sorry I'm late," she said, flicking back over her shoulder a lavender-and-green paisley scarf that was wound tightly around her head, flowing

down her back to the floor. "Have the auditions started?" she inquired. "Or have we started torturing people as a fund-raiser? Annie wasn't sure when I met her in the foyer."

"We are the ones being tortured," Doris snapped. "What were you thinking, Janet? She was awful. And she seemed to need to go to the bathroom through the whole thing, with all that jigging around."

"I know," I said to her, "but maybe we could put her somewhere in the back and ask her to sing quietly? She just has such a radiant presence."

Doris shrugged, and my daughter shook her head disapprovingly next to me. I wasn't sure if she was disapproving of my choice or just me in general.

Tanya was back on the stage. In her hand was a baton.

"I don't really see myself as a dancer, per se," she stated, her tiny fingers pantomiming air quotes as she giggled at her own joke, "but I'm a baton twirler, and I like to do all sorts of dance steps while I'm twirling."

She then galloped over to her boom box, pressed a button again, and lively band music filled the space. Tanya started marching and smiling.

"God help us," said Stacy. "I gave up a morning in bed for this."

"You didn't have to," I said. I'd wanted to say

229

that all morning, but I regretted it the minute it was out of my mouth.

Stacy looked crestfallen. That lasted for a second, and then she proceeded to anger. "If you didn't want me here, you could have said," she hissed back.

Tanya was still marching as the song "When the Saints Go Marching In" bounced around the space. She started to twirl the baton in front of her.

I backtracked. "You know what I mean, darling. You could've stayed in bed. You're still getting some morning sickness. Some people do get it this late in pregnancy."

"What? Just stay home and let you figure out how to cast this show? What skills do you have to do that?"

Before I could answer, I was distracted as Tanya yelled out a dancer's cheer and threw the baton high into the air, kicking up both her legs as she shot out her arm to catch the baton. But it didn't come down. We all looked up.

"Oh my, that can't be good," Lottie remarked.

Ruby narrowed her eyes, adding, "Interesting."

Even Stacy was momentarily distracted. Gracie leapt to her feet and started waving her magic wand at the ceiling as Doris just shook her head. We all continued to look, our attention riveted toward the flies, waiting to see when it would come down. But it didn't. Tanya, with her eyes

cast heavenward, carried on dancing. Her smile had slipped a little, and she left her arm still stretched out in front of her to catch the baton, as if some magical thing or person was going to drop it into her hand. Now this was compelling; the baton was upstaging the entertainer.

From high above, Dan's voice drifted down. He'd obviously seen what had happened from the side of the stage and had taken the stairs up into the rigging. "I've got it!" he shouted. "Hold on. It's caught in some ropes."

Tanya continued to dance. Her smile had melted into a grimace on her face. It was if someone had told her, "Don't stop; even if there's no baton to twirl, just keep smiling and kicking."

Dan shouted, "Okay."

Then the baton came down, and Tanya caught it expertly and carried on twirling it as if nothing had happened.

"Resourceful," I wrote on my clipboard. Tanya continued to march in with the saints, even though it was obvious she was thrown by the experience. She attempted the twirl-it-under-your-leg trick, and instead of the baton spinning in a neat circle, it clipped her knee and bounced off into the wings, from where someone shouted, "Oww!"

The whole production team waited, riveted. This was some show. Watching Tanya perform was like watching a slow car wreck in action.

231

Tanya continued twirling her hand as if the baton were still in it. Dan came running out on the stage.

"We're okay," Dan said breathlessly. It was obvious he had just gotten back from running down the stairs as he continued, "The third person on your list will have to go next so that the clown can steady himself before he performs."

"He's not the only clown that needs to steady himself," Lottie said under her breath.

Dan handed Tanya back her baton just as the music was crescendoing, and Tanya continued as if all of this were just part of her act. She threw it high into the air one last time for a big finish and looked tentatively up to make sure it was coming back down. When it arrived neatly in the hand behind her back, she beamed and then threw her arms into the air in a triumphant Olympic gymnast–style finish.

There was an awkward silence, so I started clapping frantically. Everyone followed along reluctantly. Tanya was ecstatic. She took the applause as a sign she was accepted and gave the group a thumbs-up as she ran offstage, saying, "I can't wait to be in a real show."

I could sense everyone glaring at me. Doris was the first to vocalize her feelings. "That girl is more trouble than a two-year-old in a china cabinet. Are you sure you want to take on that mess of trouble?"

"Yes," I said decisively. "She has a great attitude and a lovely smile. And I promise I won't put her in charge of the props or anything breakable."

Before Doris could continue to voice her disapproval, the next person was making their way onstage. It was a scruffy-looking woman wearing a beige raincoat and carrying what appeared to be a big brown plastic shopping bag. She was the complete opposite of Tanya. She looked positively depressed. She walked to the center of the stage, put down her bag, and blew her nose loudly on a Kleenex.

We all just stared at her, and she just glared back. I decided to break the ice. Maybe she was just really nervous. "Hi," I said. "I'm Janet, and you are . . . ?"

She blinked twice and said, "I am what?"

"Your name," said Doris, curtly.

"My name?" She paused, as if she were about to make one up. Then she said, "My name is June Horton." She nodded her head, as if she were sure that was her name.

"What are you going to do for us, June?" Doris asked, obviously starting to lose her patience.

"What do you mean?" said June, matching Doris's pitch of annoyance.

"Sing!" shouted Stacy from my side. "Doris is asking you what song you're going to sing."

"Sing?" She recoiled, appearing disgusted with

the mere thought. "Well, I don't really sing," she mused to herself.

"Do you dance?" I asked, trying to encourage her.

"Dance?" she said, screwing her face into a ball. "No, I don't dance, not unless someone is shooting at me."

Stacy turned to me and raised her eyebrows.

Doris was apparently done with going around in circles. "Just sing 'Happy Birthday,' then, so we can hear you."

June placed a hand to her brow to shade her eyes from the blaring stage lights and looked down at us intently. "Is it someone's birthday?" she asked.

"Crazy lady," Stacy said in a singsong voice under her breath.

"No. It's not, but we have to hear you sing if you want to do this," I stated gently.

"Oh," she said with a look of incredulity. Then she shrugged her shoulders, saying, "Okay."

She coughed twice, took a deep breath, then started a dirge of "Happy Birthday," which started out quiet and low, somewhere in the vicinity of her boots, and just got worse as she got louder. It was very slow and excruciatingly painful, a wounded animal begging to be put out of its misery. She had obviously missed her vocation as chief wailer following coffins in funeral processions.

When she finished she just stood there, blinking, and we were all speechless. I saw Doris suck in breath and knew whatever was about to come back out wasn't going to be good. So I quickly said, "Well, that was an interesting version of that song."

But Doris's comment was on top of mine. She appeared to not want to be saddled with any more of the people I couldn't help but feel sorry for. "It was awful," she blasted.

"I thought so too," said June. "I told you I don't sing."

"So why are you auditioning?" Stacy asked what everyone was thinking.

"I'm not auditioning," she scoffed. "I'm here to see if I can help out backstage or with the costumes or something."

I breathed a huge sigh of relief. "Great!" I said. "Yes, we need lots of help. Sorry, there was no need for you to come out on the stage at all. You could've just filled out a form and left your name."

June nodded. "I must admit, I did think it was a little strange, but I have never worked with artsy-fartsy people before, so I didn't know what to expect. I saw your poster in the florist's window, and I love making costumes for Halloween and thought I might be able to lend a hand."

"Absolutely," I said. "We're so grateful for any help we can get."

June mumbled back, "Is that it, then?"

"Yes, that's it," said Stacy impatiently.

June nodded her head, bent down, picked up her shopping bag, and shuffled off the stage.

Doris turned to Ethel. "Go and tell Annie to make sure she only sends performers back here to the audition."

Ethel nodded and left to do her bidding.

I started to snicker, saying, "Well, anyone is going to look better compared to that."

Lottie nodded her head, adding, "I'm just glad I'm not celebrating my birthday during the run. I don't think I could have gone through that twice."

Chapter Twenty-Six

JESSICA RABBIT & A BATTERED TOP HAT

We were all laughing heartily when Marcy walked onstage. She was glowing. A perfect goddess. Her blonde hair was coiffed into a shiny bob, and she wore a figure-hugging leotard, footless tights, and a large patent leather belt cinched at her waist. She tottered onto the stage on four-inch leopard-skin pumps.

Doris noticed them right away and announced, "She'll never perform in those. She'll break her neck."

Marcy continued to swagger like Jessica Rabbit to the middle of the stage, then carefully placed her iPad and speakers on a stool that she'd demanded Dan bring on the stage for her. Flora, who was seated a row in front of me, visibly tensed up. We continued to watch Marcy as she swaggered off the stage one more time and made her way back on with a music stand, which she took time putting up in her own sweet way. She seemed completely oblivious to the fact that she was keeping everybody waiting. Doris shouted up to her on the stage, "Are you ready, young lady?"

Marcy was having none of it. She held up a perfectly manicured finger at Doris, as if she were asking her to wait one minute, then she sauntered off the stage one more time, brought onstage a music book, and placed it carefully on the stand. Then she took her time finding the right page.

I could tell Doris was starting to boil. "Really," she said. "This is too much."

But Marcy just tottered off again and returned with a water bottle and a large designer bag in her hand and placed them carefully on the stool next to her. She finally looked up and appeared to be ready. She was totally unruffled.

"Hello," she said, her tone sweeter than apple pie. "My name is Marcy, and I would like to sing"—she paused for effect, reached into her bag, and pulled out a cowboy hat, setting it gently over her silken blonde hair—"a country western oldie for you all today."

Stacy slumped down in her chair again, saying, "God help us."

Then, from her bag, Marcy pulled out a shiny stack of photographs. "But first, I would like to give you my headshot."

Doris dismissed her. "We don't need that here. You can give that to Annie in the foyer when you leave."

Marcy did not look happy, stating, "If you're talking about the knitting woman with the tight

perm wearing a nylon leisure suit outside, she didn't seem to know a lot about talent or show business for that matter."

Now my daughter's dander was up. The one person she had a soft spot for was Annie. She sat upright in her chair and snapped back, "I'm sorry. The auditions for the Broadway show are down the road."

Marcy ignored the comment and walked off the stage one more time, and a minute later, Dan hurried down the stage steps with Marcy's photo stack in his hand. He gave them out to us, saying, "These are from her ladyship."

We all peeled off a copy and had no choice but to sit there with an eight-by-twelve black-and-white gleaming Marcy on each of our laps.

Marcy stepped back out of the wings and took a leisurely sip from her water bottle. Once Dan returned up the stairs, she coaxed him to join her with a head motion. Dan didn't respond, so she extended a long, pink fingernail toward him and beckoned to him again. Flushed, he came back on. It was obvious to us he was not at all happy playing Marcy's lap dog. Even sitting a row behind Flora, I could sense her discomfort.

"Are you going to sing something anytime in our future?" shouted Doris.

"Prima donna," sang Stacy in the chair next to me.

I liked to think I have the patience of Job, but

even I was starting to get a bit irritated. I added my own voice, "You really need to move on, Marcy. We have a lot of people to see today."

Marcy seemed unmoved by our discomfort. This was her moment, and she appeared to be milking it. She whispered something to Dan and then giggled, throwing back her head in an exaggerated fashion, causing her blonde bob to bounce around her head like a shiny, golden slinky. Dan nodded, though his expression registered annoyance as Marcy took center stage and motioned to him again.

He pressed a button on her iPod. It erupted into life with the introduction of Tammy Wynette's song, "Stand by Your Man."

As the music started, Marcy entered a different world. She locked eyes intently with our group and started singing fervently, "Sometimes it's hard to be a woman." Then, with dramatic intent, she turned her full attention toward Dan, who was still on the stage, waiting for what appeared to be his next cue. Staring straight at him, she barely whispered her next line, "Giving all your love to just one man." As she continued to perform at him, it became obvious this display was as much for his benefit as ours. The stage was hers, and it was clear she intended to savor every moment.

Stacy leaned toward me. "She's totally flirting with Dan. I thought he and Flora were dating?"

"They are," I responded. Stacy looked aghast.

Doris leaned toward me from the other side, saying, "She's not half bad."

"Hussy," snapped Ethel, the pitch and fervent delivery of her comment causing the rest of the group to nod in agreement.

Marcy hit perfect high notes with, "But if you love him, you'll forgive him. Even though he's hard to understand." She moved from her stool toward Dan, singing, "And if you love him and are proud of him." Then, placing a hand on his shoulder, she threw back her head and sang out with passion, " 'Cause after all, he's just a man."

Stacy turned to me again, her mouth open.

"How does Flora feel about that vixen in leopard skin?"

Before I could answer, someone hurried past us up the aisle, a flash of layered clothes and long hair. It was Flora. I nodded toward her, saying, "Like that."

Onstage, Marcy continued as she belted out the chorus, "Stand by your man." By the time she'd finished the song, no one appeared to know what to say. There was no way around the fact that she had an amazing voice, but I wondered if anyone wanted to deal with all that came with it.

Apparently, Doris did. As soon as Marcy finished, she jumped to her feet, shouting, "Bravo. Welcome to our show." The rest of the group just looked at Doris, but Marcy just nodded as if she'd expected it and strode catlike back to

her stool. She then took away her props, peeling them offstage in the same slow, deliberate manner she had added them. Instead of picking up her stool, she nodded at Dan, apparently expecting him to carry it offstage for her. Dan did it, but even from my seat in the auditorium, I could tell he wasn't happy about it at all.

The rest of the morning, the auditions continued, and they were pretty predictable. The Beanie Baby–juggling clown wasn't half bad. He managed to limp onto the stage and perform, even though he was obviously recovering from his encounter with the crazy twirler. The woman in the flowery hat sang opera to shatter glass but was as blind as a bat and nearly fell off the front of the stage. We decided to give her a chorus part, way in the back. Other people auditioned—some who could sing but couldn't dance, others who could dance but couldn't sing. I watched, taking notes and reminding myself and Stacy, who was getting more and more heated beside me, that this was all just a community event. After all, we were helping Annie, not putting on a West End hit.

At about one p.m., we took a lunch break. James had a treat waiting for us in the foyer. He'd asked the Crab to put together some salads and cold meat trays. Once the group finished the morning's audition, it was a welcome sight to all of us as we walked into the foyer to see him and Annie laying out the food.

"What's all this?" Doris asked, appearing suspicious as she arrived in the foyer beside me.

"James ordered food for us all," Annie said.

"I thought you might be hungry," he commented, piling up napkins on the plate.

We gathered around the table, and Flora finally joined us. She still seemed shaken, but she had put on a cheerful air, obviously not wanting to talk about it.

"There's a few people who wanted to come back after lunch," said Annie, joining us at the table. "And there was this one girl. She auditioned this morning. She wanted to do a dance audition this afternoon. She said she didn't have the right clothes and needed to get the right music."

"Marcy," we all said together. Our attention settled uncomfortably on Flora, who visibly squirmed.

"She was great," Doris added clumsily. "You also need to audition this afternoon, Flora. We could put you on right after Marcy."

You could have heard a pin drop. Everyone at the table seemed aware of what that would mean to Flora, except Doris.

I jumped to her defense. "Is that really necessary? After all, it's Flora. We know she's reliable, and I don't think we need to have her audition, do we?"

"Nonsense," responded Doris. "We don't want

it to look like there's favoritism. I'm sure you'll be just fine, Flora."

James placed a large apple pie in the center of the table for our dessert. We all offered our thanks. He dismissed it with a wave of his hand, saying, "It's the least I can do. I'm so happy to see the old place up and running again." He was just starting to launch into a story about the last time it had been used when the main doors opened and a bright shaft of sunlight cut across our conversation.

I turned to see who it was, but with the light streaming in from the outside, all that was visible to me was the outline of a man. As the door closed behind him, my eyes started to adjust, and as the man swaggered over to the table, I recognized him instantly. It was Ernie.

I couldn't believe it; he was a welcome sight! We had met Ernie on our road trip, at a jazz band dance in Medford, and he had not only been able to cut a rug but had also given the infamous Doris Newberry a run for her money on the dance floor, calling her "his little chili pepper." We had all liked him so much that we had even invited him to have breakfast with us the day before we left Oregon.

As he made his way toward us, I took in what he was wearing: a battered top hat, a set of tails that appeared to be a couple sizes too small for him, and a pair of spats. In his hand was a silver-

tipped cane. I rushed forward to greet him with a hug.

After we all had greeted him, he approached the table with a happy expression and surveyed the spread of food before him.

"I see I'm just in time for pie," he announced, showing all of his pearly white teeth and two of his gold ones. "I have an uncanny knack of knowing when someone's about to serve it up. It's my superpower."

I was intrigued about his appearance. "Ernie, how wonderful to see you again—and looking so dapper. Please join us and tell us what you're doing so dressed up."

Ernie found a seat next to Doris. She looked Ernie up and down, taking in his odd appearance. "Where did you spring from? The 1920s?"

Ernie flashed Doris another cheeky grin and grabbed her hand. "My day wouldn't be complete without a word or two from my own little chili pepper."

Doris appeared to balk at the word "own" and instantly pulled her hand away from his. He seemed oblivious to her brush-off, as all of his attention was focused on the pie in the center of the table.

"Are you going somewhere special?" inquired Annie, knitting a row of stitches.

"I'm taking myself to a very special event," he said with enthusiasm. "I'm going to audition

for a show that serves pie to the people who turn up."

James was jubilant. "Let me get you some coffee to go with that pie."

"Now you're talking," Ernie responded as James went off to organize the coffee.

Doris just continued to stare at him. "You're here to audition for our show?" she asked.

"Absolutely," he answered with conviction.

"How did you find out about it?" she continued.

"Oh, a little bird told me all about it," he said mysteriously.

Annie giggled, adding, "Ernie and I are pen pals."

"But you don't even live here," snapped Doris.

"Not yet," he said contentiously. "But this looks like a mighty fine town. Who knows what might happen? I'm retired and can afford to stick around for a month or two if I want."

Doris raised an eyebrow. "So, why are you dressed up like a dog's dinner?"

"Because," he said with emphasis, "this is my costume for the turn I'm going to perform."

"You brought this costume on a vacation?" I required incredulously.

"Absolutely," he said assertively. "You never know when you might need to sing for your supper. You should see the rest of what's in my suitcase."

Doris did not look impressed. Neither did

246

Stacy, who had just returned from the bathroom.

"And you're going to perform what, some sort of a magic trick?" Flora asked hopefully, her eyes twinkling.

"No," he said. "I'm going to sing and dance. This is my costume for the soft-shoe shuffle I'll be performing."

"Wonderful," said Flora, but by her tone and expression, it appeared she had no idea what that meant.

Stacy groaned under her breath.

"A soft-shoe shuffle," said Dan, upbeat. "Sounds great."

James arrived back at the table with a knife and a hot coffeepot. Doris sliced and handed out the pie to everyone, including Ernie, who beamed, saying, "Now, this is my kind of audition."

Twenty minutes later, the table was cleared away, and the audition team was all back in the theater for the afternoon session. Before we got started, Doris gave us some final instructions.

"We're looking for some good voices for our leads. We seem to have a lot of ensemble people, but right now only Marcy would work as a lead, so let's see if we can find someone this afternoon."

From the wings strode Ernie, wearing his hat and spats. As he entered, he took on a whole new persona, transporting us back to an era gone by. He strutted forward with his cane under one arm

and his top hat in the other. Doris tutted and Ethel echoed it.

He got himself into position in the center of the stage and hit a dramatic pose, then started singing "Mr. Bojangles" a capella. He had a surprisingly rich, deep, resonant voice that reached out to us, embracing the whole space. He had great command of the stage, and it apparently wasn't his first time performing. Even Stacy sat up and seemed impressed. He continued to sing and then went into a soft-shoe shuffle with some really fancy footwork. He was in a different world. He continued to sing and dance, ending on a crescendo that could have brought down crystal chandeliers.

We couldn't help ourselves, breaking into warm applause at the end of it. He broke into a broad grin when he heard it and took his time to complete a long, low bow. Then, as he straightened up, he added, quick as a whip, "So, where do I pick up my check?"

Chapter Twenty-Seven

GIRLY SHOWS & FLORA THE BOLD

Flora was in the bathroom, splashing water on her face as she listened to the sound of Ernie singing from the stage. It was pretty impressive, she thought. She knew she was going to have to sing too. With Dan's arrival and everything that was going on with Marcy, she'd kind of put it in the back of her mind.

But now there was no getting away from it. She was going to get up on that stage. She knew she didn't need to do it if she really didn't want to, but after Marcy's display that morning, she had felt something rise up inside her. Something she was starting to get used to, boldness and fearlessness, spurred on by her painful mixed feelings for Dan. As she looked at her dripping face in the mirror, she decided something. She was not going to sit by and let her boyfriend be seduced by another woman. He had tried to talk to her all day, and she hated herself for not being able to tell him how she felt. She was in pain all the time, so she decided that after the audition she was going to confront him, no matter what. After all, he was her boyfriend.

She stopped washing her face for a moment and looked at herself again in the mirror, realizing that was the first time she'd really thought of Dan as her boyfriend. Yes, she'd toyed with the idea of it since they'd met, even said the words out loud to Mr. Darcy, but now it was a real, taken-for-granted thought in her head. It gave her strength. She was going on that stage to show the world and the likes of Marcy Campbell that she was not afraid anymore. She dried her face, walked out of the bathroom, and practically ran into Marcy as she did.

On seeing Flora, she did not look impressed. "Oh, it's you, Florence," she said with indignation.

"Flora," she responded, swallowing. "My name is Flora." She said it with less conviction than she would have liked, but still, she was proud of herself.

Marcy flicked her eyes at her as if she were saying *whatever* and pushed past her into the bathroom, saying offhandedly, "Excuse me. I have to get ready for the dance audition."

Flora felt that new feeling of boldness. The old Flora would have slunk out into the foyer, nodding her head and cowering. But this new Flora, the one fighting for her boyfriend, found her voice, saying, "Yes. I'm getting ready for my audition too."

Marcy stopped dead in her tracks, a bemused

look on her face. "You're really auditioning, then?" she asked, saying it with such a lack of belief, it was as if she were asking Flora if she was going on a trip to Mars. Then she added with contempt, "For what?"

Flora felt the anger rise up into her chest. "The role that you want!" she said with conviction and exited the bathroom, leaving Marcy openmouthed and staring at the closed door as she went.

Flora got into the foyer and blinked. Had she said that out loud? Had she just stood up to Marcy? It felt good.

Ernie was just leaving the stage when Flora entered the auditorium. He glided into the wings with surprising agility for his age and build. Flora watched from the back and smiled. Then she saw the group taking notes on their clipboards. Annie had joined them, as only a couple of people had decided to audition in the afternoon, and she was knitting something pink, probably for Stacy's baby. It made Flora smile. Annie was a sweet soul. As she watched Annie's rhythmic clicking of her needles, she reminded herself that this was why she was doing all this—to help Annie keep her farm. After Flora's parents passed away a few years ago, the Rejected Writers' Book Club was the closest thing she had to a family.

Taking a deep breath, she marched down the aisle and then backstage to where Dan was

standing, watching. He looked almost boyish from behind, his head cocked to one side as he looked down at a clipboard Doris had handed to him. Flora thought once again how lucky she was to have him. He had just jumped in to help them with the audition, and she was pretty sure this was his first taste of show business. After all, he was a mechanic. She loved his easygoing, helpful self-confidence. Her heart softened. She wanted to reach out and give him a chance to explain what was going on. She walked up behind him and slipped her arms around his waist.

For a second he jumped back and, seeing it was Flora, relaxed, taking a deep breath. Then he took her by the arms and pulled her in close to him as he whispered into her hair, "Thank goodness it was you. For a second I thought it was . . . someone else."

Flora knew he meant Marcy, even though he didn't say her name. Then she realized he had just taken away any last doubt she had about him. Surely if his body could react like that just because he thought Marcy was hugging him, it was pretty obvious that he really didn't care for her.

Flora nodded at him, and with her newfound boldness, she walked assertively onstage. As she got into the center, she looked out into the auditorium. It was hard to see anything; the stage lights were so bright. She felt a wave of panic

come over her, but she willed herself to stay rooted to the spot.

Doris's voice floated up to her. "What are you going to sing, Flora?"

Flora stopped and thought for a minute. It had completely slipped her mind that she should have prepared something. She looked to side stage nervously, and she could see Dan encouraging her. She looked out into the lights again, but her tongue appeared to be stuck to the roof of her mouth. She suddenly felt very small. Then, as she started to panic, she heard something. It was the sound of Annie's knitting needles clicking a little melody of its own, and it comforted her and reminded her again why she was there.

She suddenly remembered that in third grade, she had learned the music from *The Wizard of Oz*, and she was pretty sure she could still remember all the words to "Somewhere over the Rainbow." Couldn't she? She moved nervously from foot to foot. Her silence was deafening her.

Another voice came out of the darkness. It was Marcy's.

"I could go next if she isn't up for it," she said. "I have my dance routine ready to go."

That was all the encouragement that Flora needed. She opened her mouth and let out the sound. It started raspy and quiet at first; then as she became braver, she started to sing "Somewhere over the Rainbow" with gusto. She

253

was surprised by her own voice. She knew she was singing, but somehow it didn't sound like her. She kept going, all the time her voice and confidence becoming stronger with each line. This was actually fun. She threw back her head as she continued to hit the top notes and hear them soar as the sound of her voice filled the stage. She came to the last line and finished on a high crescendo and took a huge breath in.

Nothing moved or stirred in the theater for a second. Even Annie's needles appeared to have stopped clicking together. For a split second, Flora thought it was so bad that they didn't know how to respond. Suddenly, she could hear clapping, slowly at first, then louder. And from the side of the stage Dan shouted, "Bravo!" She smiled and felt tears of relief prick her eyes.

She started to walk off the stage when Ernie met her halfway and extended a hand to her, saying, "You better take your bow, young lady— you were a mighty fine performer—and then allow me to escort you off."

Flora bobbed her head toward the audience and then, taking his arm, she was more than happy to leave the stage. Had she done it? It felt good. Oh, yes it did. Flora had sung, and apparently she wasn't half bad.

As she entered the wings, Dan embraced her, and Marcy, standing there for her dance audition, was boiling over with what appeared to be

jealousy. "Very nice," she spat out, though her tone did not match the sentiment.

Flora floated down into the auditorium where the rest of the girls sat. Doris nodded at her with a look that seemed to hint at a newfound respect, and Annie grabbed her arm.

"Very good, Flora," she said with a giggle. Then quietly under her breath, "You are sure going to give that Marcy girl a run for her money."

Flora smiled, and for the first time since Marcy had appeared in town, she felt her confidence rise.

Marcy didn't let Flora bask for long. She was already on the stage, standing in the middle, tapping her foot when the group looked up. Her expression demonstrated that she was more than a little put out.

"I'm ready to perform my dance audition now," she said in a demanding tone, obviously trying hard to pull any attention from Flora, who was now settling herself down in the audience.

"Oh goody," mocked Stacy sarcastically. "We'd hate to miss it."

The rest of the group sniggered. Not waiting for any further encouragement, Marcy placed her iPod and speakers on the same stool, and not even waiting for Dan this time, she pressed the "Play" button. The music exploded into life and filled the theater with the cabaret number "Hey, Big Spender."

Marcy embodied the sensual tone of the music, slinking around the stage so provocatively it even made Annie stop knitting as she watched, aghast. At one point, Marcy pulled a full-length pink feather boa from the same bag that had made an appearance that morning. She minced off into the wings, and when she came back to center stage, she had it around Ernie's neck as she pulled him back out. He looked like a more than willing victim. He chuckled as he matched her movement and tried his best to dance as she cooed, "Hey big spender, spend a little time with me."

"Well, I never," Lottie said, her pen in midair. She looked down at the clipboard and murmured, "I don't think I have a box to check for that."

Once Marcy finished, all that could be heard was silence. Even Doris's admiration appeared to be waning.

Finally Doris spoke. "Thank you, Marcy, for that"—she appeared to be fighting for the right words to frame what we'd just seen, then settled on one—"routine. We're going to talk it over, and we'll let you know which part suits you."

Marcy just picked up her iPod and clicked off into the wings, leaving Ernie still onstage with her boa draped around his neck.

He looked out into the audience and said, "I think I'm going to enjoy being in your girly show." Then Marcy stomped back on, pulled her boa from his neck, and disappeared.

At the end of the day, Lavinia talked her sister into auditioning for the witches' roles, and she pulled her onstage, where they performed a very comical version of the song "Sisters."

At the end, Lottie giggled uncontrollably, saying, "Momma used to make us perform that for our relatives every Christmas. I always thought it might come in handy one day."

After the audition, Dan approached Flora gingerly and asked if he could walk her home. She nodded, and they slipped out into the crisp afternoon together. They walked through the town in silence. When they arrived at her door, Mr. Darcy was at once at their feet. Flora picked him up and went inside. She hugged her cat defensively. She felt tired, tired because she hadn't slept much with all the excitement of the audition, but also tired of not knowing where she stood with Dan. Maybe she'd just have it out with him once and for all.

Dan stood awkwardly in the middle of the room. She knew he probably sensed that Flora didn't want him any closer as she stared blankly out the window.

"Are you going to tell me what's going on?" he asked, the concern apparent in his tone.

It's now or never, she thought. At least she would know one way or the other, and she could move on, move past this. She turned to Dan and

looked at him. Telling him was going to be harder than she thought.

"I went out the other night . . ." Her voice cracked a little, but she pushed on. Dan looked at her, bewildered. She continued, with more conviction, "I went out to the movie theater."

Dan looked surprised. "I wish I'd known," he said. "I was at the movie theater the other night too!"

She interrupted him. "Yes, I know."

Dan seemed taken aback by her response. "You saw me?" he asked.

"Yes." But she couldn't say any more. The words just caught in her throat.

Dan looked confused. "If you saw me, why didn't you say hello?"

"I didn't actually see you at the movie. I saw you afterward, when you were at the Nook with . . ." She couldn't bring herself to say Marcy's name.

Dan filled in the blanks. "Marcy," he stated. "If you saw me, why didn't you come in and have a drink with me?"

Flora turned away from him. This was going to be easier to say if she wasn't looking at him as she said it.

"Because when I saw you, you and Marcy were . . ." She still couldn't say it. Her voice cracked again as she nervously petted Mr. Darcy furiously.

But Dan knew instantly.

"You saw her kiss me, didn't you?" he said, his face now flushed. All at once, he was across the room, and he spun her around to look into her face.

Her lower lip trembled, and she fought back tears. She looked deeply into his green eyes, eyes that seemed so full of concern but also relief.

"Flora," he said with conviction, "that was nothing."

Flora's eyes flashed, and she looked out the window again, unable to keep the bitterness from her tone. "It didn't look like nothing."

Dan turned her chin gently back to find his gaze, then watched her intently.

"I love you," he said with real emotion. She felt the breath catch in her throat as he continued. "Do you not know that?"

The tears now flowed freely down her cheeks. She had wanted to hear this, wanted to believe him, but she still wasn't sure if she could trust him. She needed to know.

"If you love me, why were you kissing her?" She tried to sound angry, but she was losing steam. Dan pulled her toward him slowly and held her tightly. Mr. Darcy purred contentedly between them.

Dan whispered gently into her ear, "I wasn't kissing her. She kissed me. She took me by surprise. She was talking about a play we were in

together, and the next thing I knew she was kissing me. I have no real understanding why, because to be honest with you, I wasn't listening to her. Flora, you need to know I have no feelings for Marcy, other than as a friend. She means nothing to me. You, however, mean the world to me."

She was sobbing quietly now into his shoulder. This was what she'd wanted to hear. As he said it, she felt her whole body relax into his. It was like a large weight had been lifted from her. He held her close for a minute and stroked her hair.

"All I've thought about since I got here was spending time with you, and Marcy has just been so demanding."

Pulling away and looking around the room for a Kleenex, Flora continued to sob dispiritedly. "So why did you bring her, then?" She sniffed as she dropped Mr. Darcy onto his favorite cushion and blew hard into a tissue.

"I didn't really have much choice. She's considering moving up here, she told me, though I have no idea why. This seems like the last place in the world that would be a good fit for her to live. She thrives in the excitement of the city."

"Have you considered that she might just be here because of you?" Flora asked bluntly.

Dan appeared to consider her words. "What would I have to do with her decision?"

Then it appeared to suddenly hit him. "You think she's interested in me?" It was as if he

hadn't considered this possibility before now. He said it almost more as a question to himself than to her.

Flora nodded her head.

Dan started to laugh. "That's crazy. She's my friend's little sister, and besides that, even if that was the case, it's ridiculous and futile because the reality is, I'm already head over heels in love with someone else."

He pulled Flora into his arms again and, without hesitation, kissed her long and passionately, pulling her even closer to him. She wanted to ask him more, but she melted in response to his touch, his urgency mingled with her own.

Breathlessly, she finally pulled away, and they laughed together tenderly. He locked his arms around her waist, and her stomach rumbled. She laughed nervously. "I'm so glad that's cleared up because, as you can hear, I am starving."

"Let's go and get something to eat?" he asked. "My treat."

"I would love that."

After they had eaten at the Crab, they went out for a long walk on the beach. As they stared out at the water, Flora suddenly remembered something.

"Dan, what was the surprise you talked about? I've been hoping it wasn't Marcy."

Dan shook his head. "I can't believe I forgot to tell you this. Now, I don't want you to get

too excited because nothing is finalized yet, but it looks like I might be able to be up here in Southlea Bay for a few months."

"What?" shrieked Flora. "How come?"

"My boss has a friend who works just over on the mainland, and he needs some help right now with a car they've both been restoring. My boss has been trying to get up here to help for a while, but things have kept him busy in Medford. So, knowing you and my Aunt Karen were just a ferry's trip away from the mainland, he asked me if I might want to work up here for a few months to get the car up and running. Now, it's not permanent or anything—he wants me back in Medford once the classic is restored—but at least it would mean we could see each other every day for the next eight weeks or so."

Flora was ecstatic. She threw her arms around his neck and hugged him tightly. Suddenly, thoughts of Marcy were far away. "I would love that," she finally said, and her whole body felt as if it were glowing inside.

They spent the rest of the day enjoying themselves, chatting arm in arm, chasing each other along the sand, and giggling until it hurt. It was as if the sea air had blown all Flora's doubts about Dan away. He joked about her being on a singing reality show, and she blushed, saying she was just glad she had made it through the audition.

Later, they drove for miles, stopping at another town north of the island where a local theater was performing Oscar Wilde's *The Importance of Being Ernest*. They sat together, laughing in their own little world of intimacy. He stroked her hand and whispered lovingly to her all evening.

He drove her home then, and they held one another and kissed for hours until their kisses became more urgent, more needy.

Dan finally pulled away from her at around midnight, saying, "I have to go," and reluctantly she had agreed. They kissed one last, lingering time on the doorstep, and then he went into the night, leaving a huge void in Flora's world.

Her once happy, cozy cottage seemed empty without him filling the space. She walked aimlessly around, gathering their cups and tidying the sofa. She picked up a pillow that was still warm from his body and smelled slightly of his aftershave. She held it close to her cheek and then closed her eyes, pretending it was still him. She went to bed, taking the pillow with her.

Chapter Twenty-Eight

THE PREYING MANTIS STRIKES BACK

Dan drove back to his aunt's house, glowing, overjoyed to have spent the whole day with Flora. When his cell phone rang as he pulled into the driveway, he just knew it would be her. He smiled as he answered it.

"Hello, darling, are you missing me as much as I'm missing you?"

The person on the other end paused a beat before saying, "Danny, what a nice thing to say."

Dan realized soberly that it wasn't Flora at the other end and looked tentatively at the number on his phone. Marcy. He could have kicked himself. It was so late, he had just assumed it would be Flora. The last thing he needed to do was to encourage Marcy in case Flora had been right.

"I thought you were Flora," he said flatly, unable to keep the ice from his tone.

Marcy laughed seductively. "Don't pretend you didn't know it was me," she said confidently.

Dan stepped out of the car and paced in circles in the driveway to keep warm. The harsh chill that had been gathering in the night air was starting to settle into a hard freeze at his feet.

"What do you want?" he asked.

Marcy took a moment to answer, apparently enjoying the whole experience. "I just thought that since I'm sure I will be given a part in that little community show, I've decided to stay on this island for a while. I've nothing happening with my job at the moment, and the show opens soon. I'll go home after that."

Dan blew out a cloud of icy breath. "Why would you want to do that?" He suddenly felt very protective toward Flora and their relationship. He would have to leave in a couple of days to go back to Medford to finish things up there, and he just didn't trust Marcy as far as he could throw her. Boy, would he like to throw her right now, right off the Southlea Bay cliffs. The thought of it made him smile again.

She continued to purr. "You know, I've always loved the stage, and this seems like an interesting town." She said the word "interesting" with no conviction at all. "Then because you might be coming up again soon, we'd have more time to be with each other."

Dan stopped pacing and hung his head low. How was he going to get through to her? He didn't want to hurt her feelings. If he was honest with himself, a side of him was actually flattered by the attention. But he knew he would need to handle this carefully. This was his friend's sister, so he didn't want to be cruel, but he didn't

want to have to deal with this anymore either.

He took on a more serious tone. "Marcy, I'm very flattered that you want to spend time with me, but you've always just been a friend, and I sense you're looking for more. And I'm just not interested in that."

Marcy jumped in defensively. "You've never really given us a chance to get to know each other. I can be very sweet if you took the time to find out."

Dan shook his head; the cold air was starting to freeze his face and ears.

He tried again. "Marcy, you should know I'm in love with Flora. She's the only person I'm attracted to, and she's the only person I want to get to know better right now."

Dan kicked at a patch of ground that had already hardened to glistening ice.

Marcy didn't respond, so he continued, "I have only ever seen us as friends."

Marcy suddenly burst into tears on the other end of the phone and took Dan completely by surprise. He wasn't even sure how to respond.

Between sobs, Marcy gulped for air and spluttered out, "Are you telling me, Danny Cohen, that I'm not attractive, that I'm not the sort of person a man like you could be attracted to?"

Dan stared hopelessly at the phone in his hand. This call was not going remotely in a direction

that he wanted it to go. He was also starting to be chilled to the bone being outside, but he knew he would just have to trudge through this call to the bitter end while he slowly froze to death because there was no signal in the house. He glanced up and noted his aunt's bedroom light was already out, so he walked toward the end of the drive, as far away from the house as he could get. Marcy was starting to bawl, and he wasn't sure how far the sound would carry.

"No, no," he hissed into the phone, "I didn't say that, Marcy."

She stopped short, as if she had just turned off a hose and sniffed. "Do you find me attractive, Danny?"

He paused, weighing his words carefully. He didn't want to dig himself in any deeper or commit himself to anything, but it was hard. It was cold, and he just wanted this call to end.

He stomped from foot to foot in the driveway and responded slowly. "You're an attractive woman. And I think any man would be very fortunate to have you in his life. But—"

He never finished his thought, as Marcy interrupted him. "Oh, Dan," she said, her tone back to sunshine and rainbows. Her next words rolled off her tongue like honey. "You were just toying with me before. I knew you cared."

Dan stopped pacing, trying to figure out what was worse: happy Marcy or crying Marcy. It was

so damn cold out here. He decided the quickest route to end the call was not to get in any deeper either way.

"Of course I care," he said. "Our families have been friends for years. Now, I don't want to talk about this anymore. It's late, and we both need to go to bed."

Marcy giggled, then said seductively, "Is that an offer?"

Dan walked directly to the house. "No," he said, firmly but gently. "You know what I mean. Now, I need to go. Good night."

"Good night, Danny," she said, her tone still thicker than molasses. Then she added seductively, "Sweet dreams."

Chapter Twenty-Nine

SLUDGE SLICES &
THE MERLIN OF OOZE

The following day we met at Doris's for one of her Rejected Writers' Book Club meetings and to cast the show. Stacy came along with me. As we made our way into the sitting room, escorted by the ever-happy Ethel, I saw that the group was already assembled in the front room, circled around on the usual odd assortment of chairs. Each of them sat with a cup of tea and a plate of cake. I noticed right away that every eye was down upon the cake.

"Oh, good, Janet," Doris said as I walked in. "I have that updated script for you to edit."

Oh goody, I thought as I made my way to my usual flowery bedroom chair that had become my very own during these meetings. Stacy sat reluctantly in an orange furry bucket chair.

"Here's your tea," Doris said, pushing an English rose–patterned cup toward me. "And here," she added with much pomp and ceremony, "is my new luscious lava surprise cake."

"Lava" and "surprise" in the same sentence didn't bode well with me. Doris was an extreme cook—either very good or very bad. She didn't

mess with being middling. As she liked to "experiment," her recipes were notorious on both ends of the scales. Stacy shook her head and wrinkled her nose, confirming she wasn't even going to try it. I looked around the circle. Every head was still bowed, studying said cake as each member pushed it dubiously around her plate with a fork. Doris continued to hand out slices.

"What I don't understand," whispered Lavinia as she interrupted the communal plate scraping, "is why it's so red. When I put my fork in it, and it oozes out like this, I feel as if I've just killed it."

"I know what you mean," added Lottie. "I think I'm beginning to get an inkling of where Doris came up with the title of the script."

Doris circled back around and hovered over me, waiting to see my reaction as I gingerly dug a fork into a corner. As I did, the cake collapsed onto my plate, and bright-red goo ushered forth.

"What do you think?" Doris inquired, eager to get my response before I had even tasted it.

"Is the surprise the fact it's not really a cake at all but a pudding?" I asked, trying to use my fork to stop it flowing over the edges of the plate. "And it's very . . . red."

"That *is* the surprise," stated Doris. "I mingled my lava and a red velvet cake recipe together. I think it works."

As I stabbed at the cake, "surprise" wasn't the

word that came to mind. More like "sludge." Sludge slices would have been a better name. Lottie and Lavinia didn't attempt to eat it but just tactfully placed their plates on the side table and sat poised, holding their teacups and saucers.

Doris brought the group together by tapping her gavel.

Today would be a busy meeting because not only did they have to report on the rejection letters that they had received, but we also had to cast the show. Doris started.

"First things first," she said, banging her gavel on the table again. "Do we have any letters for the group? Any famous female failures this week?"

Gracie pulled a letter out of her pocket. "I had a rather good one," she said, chuckling to herself. She was wearing a white ball gown with a pink boa and her sparkly crown. She handed the letter to the group to read.

Doris read the part that Gracie had highlighted. "And once again, thank you for your manuscript, but for us, World War II is so 1990s. We're moving on to World War III and beyond."

Gracie giggled. "I always thought that World War II was so 1940s, but what do I know?"

We laughed as Ethel arrived with The Book, and Gracie's letter was placed inside.

Finishing off any other business, Doris moved to the matter at hand: casting *The Merlin of Ooze*.

Pulling out our clipboards, Doris handed them around the circle. She had included a cast list. "Let's start with the list of characters and see who might be the best fit. The Man in the Can?" she said starting down the list. "Ruby informs me that she has managed to find us a new music director named Olivia, who will be at our next rehearsal, and there are a lot of singing parts for that character."

We all looked down at our notes. Stacy said, "Your best choice, as far as I can see, would be somebody like Ernie."

Everyone nodded in agreement.

Doris ummed and ahhed, then eventually nodded too. "What about Dorothy?" inquired Doris. "I mean, Dorothea?" she corrected herself as she continued perusing her clipboard. "I was thinking that Marcy girl. She has the sex appeal for the audience."

"Sex appeal in *The Wizard of Oz*?" cried Lottie incredulously. "I mean *The Merlin of Ooze*?" she added in a whisper.

"She has a really good voice. We should have her for the lead role," Doris snapped back.

"Lead role?" retorted Stacy, seeming to come to life now we were casting. She actually seemed to be interested in the process. "You want your lead role in this show to be meek and wholesome. It's not *Cabaret*. That girl was like sex on a pair of stilettos."

Flora took a swig of tea and unwrapped one of her many layers. I noticed her hands shook a little as she placed her teacup back on its saucer. This conversation was obviously more than just a little uncomfortable for her.

"Who else do we have?" Doris asked, screwing up her nose as she looked through her notes.

"What about Flora or the little cheerleading girl?" I suggested. "She had the right look."

"You mean the crazy twirler?" responded Doris. "I'm not sure I could trust her to get herself on and off the stage on her own."

"She's very willing," I chirped in.

"But she appeared to be tone deaf," Doris said. "She was terrible once that music changed key."

"That might just be her ear," mused Annie as she looped stitches onto her needle. "With the right training, she could be taught to hear the notes better."

Everyone looked at Annie. She seemed to understand what she was talking about.

"How do you know?" asked Doris, suspiciously.

Annie pulled on the ball of pink wool she was turning into a matinee jacket as she spoke. "When I was young, my mother made me take singing lessons for two years."

"You had a singing career?" inquired Doris.

Annie frowned. "I didn't say that. But that didn't stop my mom from having high hopes of me having one. I always remembered my teacher

saying anyone can sing if they train their ear to hear the music. She might just need some help with that."

"That might be the case," said Lavinia, "but the problem you have is that her ear is attached to the rest of her, and she was a walking disaster. I agree with Doris. I wouldn't trust her not to fall off the stage."

Lottie nodded beside her sister. "I have to agree with Lavinia. I think she could be trouble."

"You agree with me?" stated Lavinia incredulously. "I must be slipping."

Annie also nodded. "It would take too long to train her." She stopped knitting and looked over at Flora. "What about you, Flora? Would you like to play the main role?"

Flora choked on her tea and stammered, "I don't think I could. I am happy to take a minor role."

"Why don't you step outside of the room and let us discuss it?" ordered Doris. Flora did as she was told, clutching her cardigan as she went.

"I think Flora would be perfect," piped up Lavinia. "It would do her confidence a world of good."

There were general nods around the table.

"But could she pull it off?" Doris inquired sternly.

Stacy picked up the thread. "I think with the

274

right training, her confidence would grow. Who do you plan to have as your music director?"

The entire room looked at her blankly.

Doris narrowed her eyes at me.

"Don't even think about it," I responded. "I have enough to do trying to cobble together this story you've created, and I know nothing about singing."

"I might be able to help you out there," Ruby announced wistfully. She was dressed from tip to toe in a blue sari. She called the outfit an "avant-garde hurrah to Van Gough." "I have a friend from my midnight moon bathing group that does that. I'll call her."

We finished casting the show. Ruby would help with costuming, Annie would work the ticket booth, and Doris wanted to be stage manager. Flora would play Dorothea, Marcy the Goddess of the Corn, Ernie the Man in the Can, the crazy twirler would be the Scaredy Lemur (a smaller, easier part), and Lottie would be the Pink Witch of Light and Love. Her sister, Lavinia, was excited that she was going to be the Green Witch. "I will be positively organic," she retorted.

Chapter Thirty

SAGGY OLD CATS & A VISIT FROM MORTICIA

The following week, we began the first week of rehearsals, or "collective craziness," as I nicknamed it. Things were also busy at the library. We were creating a whole display for Big Bird, who was coming to read to the island children, and alongside that, we had all sorts of craft days and book drives planned. It was an absolute hive of activity. Between the library, taking care of the ever-demanding Stacy, and planning the show, I was exhausted.

"Do you think warm-ups are really necessary?" I asked Stacy, handing her the book that I'd brought from the library as I prepared for the first rehearsal.

Stacy eyed the picture of people in their dated black leotards stretched into weird positions. "Er, yes," she said indignantly. "Unless you want one of the old ladies to throw a hip out."

I gave her a disapproving look, saying, "Those old ladies you're talking about are only a few years older than me."

Stacy rolled her eyes as if she were saying, *If the shoe fits . . .*

The next day, I talked to Ruby. I knew I wouldn't be the sort of person that could do warm-ups; maybe she could do some yoga. When I entered the Emporium, she was up a ladder, draped in fabric and dried fruit.

"I'm decorating the Roman goddess, Terra Mater, for Earth Day," she announced as I entered the shop.

"Any chance you could do warm-ups for the rehearsals?" I asked her.

She threw down the multicolored garlands of apples and oranges she was using to drape around the model and clambered down her ladder, saying, "I would love to. I'll bring my own little pink mats, and we could do some beginner's yoga. That should help our whole group get loose."

A picture of Ethel flashed into my mind. We would need a rack and a bottle of Scotch to loosen that one up, I thought to myself.

I saw the twins that afternoon at the library and told them about my plan.

"I don't really do exercise," Lottie said as she slid a copy of *A Closer Walk with God* across the desk for me to check out. "I prefer to walk or garden," she added.

"Come on, Lottie," said Lavinia. "It sounds like fun."

When I dropped by Doris's to inform her on my way home, she and Ethel were up to their

elbows in creating props for the show. Scattered all around them were glue guns, glitter, and strips of papier-mâché. Ethel, as I had predicted, looked horror-struck at my announcement.

Gracie, who was using the time to add more glitter to a pair of pink tulle wings, clapped her hands together. "Wonderful," she said. "I have the perfect outfit. I always wanted to be a ballerina," she added.

Doris looked at me through narrowed eyes that suddenly registered something. "I know," she said. "Those hot-pink jogging pants I bought for California." She had apparently been reviewing her wardrobe.

Oh no, I thought to myself. I had hoped they would never see the light of day. She'd bought them for our trip to San Francisco to blend in, but the reality was, she never had a chance to wear them. Thank goodness. Now, apparently, they would be making their world debut.

That evening, the cast arrived to warm up. We stood on the stage in a wide array of outfits. Flora obviously had nothing that resembled exercise gear, so she was in a long, flowing skirt and a blouse and still had on a pair of Victorian boots, plus many petticoats. But she did have her hair up.

The twins were dressed in pale-blue jogging suits with white sneakers.

Doris turned up in the infamous pink jogging

bottoms. Good grief, I thought to myself. I couldn't believe she'd left the house that way. Somehow she'd managed to squeeze her whole bottom half into very tight, shiny spandex, which popped the rest of her up into a round, layered, blobby ball. She looked like a lollipop on a Pepto-Bismol stick, a luminous balloon the day after the party, all stretched and round in one area and all saggy in the other. She seemed utterly oblivious to how ridiculous she looked.

I had opted for a pair of black jogging pants and a white T-shirt, as I thought I might as well get some exercise. I had never tried yoga before.

We all stood in front of little pink foam mats Ruby had rolled out onto the stage. It was obvious she was taking her job very seriously. She appeared in her leotard, tights, and bare feet. But the usual flamboyant character had calmed herself into a meditating goddess as she stood with her palms pressed together, her toes on the tip of her pink mat. We stood reverently, waiting for her to begin.

"First," Ruby said in a very ethereal tone, "we need to clear the room so the spirits can come and cleanse our auras."

"No need for that," piped up Lavinia. "Some spirit cleared my aura last night."

"Lavinia," said Lottie, exasperated. "No one needs to hear about your drinking habits."

Ruby seemed unmoved by the distractions. She

279

continued to breathe deeply, encouraging us to do the same. Then she tapped a little pair of finger cymbals together, telling us to breathe with the sound of the chimes.

This is very entertaining, I thought. Not what I'd expected for exercise.

She then started to flap her arms in big circles, encouraging us to do the same, telling us to breathe deeply. We huffed and puffed and windmilled our arms.

"Bring your palms back together," she said gently. "Now, we'll kneel."

"Now we'll what?" boomed Doris, incredulously.

Ruby ignored her and kneeled down on her mat. We all clambered down as best we could.

"I'm getting down," said Lottie, "but I'm not sure how I'm getting up again. Let me know what else you need me to do while I'm down here."

"Maybe the spirits will float back and lift you back up," Lavinia joked.

"First," continued Ruby, "we will attempt downward dog." She placed her hands firmly on the mat in front of her, bending her body so her rear end was pointing up in the air, like a dog stretches.

Lottie looked horror-struck. "I'm not sure I want to even attempt that. I'm not sure any Southern woman should attempt that," she added, shaking her head.

Lavinia was already ahead of her in downward dog, her own patootie up high.

"Come on, Lottie," she said. "It's fun."

Lottie looked at her twin and scowled at the vision before her. "As our patooties are identical, I just got a glimpse of what I would look like, and there's no way I'm doing that. Can't I just do upward cat?" she said and sat back on her heels and pawed at the ground.

Annie, who was stretched neatly into the position, started barking. "It seems to work for my dogs," she said. "They do this every morning."

As I looked around the room, downward dog was not what went through my mind—more like saggy old hanging cat.

Ethel looked mortified. She was having none of it. "I think I'll go and check on what needs to be done in the theater," she said, clicking her tongue and leaving the room. Ernie had decided to sit it out and sat chuckling at us from the audience while Tanya made excited whooping noises every time we changed position.

Ruby continued to direct the class as we all stretched and puffed and panted into different positions. She moved the group through several of them till she eventually told us to stand with one leg wrapped around our knees and both hands clasped together above our heads. This produced people falling over in every direction.

"Don't tell me," said Lavinia. "This is called falling-down tree?"

"I'm not sure my leg wraps around like that," added Annie as she attempted to do it two or three times.

Gracie just turned in circles in her ballerina costume, in her own little world.

Flora got her boot stuck in her skirt and ended up falling flat on her face.

Surprisingly enough, Doris was very adept at the movement and stood straight up, like a misshapen Pepto-Bismol ice cream cone. As I watched each person attempting the positions, I thought that maybe it wasn't such a good idea to do yoga before we rehearsed. We all hobbled back into the audience to recover.

As I began organizing the scripts, a strange woman walked onstage and established herself there. I had missed her entrance, so as I looked up, it was as if she had just magically materialized. She was a tall, wiry string of a woman, wearing a long black lace dress that wouldn't have looked out of place on the bride of Frankenstein. Around her shoulders hung a short silk jacket trimmed with peacock feathers. Her figure-hugging ensemble brushed the tops of glove-tight snakeskin stiletto boots. Her long fingers were adorned with bulky rings and an oversized silver charm bracelet dangled on her wrist. Her hair was arranged in heavy, rich layers—black, shiny

coils rolling all the way down to her tiny waist. On her head was a peaked cap, a cross between a Victorian soldier and a costume from *The Music Man*. Positioned at a rakish angle, it was made of soft black leather with heavy swags of gold braiding draped around the band.

She stood there, a quiet but commanding presence, her weight thrown suggestively onto her left hip, and her eyes firmly closed. She seemed to be there for a very long time. I waited awhile patiently and then decided to break the ice.

"Hello," I said, "my name's Janet—"

I didn't get any further than that because she responded instantly by moving both her hands in my direction. Her long thin white fingers extended forward, displaying shiny black nail tips. She appeared to be demanding silence.

I found myself hovering with my mouth open in midsentence, not entirely sure what to do. She continued to stand there, rooted with her hands in the air for a moment. Then she balled them into fists, slowly turned them over, and opened them, one finger at a time until they were splayed, outstretched as if she were reaching out to grab some external power.

Lottie leaned forward and commented over my shoulder, "I don't remember casting Morticia."

I found myself whispering back, afraid to further disrupt her odd meditation. "I think she

might be the music director we've hired."

We all continued to watch, mesmerized, as the woman drew in a sharp intake of air, as though she had been woken from a nightmare. Then she balled her hands into a fist again, brought them down to her sides, and dropped her head to her chest as if she had just finished a performance.

"What a lot of nonsense," Doris said with a huff as she arrived back down the aisle. "What is she doing?"

"I'm not sure," I answered honestly. "But I think she may be ready to talk now."

We both looked toward the stage. The woman filled her lungs with air again, then said in a very ethereal voice, "Yes, this will do nicely. I feel an intense, pulsating vibration that I'll be able to connect with here."

Only then did she open her eyes and acknowledge us all with a deep bow.

She announced in a booming stage voice, "I'm Olivia. I'm here to bring music to fill this house."

We all just stared back, and I suddenly felt very underskilled and underdressed. The rest of the team seemed speechless.

Olivia steepled her fingers together in front of her as her treasure trove of rings glinted and glistened in the stage lights. She pierced me with her commanding gaze. "And where is my piano?" she asked with a sharp, accusing air, as if she suspected me of hiding it from her.

I stared up at her, feeling about ten years old, trying to remember why I hadn't thought to bring a piano to the rehearsal with me before realizing how ridiculous that was. Suddenly, I remembered seeing one when I had been clearing costumes.

"Um, well, there's one on the side stage. I'm not sure if it's a good one," I babbled, "and I'm not sure even if it's in tune or anything. We didn't really get a chance to clean it yet."

Olivia silenced me again with her long bony white hand and floated off in a cloud of feathers to the side of the stage to find the piano.

Doris looked at me and shook her head. "What the devil was that?"

I shrugged at Doris just as the sound of a piano coming to life started to fill the air. The music was enchanting. The empty stage was magically transported by her exquisite rendition.

The melody must have traveled into the foyer, because I turned to see that James and Annie had gathered at the back of the auditorium.

Olivia broke into a beautiful rolling arrangement of "The Swan's Theme" from *Swan Lake* that wouldn't have been out of place at Carnegie Hall. Annie, the twins, and I all wandered closer to the stage, drawn by the beauty of the sound. She finished her incredible rendition with a dramatic cascade of notes, causing everyone to burst into spontaneous applause.

As the clapping petered out, someone continued

to clap heartily from the back of the room, shouting in deep dulcet tones, "Bravo! Bravo!" I looked back to see Ernie making his way down the aisle. Olivia walked back out onstage and gave a small bow in his direction.

"Yes, I think this will do fine," she said calmly. "It seems to be in tune and in good shape for an instrument you said hadn't been touched for a long time."

James walked forward and chimed in, "Actually, I only just had it tuned this week. I thought someone might need to use it. I'm so happy to hear it making such wonderful music again."

"I need someone to wheel it out for me, if you please," Olivia informed us.

James nodded, and Ernie joined him backstage. They pulled it out onto the stage.

Olivia took control as she stood at the piano and said, "I am your music director, and I'll need your cast gathered on the stage here with me, please."

Doris, not wanting to be upstaged, announced to the cast, "Everybody, this is Olivia . . ."

She looked to Olivia to help her fill in the blanks, but Olivia responded, "Just Olivia."

Doris looked as if she didn't know what to do with that information, so she just said, "This is . . . Ms. Olivia."

As the cast gathered, Olivia moved to the front of the stage and addressed the production team.

"I have been made aware of the nature of this endeavor, and I understand that at this point, you have no music."

I was just about to make up an excuse when Doris chimed in. "I have been playing with a few ideas at home."

Olivia paused before repeating Doris's words with disdain. "Playing with a few ideas . . . at home?"

Doris pulled out some scrappy-looking music pages from her bag and held them up toward the stage. Olivia took out a small pair of sparkly glasses hanging on a diamante chain and peered at the sheets Doris handed her. She screwed up her face as she read, communicating that this was not exactly the Brahms she had hoped for.

Giving them no more than a customary glance, she handed the sheets back to Doris, saying, "I have a degree in music composition and I know of Annie's work, and I love animals. If you would permit me, I would be willing to write music for this show."

"Good," said Doris stolidly. "You can help me."

Olivia narrowed her eyes before forming and drawing out the word "yes," with more than a hint of disapproval etched in her tone.

She moved back to the group that now hovered around the piano.

"I'm not sure about her," Doris said to me under her breath.

"I think she's perfect," I said. "She's a little odd, but most creative people are. Let's see how she does."

Doris shrugged, puffing out her cheeks as if to say, *We will see who's right* and sat down in her chair.

Marcy arrived late and clicked her way toward the group in extremely high black pumps, wearing a long angora sweater and footless leopard-skin tights that accentuated her curvaceous hips. She seemed to enjoy drawing considerable attention to herself as she went. The cast, sensing greatness, parted like the Red Sea. Olivia, who'd been looking at her own music sheet, caught sight of Marcy over the top of her reading glasses. At the piano, Marcy flipped back her glossy curls, clicked her cherry-red lips together, and just posed.

Olivia sat way back on her piano seat and said, "And who might you be, young lady?" It was obvious from her tone that she wasn't the least bit fazed by Marcy's need to make an entrance.

Marcy looked over her shoulder before answering, then, placing an elegant hand to her chest, inquired in mock surprise, "Who, me?"

Olivia just stared at her and raised one eyebrow as if to say, *Who else?*

Marcy giggled and threw her head back again. "Oh, I'm just Marcy." She then extended a hand

toward Olivia, saying, "I'm pretty sure I'm playing the lead."

Olivia smirked a little and shook just the tips of Marcy's fingers, saying, "Well, Just Marcy, can you sing?"

Marcy opened her eyes wide, responding, "Of course I can."

Before Olivia could answer her, Flora arrived from the bathroom, out of breath and red-faced from stripping off what seemed to be the whole of the thrift store; she fell up the stairs and splayed out onto the stage. Ernie rushed to help her, saving her embarrassment by joking with her, "Hey there, Flora, don't go falling for me just yet." He then broke into a little soft-shoe shuffle, dancing and singing.

Flushed, Flora was on her feet quickly and brushed herself off as she limped to the piano. Ernie continued singing and dancing beside her.

"I'm fine," she said dismissively as the group watched.

Olivia was about to speak again, when suddenly an imp-like character bounded up the stairs, shouting, "I'm here. I'm here. So sorry, I was waiting in the foyer."

Then she collapsed into peals of laughter at her own incompetence and hopped and skipped toward the piano. It was Tanya.

"It's like a zoo," remarked Doris.

Ethel, by her side, responded, "Monkeys and kangaroos."

Olivia quickly took control, and soon they were all warming up, singing scales that actually sounded quite good. She also took them through a number of popular songs, letting them know she was assessing their range. After an hour, Olivia stopped, placed her hands gently on the top of the piano, stood up, and took in a deep breath as she slowly made eye contact with the whole cast.

"That was adequate for a first rehearsal," she said. Then she turned to the production team, inquiring, "Who is doing your choreography?"

I was dumbstruck and then glanced helplessly at Doris. There hadn't been any discussion about choreography.

"Do we need a choreographer?" Doris asked bluntly.

"Of course you need one," said Olivia. "This is a musical."

Stacy struggled to her feet. "I could do it," she said calmly.

"Splendid," said Doris and then announced the rehearsal was over.

Chapter Thirty-One

STEVE MCQUEEN RIDES AGAIN

Annie had finished exercising the dogs and was just settling down to watch her favorite soap on TV while she knitted a couple of rows when someone knocked at the door. John Meyers stood on the doorstep. Gone was all the charm of his last visit. In his hand he held out a letter.

"Hello," he said, abruptly, his demeanor void of any lightness; he was apparently in work mode. "I have to inform you that, because you didn't come up with an alternative repayment plan and per the documents you signed, your property is to be acquired by developers, and they'll be moving within the next week to start preliminary work on removing the buildings and accessing the trees to be taken down."

Annie just stood riveted to the spot in shock, and her whole body started to shake. Had she heard him right? Did he say that they were going to bulldoze the farm? The one thought she'd had when all this started, the thing that kept her going, was that maybe some wonderful family would buy the property. She had visualized being able to have them come and visit before they moved in, take them around and show them

some of her favorite places. Maybe they would have let her stop by occasionally and take a walk in the woods. Now what was he talking about? Developers?

"What do you mean?" she cried, unable to keep the panic from her tone. "What do you mean, developers? I thought we were working together."

"We didn't hear back from you by the requested date as set out in the document page 732, paragraph four, that you signed last time I was here. So, we moved the farm into foreclosure, and it will be sold at auction quickly. This is prime land," he added stiffly as he scribbled notes into a file. "We will get a good price for it, and potential developers want to come here and do an initial inspection. It's perfect acreage for a fair-sized housing community."

"Page 732?" said Annie, confused and desperate. "You can't just knock down the farm. It's over a hundred years old, and these trees are even older than that."

"Exactly," he said, signing something. "Good money. We'll get a small fortune for these trees."

Annie became protective. "I won't allow it. This is my farm."

"That is now in foreclosure," he corrected her pointedly. "So this is the bank's farm."

"Not yet," said Annie, lacing her words with all the indignation she could muster.

"Eleven days, to be exact. Here's the paperwork outlining the dates of the inspection and when they will be setting up their heavy moving equipment. They'll be here within the next week."

He started to walk away, and Annie just followed him to his car absently, saying, "You just can't do this. Do you people have no heart?"

Apparently sensing something desperate in her tone, the dogs in the barn started barking hysterically. For a minute, John looked regretful, then the shutters were back up and he said gruffly, "I'll see you again soon," and drove away in his red sports car.

Annie just stood in her driveway, staring after him, the letter in her hand, tears rolling down her cheeks.

Chapter Thirty-Two

EXPLODING WITCHES & ETHEL THE SWINGING STARFISH

Martin accompanied Stacy and me to the next rehearsal. He had been summoned by Doris to lend his expertise to some sort of a balloon contraption she was building. She had some bizarre notion of flying the cast off the stage at the end of the show.

It didn't take much to talk him into coming. Normally giving a wide berth to any of my "projects," from his latest comments at home, he seemed more than a little intrigued to taste the stew we were all brewing at the old cinema.

"Just what every artistic production needs," he had joked in the car on the way there, "an aerospace engineer."

As we entered the theater's front doors, Stacy went off to the bathroom. Even in the foyer, the sound of the opera singer from the audition greeted us from the stage. It sounded like fingernails down a blackboard. She was screeching out her high notes as Olivia accompanied her on the piano.

Martin's face broke into a roguish grin as he asked, "Is that what happens to cast members who don't do what Doris wants?"

I punched him playfully on the arm. "Behave yourself," I demanded. "This is a serious rehearsal."

But all illusions of that were lost the minute we entered the auditorium. I couldn't believe what I was seeing. Ethel was dangling about six feet off the ground from a rope hanging down in the middle of the stage, hoisted up on some sort of rigging dangling from the flies. She was encased in a hefty harness that looked like an enormous buckled leather diaper. She swung back and forth, her body splayed out like a starfish on a pendulum.

Martin couldn't help himself. "What did *that* one do wrong?" he asked in a mischievous tone.

I purposely ignored him as I moved to join Doris's side.

"Did I miss something?" I asked quizzically as I started to scan through my script.

Doris responded, overtly excited, "Isn't it wonderful? Look what we found."

"That you can swing Ethel back and forth for entertainment? Or are you planning on using Ethel on a string to hypnotize the audience into handing over their cash?" I asked sarcastically.

"No," she said with obvious irritation. "We found this rigging in the prop room, and apparently James knew a person who knew how to work it. He's backstage on the other end of that rope."

"What are you planning to do with Ethel on a rope?" I inquired, my tongue firmly in my cheek.

"Ethel is testing it for Lottie. I thought we could fly the Pink Witch of Love and Light in and out of her scenes this way."

I was just about to voice my disapproval when the swinging Pink Witch herself arrived, along with her twin and Gracie.

"Oh my," remarked Lottie as she observed Ethel rocking from side to side and looking about as happy as a pig chewing on a barbed wire fence.

As we all continued to watch the hypnotic display, Martin whispered into my ear, "I don't think it will matter how hard you hit that one with a stick. There won't be any candy coming tumbling out of her."

"What do you think about that, Lottie?" asked Doris enthusiastically. "How would you fancy learning to fly for this part?"

Lottie looked desperate. "Don't I need a license or something? And how am I supposed to perform with all those straps and buckles between my legs?" she inquired. "I'm pretty sure this is very un-Southern."

"Nonsense," stated Doris sharply. "All the rigging will be up under your dress, with a hook under your wings."

Lavinia started to laugh. "That will be a first for you, sister dear. You can see what it's like to be an angel." Then adding a huge glob of sarcasm,

she said, "I'm so sorry that I get to miss out on all the fun."

"But you don't," remarked Doris merrily. "Come with me."

She marched up the stairs and pointed at a hole that had materialized in the stage. Martin trotted behind us, and I could tell he was having way too much fun at our expense.

"What is that?" asked Lavinia as we peered down into the gloomy void.

"That," said Doris buoyantly, "is your entrance."

"My what?!" exclaimed Lavinia. "How am I supposed to get up through that? On a rope ladder?"

"Maybe there's a trampoline down there," added Martin ruefully.

"No," Doris said. "Under the floor is a trapdoor. You stand on it, and it springboards you onto the stage. Lottie will come from the flies, and you can come from down there."

"The bowels of the earth," stated Lottie soberly. Then she added playfully, "And then you, sister dear, can see what it's like to play a demon. And unfortunately for you, that *won't* be a first."

Lavinia clicked her tongue in response.

"Is this really necessary?" I asked with thoughts of insurance claims and hospital visits whirring through my mind.

"I want this to be an extravaganza," stated

Doris sternly. "I want people to come from every town around to see this show, so we're going to make it as dramatic as possible. I think the twins will be perfect as our witches. They will appear out of thin air through a detonated blaze of exploding smoke and sparks."

"A detonated blaze of what?!" screeched Lottie.

"Ditto!" screeched Lavinia.

Gracie clasped her hands together. "Oh, can I do that?"

"You can take our places," Lottie quipped back sharply.

Doris seemed annoyed at their lack of enthusiasm. "It's perfectly harmless," she stated, as if addressing small children. "People have been blowing up witches onstage for over a hundred years."

"And where, exactly, do you get those explosives?" snapped Lavinia. "Salem?"

Ignoring her comment, Doris continued, "I want you to meet my neighbor's son. He will be in charge of the pyrotechnics."

Before anyone else could protest, she marched off to the side of the stage to find him.

As we stood with our mouths agape, Martin looked around our circle and shook his head. "Wow, this is some book club you girls have got yourself here. Makes me want to read more."

"Makes me want to stop," snipped back Lavinia coldly.

298

Doris returned with a young man who was so tattooed and pierced, he was his very own walking work of art. He wore black ripped leather pants that revealed a chain attached to his belly button by a ring that then affixed to his belt buckle. A short, tight sleeveless T-shirt was stretched across his muscular chest with the words "why bother" splashed in an anarchic fashion across the front.

Doris introduced him.

"This is Jimmy."

He had a mild and pleasant demeanor as he stretched forward and shook all of our hands. He then dove into a long and informative description about his pyrotechnic experience, but to be honest, I didn't follow much of what he was saying. I was too mesmerized by a large silver ball stud protruding from the middle of his tongue that bounced around as he spoke. That and trying to work out how he had managed to insert a fair-sized bolt that seemed to be growing out of either side of his nostrils. He was very entertaining to watch—a glistening, studded show all of his own. He finished his spiel by announcing jocularly, "So, in a nutshell, I'm the guy who is going to be blowing you up!"

I heard Lottie suck in a breath behind me as he nodded to us, announced he had powders and potions to mix, and disappeared back into the wings.

As soon as he left, Lottie erupted. "I'm not going to be blown up in a nutshell or any other shell. That just doesn't sound safe."

"That's ridiculous," scoffed Doris. "Jimmy may look a little unusual, but he has a lot of experience in explosives. I'll show you how safe it is. As soon as he's ready, I'll have him detonate under me first so you can see just how harmless being blown up can be."

I pondered her words. I never thought I would hear that sentence in my lifetime, and I could feel Martin twitching by my side. This was going to be comedic fuel for him for a long time.

We had just finished the medieval tour of Doris's theatrical torture chamber, with the exploding, spring-boarding witches and the dangling piñata of gloom, when the seamstress, June Horton, arrived. She had a box containing a heaving mass of fabric, tapestry ribbons, bows of every description, and plastic flowers. Everyone watched with interest as she paraded down the aisle like a towering ice cream sundae. When she got to the front, she slung the mounded heap onto the stage, saying, "Is the hippie joining me? The one from the wool shop? We need to try some of this stuff on the cast, and I'm not feeling great, so I need her help."

We all took a step back as she punctuated the end of her sentence with a rallying, chest-wracking cough. Then, to stress the point, she

blew her nose loudly on a tissue and popped a cough drop into her mouth.

Stacy arrived from the bathroom and had changed into her exercise gear. She climbed the stairs onto the stage, puffing, blowing, and saying, "I thought we could start to work out some of those dance numbers today, as I'm not feeling so sick. And they don't have long to learn everything."

June clambered up the stairs onto the stage as well and started fishing through her enormous pile, throwing costumes hither and thither. She pulled a pink tutu and plopped it over Stacy's head before either of us had a chance to speak. Stacy was so livid, she was dumbstruck.

"You're quite a pudding, aren't you? Are you the Pink Witch?" she said as she tried to pull down the costume's sparkly ruffle over Stacy's belly. "You should probably think about going on a diet before the show."

When the rest of the dress cleared Stacy's face, she was blood red.

"How dare you!" she fumed.

I jumped to my feet to stop the flow that was about to issue forth from my offspring's mouth. "Stacy won't be needing a costume. She's just helping me direct."

"Good job, really," muttered June. "She would have been better as Tweedledee or Tweedledum in *Alice in Wonderland*."

301

I joined them both on the stage, saying, "She's pregnant, not fat."

"That would explain it," said June, attempting to yank the costume back over Stacy's head. "So, who is the Pink Witch then, if it's not tubby here?"

I helped Stacy out of the constricting costume as I spoke. "The Pink Witch is just being fitted for her harness, I believe."

"Harness?" asked June. "What is she, a horse?"

June then called the cast to line up on the stage, so she could, in her words, "kit them out." Then she started thrusting hats on each of their heads to see what she liked. Just then, Ruby arrived down the center aisle. She had a box as well, but hers contained waves of beautiful fabric, silver braiding, and precious bracelets from her own collection. She slid the box onto the stage and seemed to ponder what June was doing.

I looked at the lineup of actors, each wearing an odd collection of hats, feathers, and plastic flowers. They looked like a police lineup from a Buster Keaton movie: hats that were too small on big heads, huge hats that were swamping tiny heads, and Flora was wearing one that was wedged down on her head so tightly that it was making her ears protrude like Dumbo. June handed a hat to Marcy, who took it reluctantly and refused to wear it, deciding instead to dangle it unceremoniously off her forefinger.

"Oh, there you are," June sniffed at Ruby. "What do you think?"

We all looked over at Ruby. I was secretly hoping she would save me the job of saying something honest.

"Yes," said Ruby, narrowing her eyes. "I can see where you're going."

To Toy Town? To the Land of Misfit Performers? I wanted to ask but bit my lip.

Ruby bounded up the stairs as June started another round of coughing. All the actors took an automatic step back.

"I'm not a well woman," stated June as Ruby joined the group.

"Why don't you sit down? I can do this," Ruby said tactfully. "You can list the costumes as we decide on them."

June huffed, unwrapped another cough drop, popped it into her mouth, thrust her hands into her mushroom-colored ribbed cardigan, and shuffled down into the audience. Ruby, now left to create, started to pull out bolts of luxurious fabric and draped them in spectacular swaths around the shoulders of the cast.

June seated herself in one of the red velvet auditorium seats and pulled out a scruffy notepad from her plastic shopping bag. "Okay," she said, removing the extra ink off the nib of her pen by wiping it on the sleeve of her cardigan. "I'm ready."

303

Ruby started with Marcy.

"I was thinking, for the Goddess of the Corn, of something in a textured azure. It's ethereal, and I see her as the spiritual mother of the group. Blue is the color of the sky and sea. It is often associated with depth and stability. It symbolizes trust, loyalty, wisdom, confidence, intelligence, faith, truth, and heaven."

June blinked twice, her newly cleaned nib in midair. I could tell that everything Ruby was saying was not only going over her head, it wasn't even in the same stratosphere.

Ruby continued to drape extravagant yards of fabric as Marcy stated in an indignant tone, "Nothing too old ladyish. I want to look cute and sexy, not like a nun."

Ruby looked a little sternly at Marcy and continued her presentation. "Then I like the idea of contrasting the cool palette of the azures with an accent of a dramatic fire color. The color of passion, strength, and power, to show determination and an energetic demeanor, emphasizing that she is a strong, ambitious woman with an unequivocal nature."

June nodded stiffly, then commented, "Blue and red, then."

Ruby continued down the line, each time going to great lengths to describe her thoughts behind the costumes, and each time June boiled it down to just a couple of pointed words.

This was going to be an interesting partnership, I thought to myself.

By the end of her demonstration, Ruby had draped bolts of fabric around each person and had positioned contrasting bindings and ribbon over each of their shoulders. I watched the display before me as we moved from Buster Keaton to *Lawrence of Arabia*.

With the wardrobe fitting apparently over, we moved on with the rest of the rehearsal. Ruby moved the group through more yoga, to the great enjoyment of Martin, who couldn't help jumping in front of a mat and joining in. Then, while the cast went through a music rehearsal, Martin went to look at Doris's contraption.

Just as I was getting ready to wrap up the rehearsal, Jimmy arrived on the side of the stage and announced all his flash boxes were loaded, and he was ready to test them.

With those words, Doris jumped to her feet and marched onto the stage.

"I am your willing victim. Feel free to blow me up with your explosives," she stated in her commander-in-chief voice.

The rest of the cast cleared the stage at the word "explosives," and Martin found a seat next to me as Doris took her mark.

"It's so exciting," he stated impishly. "Will she make it, or won't she?" he added with an expectant air.

Even Dan moved from the side of the stage to join the cast in the audience.

"I wish I had some popcorn," added Martin. "How many people would love to be here for this? This is what you should have sold tickets for, to see Doris Newberry get blown up."

"Fire in the hole!" shouted Jimmy from his command center on side stage.

Suddenly, there was a boom and a crack of white exploding light, and Doris's bulky silhouette and wavy brown hair lit up like a Christmas tree for just a second. Then a cloud of choking black smoke issued out into the audience, and we all started to cough. We waited with bated breath for the smoke to clear as we wiped at our eyes.

"She's still there!" cheered Martin. Then, in a quieter tone for my ears only, he said, "You missed your chance there. You could have paid that guy to send Doris out in a blaze of glory."

As I regained my composure, I noted Doris's face was slightly blackened, and she looked a little off-kilter. Jimmy came onstage to study his handiwork. "Maybe a little less powder? Do you think?" he inquired.

"What?" Doris shouted back. "I can't hear a thing."

Chapter Thirty-Three

A HEAD ON THE STAGE &
A CRAZY CANINE

I entered the theater, and bustling all around the foyer were the members of James's work crew who were fixing it up. I pushed past several carpenters, plasterers, and laborers as I made my way into the auditorium. Walking down the aisle, a strange sight greeted me.

"There's a head on the stage. Did you know that?" I asked Doris as I arrived and threw down the huge box of props I'd been working on at home.

"Of course I know there's a head on the stage," Doris snapped. "It's attached to Lavinia."

As I got closer, I recognized Lavinia's impish grin.

"Hi there," she said.

"Lavinia," I asked, "what are you doing?"

"We were testing this, and I got stuck," she said. "I've been here for twenty minutes. John, a member of the backstage crew, was hoisting me up through the trapdoor when something snapped, and it's not working, so here I am, just a little head on the stage."

"We can't just leave her here," I said to Doris.

"How are we going to do the rehearsal? What are we going to do with a head in the middle of the floor?"

"Oh, just put a bucket over me or something," said Lavinia. "You won't even know I'm here after a bit."

I looked at my watch and back at her with concern. "We need to start the rehearsal. Are you sure you'll be okay, Lavinia?"

John shouted past her from the pit, "We had technical difficulties. We should have her down and reloaded in about ten minutes. Then we'll be ready to fire her up again."

He made Lavinia sound like a canon.

"I've been through worse," she said confidently. "Besides, I have a ringside seat of the action right here."

I looked at my watch again nervously and called the cast together. "Places, everyone, please. And don't forget to be mindful of Lavinia."

The cast shuffled around the hole to get a good look at the oddity.

"Hi," Lavinia said, nodding from person to person as the rest of the cast looked down at her.

"I think we need to put something over it," said Flora. "I mean, her," she corrected herself. "I don't want to trip over her."

"Okay," I said, flustered. I made my way to side stage and found a prop table, which I cleared

off and then dragged into place over the top of Lavinia.

"Places again, everyone. We need you to go from the top of scene three, the scene where Tito moves everyone toward the blue sparkly road."

Suddenly, hearing the name, Tito slipped her lead and raced into the middle of the stage and started licking Lavinia's ear enthusiastically.

"Oh my God," hollered Lavinia. "Get this dog offa me."

"Sorry," Annie said, running from side stage and slipping the leash over the head of the small dog. "She's just never seen a head on the floor before." She yanked at the dog's collar and pulled her back to the side of the stage.

Lottie suddenly appeared, clanking in her harness. She pulled out a wet wipe from a packet and started cleaning off her sister's face.

"Get off me, Lottie," Lavinia yelled with irritation. "Stop making such a fuss."

"You've got to stay clean, honey. You don't know where that dog's been. I saw her out there licking her whatnots just a minute ago."

"Okay," Lavinia said decisively. "Keep on wiping."

We started the rehearsal.

Dan pulled the curtains, and we opened on Nebraska. Flora came onstage dragging the dog, who was pulling hard at her leash. Flora was wearing a flowing affair Ruby had created and

some ridiculous wig June had put on her. She started her lines.

"Oh," she said. "Where do I go? I don't know. Tito, Tito . . ." She stopped, trying to remember her line.

The head looked up. "I think you say, 'Show me the way to Ooze,' remember?"

"Oh yes," said Flora. "Thanks very much." She patted Lavinia on the head and carried on once more. "Tito, Tito, show me the way to Ooze."

Suddenly, there was a scream, and Lavinia disappeared. We all stopped dead for a second, and I raced to the front of the stage.

"Lavinia?" I shouted. I couldn't hear anything. I raced up the steps and onto the stage itself and ran to the hole. "Lavinia! Lavinia! Are you okay?" I shouted down to her.

"I'm fine," she said, waving up as I shined my flashlight down toward her. "But I think your next line should be, 'Where did the head go?' "

As we stopped to reload Lavinia, Marcy stomped onstage in her costume of blue-and-red silk. She clicked up behind me in her red pumps. "I have to talk to you," she said. "I hate this costume. It looks ridiculous, like a huge, fluffy, old-fashioned ball gown."

"I think it looks fine," I said as Ruby moved onstage.

She looked over at Marcy and exclaimed to

me, "I'm having a lot of trouble with Marcy's costume, and she's very unhappy."

"It looks okay," I said. "Marcy, you need to get off the stage, and we need to start this rehearsal. We're on a tight deadline. Please get to your place."

Marcy folded her arms and stomped off the stage, huffing.

Ruby shook her head as she walked off too. "She's not the only one I'm having problems with," Ruby said as she went.

As if on cue, June also appeared on the stage with a bunch of costumes in her arms. "I'm looking for the sewing machine," she said as she sniffed loudly. "And I'm not a well woman. I think this cold is starting to turn into something else."

Ruby lifted up her arms. "You see what I mean?" she commented from the wings. "It's not easy."

I shook my head and took myself back to my place in the auditorium. Grabbing hold of my script, I took a deep breath. "Okay, let's get going. Is Lavinia loaded below stage?" I asked.

"Yep," shouted John from below.

"Jimmy!" I shouted.

From the side stage, he poked out his head. "Yeah?"

"Are the flash guns loaded?"

"Ready," he said and disappeared again.

"Okay, let's practice the witches' entrance then, shall we? Lottie, are you set?"

"I am," came a distant voice from offstage.

Olivia nodded her head at me, and I cued the music. Olivia started to play the entrance of the witches.

Suddenly, I heard a whooshing sound. Lottie came across the stage at such a speed that she nearly took the head off the Green Witch, who had just popped up through the trapdoor.

"Whoa!" shouted Lavinia.

"Whoa!" shouted Lottie.

"I think someone needs to get hold of those horses," said Ruby, who'd appeared by my side to take costume notes. We watched in amazement as Lavinia ricocheted off the side curtain and swung back across the stage, attempting to land gently on the floor. Instead of that, she bounced up and down like a big pink fluffy blancmange, finally finding ground just to the side of her sister. As they both hit their marks, Jimmy set off the flash powder, and there was an almighty bang.

"Good grief!" shouted Lavinia. "I hope it's not going to be like that!"

As she coughed her way through the smoke, Jimmy came running onstage. "Sorry, Lavinia. There was a malfunction. Are you okay?"

"I'll let you know when I've stopped choking," she said, using her wand to waft away the smoke. On the other side of the stage, Lottie limped over

to join her, and they continued with their lines.

Doris, who'd been watching from the back of the auditorium, came forward and nudged me, saying, "I think it looks great!"

To who? I thought. It was like a comedy of errors.

We continued the scene and got to the part when the crazy twirler was due to enter as the Scaredy Lemur. But no matter how she tried, Tanya could not seem to stop smiling.

"You're supposed to be scared," I kept saying to her.

"I know, but it's so much fun," she said as she skipped on the spot.

Ernie did a masterful job as the Man in the Can, and that was about the highlight of the piece. However, whenever he forgot a line, he would suddenly break out into a soft-shoe shuffle around the stage.

I had Ethel stand in as the dog, as the real Tito was having issues, Annie informed me. Ethel wasn't happy being a dog, but she knew how to stand on the spot. We managed to get through about half of the show before we called it quits. Even though it had been a mess, I just put my thumbs up and said, "That was great! Let's see if we can improve a little bit tomorrow, eh?"

Chapter Thirty-Four

THE DRESS REHEARSAL
FROM HELL

Arriving early for dress rehearsal, I was pretty nervous. During the last few weeks, we had made some progress, but I never knew what to expect. When I got to the theater, Jimmy was already setting up his flash boxes.

"I think I've got it right," he said. "This time I promise not to blow up Ms. Lavinia."

"I'm sure she'll appreciate that," I acknowledged with a nod.

I just hoped she would be coming back after all of her pyrotechnic adventures.

An hour later, the whole cast was assembled on the stage in their first costumes. June Horton sighed as she sewed Lavinia into hers. She took a moment to blow her nose hard on one of her many tissues that she kept stuffed in crevices and corners of every outfit she wore.

"How are you doing?" I asked. "We go up in ten minutes. Will you be ready?"

"Maybe," she said, "if I don't die first. I diagnosed myself on Google, and I'm sure I've got walking pneumonia. So I might not be around for the second half of the show if I pop my clogs."

I bit my lip and tried not to be cynical. Since we had started rehearsals, she had Google diagnosed herself with shingles, scabies, scurvy, gout, and a brain aneurysm, only to come back the following day with a new Google disease and set of symptoms that perfectly aligned with it. Now it was walking pneumonia. More like walking old moaner, I thought to myself.

I checked in with Doris on side stage.

Ruby was also in the wings, her sewing machine whirring ten to the dozen as she attempted to finish her creations. She called her latest design "Heliotrope Heaven," for the citizens of Amethyst City. She was swathed in yard upon yard of shimmering purple fabric that rose from the side stage like a voluminous mulberry mushroom cloud.

"Will you be ready in time?" I asked desperately.

"Maybe, but the planet Mercury is in retrograde, so who knows what could happen?" she said with the tone of impending doom.

I shook my head and went back out onstage. June was still sewing Lavinia into her costume.

"Are you nearly done?" I asked, noting that we were already ten minutes late.

"Well, maybe you should have starved this one," June said sarcastically.

Lavinia tutted her response; she was having none of it.

"Maybe you need to check your sizes in those costumes again, I have always been a size six."

June looked up at her incredulously. "Well you might be on this side," she said, patting one of Lavinia's hips, "but what about the other side? What about your twin? What size does she pretend to wear?"

Lottie puckered her lips. "Well, I think I'm about a twelve."

"I rest my case," said June through a forest of dressmaking pins that were sticking out of her mouth.

"She's older," said Lavinia. "She must have spread."

"Spread?" balked Lottie. "I have done no such thing. Besides, I'm only your elder by two minutes. How much spreading could I have done in just two minutes?"

"Look," I said, impatiently interrupting their banter. "We need to get going. We're going to go from the top, and we're not going to stop for anything today. We are *trying* to keep the show to two hours. Do you understand? This is dress rehearsal. Right, Stacy?"

Stacy nodded her head. "It *is* really important," she said.

"Ethel's going to be timing the show."

Ethel nodded. She sat in front of the stage with a clipboard and a stopwatch hanging around her neck.

Doris added, "Yes, I'm stage manager. I will be in charge of the props on the sides of the stage. I will tell you when to come and go and what to do."

Typecast, I thought to myself.

Olivia started playing the music for the overture, and everybody left the stage. The curtains were pulled shut, and we were off. The stage opened on Nebraska, and in shuffled the cast.

Suddenly, the dog leapt out of Flora's basket and ran across the stage and off into the wings. Barking could be heard from the side of the stage, then Doris's abrupt voice. We heard snippets of, "Get off that" and, "No, put that down."

Suddenly the dog appeared with a long string of scarves that she had pulled off the prop table and run with across to the other side of the stage.

Flora was completely thrown off balance and stood in the center of the stage like a deer in the headlights. Finally, she started her lines, faltering at first and then picking up as she went along. The rest of the chorus stood bemused as they watched the dog run back and forth across the stage with Doris chasing it. It finally ran circles around everyone, knotting the scarves around the cast and almost tripping them. I shook my head as I watched.

The Goddess of the Corn entered from a cloud of dry ice that Jimmy was pumping out from the

side stage. As she walked forward, I had my head down over the script reading when I heard Ethel gasp beside me. I looked up to see what had caught her attention and couldn't believe what I saw. Marcy's costume had been completely altered. Instead of the long blue satin robe that Ruby had designed for her, all I could see were legs, red pumps, and underwear. She had apparently taken a pair of scissors to her costume and made a maxi into a mini. The skirt was so short, I wasn't sure if she was wearing it or was just using it as a long scarf.

Oh no, I thought, the Goddess of the Porn has just made her entrance.

She started her lines upstage, stepping in front of Flora every chance she got. It was very discomfiting to watch, and I could see it was throwing Flora for a loop as she scrambled to fight for her place in the spotlight.

Lavinia suddenly made her entrance. She popped up from under the stage and came in beautifully as Lottie floated in, too, maybe a little abruptly, but much better than the last rehearsal. There was a flash. Lavinia prepared herself for the worst, but it actually worked wonderfully. Then, suddenly, a second flash nearly took her off her feet.

"Oops," said Jimmy from the wings. "Sorry, Lavinia. I must have double loaded it."

"I'll double load you when I get hold of

you," said Lavinia, shaking her green fists into the wings and stomping out sparks that were still alight on the stage. "Thank goodness my underwear isn't flammable."

Things continued to fall apart as we went on. Ernie forgot his lines and started a soft-shoe shuffle in the middle of a serious moment in Ooze. Tanya tripped on her costume, falling into the wings and nearly taking Doris out on side stage. Marcy played her character like a prima donna reality star and just posed, mostly in front of Flora. This made Flora so nervous that when she was supposed to kill Lavinia with a bucket of water, she missed her completely and drowned the rest of the cast instead. The dog, who had been deemed three parts crazy, had been fired. So her understudy, Ethel, had to stand in again. She stood in the center of the stage barking on cue, begrudgingly, whenever Flora spoke to her as she continued to watch her timer.

The cast gathered on the stage for the finale. They all stood there, a shocked, bedraggled, wet mess as they sang the ode to the blue sparkly road, accompanied beautifully offstage by Olivia on the piano.

I called the cast together as we finished, and I asked Ethel for a running time.

She checked her watch.

"Four hours and twenty minutes," she said decisively.

I dropped my head into my hands. At least the audience would be getting their money's worth.

I looked around at the cast. Lavinia's face was blackened from the flash powder. Lottie looked rattled from being lifted up and down and hobbled to the front of the stage, mumbling to me, "I think those ropes are chafing me." The cast, still wet and dripping makeup, looked like a haunting Van Gogh portrait during his ugly period. And still the dog skipped around the stage.

This was going to be a disaster.

"On the positive side," noted Stacy as she sat by my side, "they do say bad dress rehearsal, good show." I looked at her and lifted my eyebrows. I couldn't see how we were going to pull this off.

Chapter Thirty-Five

BRINGING DOWN THE HOUSE

Opening night, I arrived early at the theater, and it was already a hive of activity. In the foyer, James was busy organizing the snack counter and last-minute cleaning jobs. Displayed in a prominent place was a large announcement board, and pinned to it were black-and-white headshots of all the cast that James had taken during one of the rehearsals. Above their smiling faces were the words, "Your Cast of *The Merlin of Ooze*."

As I moved to the main auditorium, I was greeted by Doris. "We're having trouble with that dog again," she snapped. "I think we should put Ethel on instead. She's learning her lines as we speak."

I nodded as I strode up the aisle. On the stage, a volunteer with a script stood next to Ethel, feeding her the lines while Ethel barked begrudgingly on cue. She was standing between Ruby and June, who were both busy sewing her into a dog costume with white-and-brown liver spots. As June sewed on a floppy velvet ear, she coughed and sniffed.

"Google told me this might have developed into double pneumonia," she said as she blew her

nose, and Ruby mumbled something about "using yellow to bring out Ethel's clarity of memory and fend off Mercury's reversal" as she sewed reams of the color into Ethel's dog collar.

As I noted the face of the peeved puppy, I wondered what color we needed for the appearance of joy.

I walked backstage to see how everyone else was faring. John met me in the wings. His hands were black with grease, and he was holding an old rag and oilcan.

"How are things with the trapdoor?" I asked.

"All ready to go," he said optimistically. "I've had my young boy up and down on it two or three times already. It's running slick as a whistle. Ms. Lavinia is going to have the smoothest ride of her life."

I then spoke to the crew in charge of winching up Lottie on the other side of the stage. "How are things going back here?" I inquired.

They also gave me the thumbs-up.

My last stop was over to Jimmy. He was busy on side stage, listening to music on his iPod as he did last-minute alterations to his mixtures. "Tell me you've got it right tonight," I implored.

"Oh yes," he said brightly. "I've been here most of the day blowing things up. I've mixed it perfectly this time." The hardware on his body jangled and glistened merrily as he nodded his head with enthusiasm.

I started to relax. Maybe Stacy had been right about dress rehearsals.

I moved through to the dressing rooms. Lavinia was already busy plastering herself in her green makeup, and Lottie was fluffing up her hair, which she had just released from hot rollers. A pink, sparkly tiara was being lovingly placed on her head by Gracie. "How are you doing?" I asked them both.

"Great," Lottie and Lavinia said in unison.

I found Flora. She sat, pale and anxious, looking into her mirror. I put my hand on her shoulder.

"Flora, you're going to be great," I reassured her. "Please don't worry. Remember, we're doing this for Annie, and the community knows that."

Giving me a half-hearted smile, she nodded her head as she started to put on her makeup.

Marcy stomped into the dressing room and huffed loudly. She hung up her costumes on a rail and then, putting one hand firmly on her hip, she pierced me with a look in the mirror.

"That hippie has added back a piece to my opening costume and I'm not wearing that ballooning affair in the second act," she said willfully. "I can just about tolerate my first-act costume, but I hate the one in the second act. I just look ridiculous. I want to wear something else. I've brought something from my own wardrobe." She held up a jumpsuit that looked

like it would fit so tight, she would have probably had to jump off the roof to get into it. "So, where can I find something else?"

I sighed deeply. I'd given up arguing with Marcy. "There are more costumes up in the flies in a little room at the back. As long as you approve it through Ruby, then that's fine. Just make sure that you find something that covers all of your body," I stressed.

She huffed again and took her place in front of a mirror and started unpacking numerous bags of makeup.

I went back to the front of the house to see how things were coming together. Annie had taken it upon herself to clean out the box office, and it positively sparkled. I poked my head through the ticket office door and noticed she was dressed in a long black velvet dress and pearls as she sat on a high stool, merrily taking money and giving out tickets. "How are things, Annie?"

"Great," she said. "Look at the line down the street. I think Doris must have threatened everyone in town," she giggled.

I looked out the ticket window, and the queue did indeed stretch around the building.

"People have been so generous," she stated, showing me the growing pile of bills in her cash box. "Many of them know about the farm and have offered me so much support. I feel so

fortunate to live in such a warm and wonderful community."

I noticed tears creeping into the corners of her eyes, and I squeezed her arm.

As I arrived back in the foyer, Martin greeted me, with Stacy on his arm. He was dressed in a dark suit and tie, and she was wearing a chic pregnancy gown in black-and-cream silk taffeta.

"Here we go, then," he said jovially. "Opening night. How are you feeling, Madam Director?"

"I will feel much better once we are at the end of act one," I responded as I walked them down the aisle and showed them to the seats I had saved for them at the front of the auditorium.

The rest of the cast and crew arrived, including Olivia, who was to play all the accompanying music on her piano from the wings. She was dressed in an ankle-length black sequin gown, with long black gloves and a velvet-and-diamond choker, and her hair was whisked up high, Audrey Hepburn–style.

As Doris finished her last stage preparations and Ruby pulled and cut the last thread of Ethel's costume, the cast gathered on the stage. I encouraged them to do their best and make us proud. As they all filed off, Dan pulled the curtains closed. James opened the house.

I sat next to Martin and Stacy in the front row, waiting nervously for the start of the show as Olivia filled the house with pleasant preshow

piano music. The anticipation and excitement in the theater was palpable as people filed in and packed the building. Doris was backstage and in charge now as the curtains opened. I was brimming with joy and anticipation, and the crowd clapped loudly.

Flora came out onstage with Ethel dragging behind her, along with some of the rest of the cast. Her first words were quiet, but as she was encouraged by the laughter and clapping of the audience, she grew bolder by the minute. Marcy did her entrance, parading on like a regal princess. As usual, she sucked up all the air on the stage, but once she was in front of a real audience, seemed to forget about upstaging Flora and just reveled in the response of the crowd. At least no one forgot their lines, including Ernie, who looked very dapper in his can suit. Even Tanya seemed calmer and more in character as the Scaredy Lemur.

I started to breathe a sigh of relief.

Martin leaned over to talk to me. "Not half bad," he said. "It appears all your hard work has paid off."

"We haven't had the witches' entrance yet," I commented.

The Minchkins filed onstage, and all of a sudden, the flash box went off. I held my breath, but it turned out just about perfect. Enough of a dramatic demonstration to draw joyous gasps

from the crowd but not too much to knock Lavinia off her feet as she slid successfully up the trapdoor to emerge through the cloud of exploding smoke. The crowd clapped their approval as Lavinia confronted Flora with her wand lifted high.

Just one more witch to go, I thought.

From the side stage, the Pink Witch of Light and Love swooshed onstage as if she had been flying all her life and floated down perfectly, landing on her mark. Could this all be going so right? I couldn't believe it. The audience loved it, the costumes looked great, and the cast seemed to be pulling it off.

As the show continued, I started to relax and enjoy it. We got to the end of the first act, and by the enthusiastic applause from the auditorium, I realized it was going really well.

During the break, Martin, Stacy, and I went out into the foyer to mingle with the Southlea Bay crowd. Suddenly, Annie was by my side.

"We've got a problem," she said breathlessly. "You have to come backstage."

I excused myself from the people I was chatting with and raced down the aisle. Before I even got to the front, I knew what the problem was. Plumes of black smoke came out from under the closed curtain. I raced up the stairs and found my way backstage.

"It wasn't me this time," shouted our pyro-

technics expert as he raced across the stage with a fire extinguisher in his hand. I followed him to the scene in the wings.

I noticed right away what the problem was. A velvet curtain had somehow become caught and draped itself across one of the lights.

"That curtain went up in a flash," Doris shouted to me as she threw the bucket of water set for the end of the show on a flaming piece of cloth that had landed on the stage in front of her. "Once the curtain went, it quickly spread out along all the rigging in the flies," she continued, stamping on the blackened cloth to ensure it was out.

Dan was there. So were James and Ernie, all of them working in vain to put out the fire.

"We have to clear the building," I shouted. "I'll go to the dressing rooms," I yelled at Doris. "You and Annie should start clearing the foyer."

"I've already called the fire department," said Annie as she caught up with me in the aisle.

I raced to the dressing rooms and let everybody know what was going on and that they needed to leave as fast as they could by the stage door exit. Everyone grabbed robes, costumes, and scraps of clothing—anything to make themselves decent—and raced to exit the building.

Then James and I swept through the building one more time to check it was empty just as the fire department arrived. I turned to see the stage starting to become consumed in flames.

I found Stacy and Martin, and we all gathered on the street as the building started to succumb to the fire. I suddenly thought of something. I turned to Annie. "Annie, did you grab the cash box?" I asked, panicked.

She looked crestfallen.

"I was too busy getting everybody out," she said. "I left it in the dressing room for safekeeping. I didn't even think about it."

I put my arm around Annie as we both turned to the flaming building, and Annie started to cry.

As we huddled together, the smell of burnt, acrid rubber permeated the night air as thick black smoke pumped out into the dark night's sky. Fingers of angry yellow and orange flames broke windows as the fire attempted to fight its way out of the building. Once free, it licked its way angrily around the walls and doors, blackening and consuming everything in its path. We watched hopelessly as the mock Tudor front doors changed rapidly from white to gray, and the paint bubbled up and peeled away. The little glass ticket booth filled with smoke.

Doris arrived at our group with her clipboard. "Marcy's missing," she said seriously. "Did anyone see her leave the building?"

Everyone looked blankly at each other and shrugged.

"I checked everywhere," I reassured her. "Backstage, toilets, everywhere."

"The last time I saw her," responded Lavinia thoughtfully, "was about ten minutes before the end of the first act. She was moaning about her costume and said she wanted to check out some costumes behind the stage."

I froze as Flora's eye caught mine, and we said at the same time, "The door!"

I raced to the fire chief, saying, "Marcy may still be in there. There's a place she could be trapped."

I then hurriedly gave him instructions about how to get to the attic above the stage. The fire chief got on his radio, and firefighters raced into the building with a backboard.

I just felt awful. What if Marcy was still inside? What if she was trapped in the same room Flora and I had gotten stuck in? It was hard enough being in there when there wasn't a fire. Imagine how terrified Marcy would be with the smoke pouring up the stairs toward her.

As we stood waiting for what seemed like an eternity, an ambulance horn blared and drew up close to the scene. The firefighters' activity increased around us as people ran around, shouting instructions to each other.

"That can't be good," commented Lavinia, and I noticed Lottie's mouth was moving silently in prayer.

The fire chief approached our group, saying gravely, "Yes, we found her. She was where you

said she would be. Do you know her next of kin so we can call them? We need to let them know we're taking her straight to the hospital."

Dan nodded, saying, "They're out of state. Let me do it. I think it will be easier on them if it comes from me." He walked away from us to make a call to her family.

From the building, two firefighters emerged with Marcy's limp and gray body strapped to a backboard and hurried her to the waiting ambulance.

Annie collapsed in tears in my arms, not only for Marcy, but for the farm too. This had been her last hope.

Chapter Thirty-Six

A CAST AT THE HOSPITAL

Martin took Stacy home, and I went to the hospital. When I arrived at the emergency entrance, I found most of the book club seated in the waiting room. Marcy's local family members had already arrived with the ambulance and had been whisked away to speak to the doctor. About an hour later, a nurse came out to update us. She informed us in a professional and somber tone that Marcy had inhaled a lot of smoke, and they would know more in the morning. If she made it through the night, she had a good chance of survival, but the next twenty-four hours would be critical.

We passed the time the best we could. James plied the group with vending machine coffee, Doris paced, Ethel slumped in a chair, and Annie stared into space with half-knitted pink booties in her lap. Flora sat with her head on Dan's shoulder, the twins beside her, and Ernie was doing magic tricks for a young kid who was waiting for stitches.

At three in the morning, a nurse came out to tell us that Marcy's eyes were open, and she was asking for her boyfriend, Dan.

The relief was palpable in the room as we started to hug one another with relief. Only Flora froze. The nurse continued to ask cheerfully if Dan was in the waiting room.

"She has to be delusional," Lavinia said quietly to Flora, who didn't seem to know what to do. Half of her looked relieved, the other half terrified, as if she appeared to be wondering if Marcy had somehow planned the whole thing. Dan looked at Flora for guidance. She tapped his hand, saying, "It's okay. Go and see her."

The nurse nodded expectantly as Dan stood up.

"I'm Dan," he announced, "but we are only—"

He was about to say "friends" when she cut him off saying, "Oh, good, if you could follow me this way."

He walked away, giving Flora a shrug as he went.

Dan followed the nurse through the corridors, past hospital rooms that were dark and still. The various monitors and machines pulsating a methodical beep as he walked by were all that could be heard emanating from the rooms. Outside Marcy's door, he was met by a doctor who confirmed that she was, in fact, awake and doing very well for someone who had been through this sort of trauma. He cautioned Dan

that it was early, but if she continued to recover in this way, her outlook was very optimistic.

"It's good they found her when they did," the doctor assured him. "A few minutes longer, and who knows what we would have been facing?"

As Dan walked into the room, Marcy's uncle stood up and walked toward him.

"She's been asking for you, son," he said as he stretched. "I'm going to go and get a coffee and give you two young people some space." Then he winked, implying they would want to be alone. Before Dan could set him straight about his and Marcy's relationship, he was gone.

Dan approached the bed. Marcy was surrounded by a mass of machinery and was wearing an oxygen mask. Her golden hair was a dusty yellow from the smoke, and her face was gray. He walked to her side, and she fluttered her eyelashes and then opened her eyes. When she saw him, her face seemed to light up.

"Danny," she said. Her voice sounded raspy and dry. "You came to see me."

Dan pulled a chair close to her. She looked like a little girl, so small in this huge bed. For the first time since their childhood, she sounded more like the girl he remembered: innocent, sweet, and vulnerable.

"Yes, of course," he said.

She stretched out her hand for him to take, and he hesitated for a moment, weighing whether he

wanted to be this intimate with her. He decided she wanted to be friendly and he gently took her hand.

"I was dreaming about you," she said. "I was dreaming about when we were children, and your parents made you that tree house. Do you remember?"

Dan nodded. It was a distant but pleasant memory. "I painted a sign saying 'No Girls Allowed,'" he said, "and you and Ruth Tamaler stole it."

Marcy closed her eyes. "Yes," she said. "Those were good memories. You still let me into the tree house behind her back. Do you remember?"

Dan chuckled. He had completely forgotten about the incident until she brought it up, but now it was vivid in his mind. Ruth leaving for dinner and Marcy creeping back to his yard, her wispy blonde hair tied up in two bunches. She had worn a Mickey Mouse T-shirt. He'd remembered that because she'd told him she had bought it on a trip to Disneyland, and he'd wanted to go there so much.

Suddenly, there were tears in the corners of her eyes. "We were such good friends as children. Do you think there's any way we could be that way again?"

Dan was taken aback by her gentle longing and her need to be close to him, need for friendship. Surely he could do that for her. Wasn't that what

he had always wanted? Flora was still his girl, but it was possible to be Marcy's friend, too, as long as they kept it on that level.

"Of course we can be friends, Marcy. I always wanted that."

Her eyes opened wide and she seemed so hopeful. "We'll be good friends?" she said. "That would make me so happy."

"Yes," he said. "It would make me happy too."

Marcy's uncle returned, and he nodded at them both, saying, "Don't let me interrupt you two. I'm just going to find myself a spot over here until Marcy's parents arrive. They're driving up from Medford."

"We were just talking," said Dan, suddenly feeling weird holding Marcy's hand. "I should probably get back anyway."

Marcy looked grief-stricken. "Really?" she said. "You haven't been here very long."

Her uncle interrupted her. "You know, your doctor *did* say not too long, as you need to get your rest."

Marcy's eyes fluttered closed again, as if responding to the need to sleep.

Dan gently withdrew his hand and nodded at her uncle. He wasn't sure whether Marcy had fallen asleep or was just resting, but he crept toward the door.

Her eyes flashed open again as she called out to him, "You'll visit again tomorrow, won't you,

Dan? I'll need your support if I'm to get well again."

In the first time since he'd entered the room, Dan sensed the old Marcy. Her request had been couched in a manipulative way, less need and more want. He decided to let it go.

"Of course I'll come tomorrow," he said, and then he slipped out the door and made his way back up the hospital corridor.

He reflected on the conversation. He just wasn't sure how he felt about tying himself up with Marcy again, having just freed himself from her clutches. But was he being selfish? She didn't know many people in town. How much would it cost him just to spend an hour with her the next day? He was sure Flora would understand. Maybe they could visit Marcy together. He cheered up at the thought of that. He liked thinking about doing things with Flora.

He pushed through the double doors into the waiting room, and Flora was there, smiling at him.

"How is she?"

"Okay," he answered. "Groggy, but she seems okay."

The whole group all looked relieved. Doris took control. "There's nothing more we can do here. I suggest we go home and try to get some sleep. We've got a lot to talk about in the morning. We have to decide what we're going

to do, and who knows, maybe the damage to the theater is only superficial, and we can still open as scheduled."

Everyone nodded, but it was obvious that no one appeared to share her optimism.

Chapter Thirty-Seven

WRECKING BALLS & FREEDOM FIGHTERS

Doris called me the morning after the fire to say we needed to meet at Annie's because there was an emergency to deal with and to wear warm clothes and bring water. Apparently Annie had received an alarming visit from the bank that she hadn't wanted to tell anybody about before the show, but now it seemed the farm could go up for auction very soon. Doris was also concerned that something underhand was afoot, because even though the house was still Annie's, the bank appeared to be proceeding as if the farm had already been sold.

"We are putting Plan B into action," she stated in her getting-things-done tone. "You need to meet us all at the farm this morning."

Martin met me in the kitchen as I poured tea into a flask. I was wearing two layers of fleece and my thick socks and boots.

"Leaving me to live in the woods?" he inquired, looking at my getup.

"I've been summoned by Doris," I stated flatly as I secured the thermos flask stopper.

"Don't tell me," he said. "You're off to the

Arctic to scout for polar bear or maybe trekking up Mount Hood to sing together in an ice house Doris plans to build by hand."

I shook my head as I pulled a pair of warm woolen gloves out of a drawer. "Apparently we are moving to her secret Plan B."

"Ahh," Martin nodded in response, as if acknowledging a secret society. "The infamous Plan B, which could be any of the above or worse."

I raised my eyebrows in response, grabbed two bottles of water, and trudged out the door.

I arrived at Annie's and couldn't believe what I saw as I drove up. What had once been a sweet and peaceful avenue of trees was now surrounded by a line of heavy construction equipment. I knocked on the front door and set off a cacophony of desperate barking from inside.

While I was still on the doorstep, I noted that many of the other rejected writers' cars were parked in the driveway. Ethel opened the door. The woman always seemed to be opening doors.

She clicked her tongue and said, "You'd better come in."

Inside was a zoo. Every single one of Annie's dogs was in the house, all fifty of them. And they all decided to greet me at once. After about ten minutes of furry love, I finally waded my way

through hairy bodies and into the front room, where the rest of the group was gathered.

Annie stood at the table. Exhaustion showed on her pale face. She was using her nervous energy to wrap newspaper around blue china plates. As she did, she mumbled to herself, "I don't even know where I'm going to keep them until I move. But it's all got to be packed."

Also at the table was Doris, her infamous clipboard in front of her. I greeted everybody. They all moved somberly around the room, deep in thought as they gathered things to be packed. There was another knock at the door, setting the alarm dogs off once more. The barking was deafening.

"Are all the dogs in here for a reason?" I shouted, trying to be tactful.

Annie wiped stray tears from her face. "They couldn't stay outside. They were too upset with all the noise that's going on out there with that equipment. I had to bring them in," she sniffed. "And besides, we all want to be a family together."

I looked at the dogs that were now returning to lie down in the sitting room and noted that they all hung their heads and seemed to have the same despondent expression. They obviously sensed something wasn't right.

Ruby appeared in the room with an energetic crew of odd-looking people, some with short hair, some in military jackets, some wearing peace

signs and peace T-shirts. They strolled in like an army of freedom fighters from the retirement home.

"I'm here," she said. "We're going to build a picket line. A human chain against injustice."

I looked at the scrappy, wiry mess of them and hoped a large wind didn't blow them all away.

Doris jumped to her feet. "Perfect," she said. "Follow me."

I was intrigued. I followed them outside.

In the driveway, Ruby pulled out a megaphone and a huge bundle of brightly colored material. She had it all hoarded up in a Mary Poppins–sized bag that had "Save the Whales" on the outside and that was big enough to actually keep a saved whale in it.

She handed one line of the jumble of colorful pieces of cloth to a stocky woman with short, white, spiky hair. She was wearing a green quilted bomber jacket, and the pieces started to unravel. As they did, I realized what they were.

"Tibetan prayer flags?" I asked.

"Yes," she said. "This is going to be a holy picket line. Let's see if they'll have the gall to break this."

I tried to imagine the burly guy I had just witnessed hanging off a tractor at the bottom of the drive and smoking a cigarette being confronted by a bunch of gray-haired old ladies in freedom fighting gear with a picket line of

brightly colored flags. I wasn't sure he was going to be too worried about it; all he would probably need was a pair of scissors.

Once their line of defense was unraveled, the spritely group jumped into action. Picking up her megaphone, Ruby started chanting, setting all the dogs off once more.

"Hell no, we won't go. Hell no, we won't go."

The woman with the spiky hair pumped a fist into the air as the group started to follow suit, striking out in strained, tinny voices as they carried their flags high and started to pin them on posts at the end of Annie's driveway.

In the midst of this display, the twins arrived, dressed differently from one another for once. Lavinia jumped out in a pair of jeans and a sweater, while Lottie was in her usual skirt and blouse.

"I'm here!" said Lavinia. "I'm here to lie in front of a bulldozer if I need to."

"And I'm here to pray that it doesn't run over her," said Lottie, shaking her head.

Lottie made her way into the house while Lavinia took up the cry, "Hell no, we won't go."

I shook my head. If Martin were here, he'd be laughing his head off.

Doris started handing out emergency supplies. She had water bottles, granola bars, and of course, her famous concoctions, all packed into little white plastic containers. This particular

recipe, she told me, was called Freedom Pie, followed by Sit-In Scones. "They have extra ginger in them," she informed me as she handed out boxes. "Keep the group spiced-up and peppy. We're all good. We can go all night if we have to. I've got candles too."

As some sat on the ground, the rest of the rejected writers filed outside, apparently ready to do their duty. Ethel climbed inside the bucket of the bulldozer, and Doris chained her to it.

Within an hour, the rest of the construction crew arrived. It sent quite a bit of excitement through the troops, and the dogs started barking again. The head construction honcho walked toward us. He was an overweight man with a stubbly chin and a pair of jeans that were so dirty it looked as if water was against his religion.

"Look, you lot," he said, rubbing a club-like fist through his graying, greasy hair. "We're just here to do our jobs."

"And so are we," responded Ruby, shouting through her megaphone very loudly, right in his face. "We are not going to let you near the farm." And then, with that, the entire group surrounded the bulldozer.

"So, it's going to be one of those days," he said as he jumped up onto his truck.

"You have no weapons that work against injustice," shouted Ruby through her megaphone again as the group of freedom fighters paraded

around in a little circle, donning banners and flags they had made.

"Oh, I do," he said as he pulled out a mobile phone. "I have this."

Twenty minutes later, Sheriff Brown arrived and, pulling up at the farm gates, stepped out of his patrol car and shook his head. "Doris Newberry," he said with the tone he reserved for finding criminals in expected places. "What are you getting yourself into now?"

Doris stepped forward and pulled herself up to her full height.

"Sheriff Brown," she responded respectfully, "we are saving this beautiful farm from being bulldozed. These men are here to start taking down trees and digging up land that doesn't belong to them."

The guy in the bulldozer jumped down and passed a work order to the sheriff, who then huffed and puffed his way through reading it.

He finished the document, then eyeballed the ladies, saying, "So, this man has a right to be here. What do you want me to do about it?"

"We will fight to the death," Ruby shouted back through her megaphone.

"Well, that might not be so long," stated Sheriff Brown. "I hear we have a storm blowing in tonight that threatens to take you all with it. Now, come on, ladies. You know I only have two cells, and my deputy had a baby, so he's over on the

mainland with his wife today. Please don't make this hard for me."

Doris straightened up again and looked him squarely in the face.

"Robert Brown, we have known each other since high school. Have you ever known me to back down on anything?"

The sheriff took in a long, slow breath and shook his head. Handing the work order back to the site manager, he said, "Looks like there is no work for you here today, and with a storm brewing, that might give you another couple of days on top of that. My advice would be take off now, give them all a chance to get pneumonia or chain-chafed, and come back next week."

The guy nodded and stood toe-to-toe with Doris. "We *will* be back. Don't you worry."

"And we *will* be here," boomed back Doris.

The crew filed out, got into their cars, and left the farm as the band of freedom fighters cheered.

"End of round one," shouted Doris. "Now, let's leave one person to keep guard and the rest of us can go up to the farmhouse. I'll make us some tea, and we can eat our Sit-In Scones in comfort."

Chapter Thirty-Eight

TWO BABIES, THREE WISE MONKEYS & A WHALE

The next day, Doris summoned the whole cast to meet in the evening to discuss possibly changing the location of the show. They had to gather at Annie's instead of Doris's, as the majority of the Rejected Writers' Book Club was still manning an active picket line there against the bulldozer crew.

Flora looked out the side window as she and Dan drove to pick up Marcy, who had insisted on coming but felt too fragile to drive herself. Marcy's parents had returned to Medford once she was out of the woods, but Marcy had insisted on staying. Flora wondered what possible reason she could have for staying, except continuing to pursue Dan. Flora noticed that the clouds were darkening, and because the island was under a storm watch, she felt some concern. But Doris had classed this emergency meeting as imperative, and no one dared cross Doris when it was imperative.

They arrived at Marcy's, and she dragged herself out of the house, looking very pathetic indeed. Gone were the swishy curls and the

347

poodle trot. She was dressed all in white, her hair was pulled back in a sad-looking rubber band and she was wearing hardly any makeup. She carried a pillow and a bottle of water. She had apparently given up playing vixen and was now going for Mother Teresa, Flora mused to herself.

Marcy arrived at the car and stood there waiting for Dan to open the door. He glanced at Flora and rolled his eyes. Eying Flora in the front seat, she placed her hand on her neck, whining, "Dan, I wonder if it's possible that I could travel in the front seat. My back is still not quite right, and I need to stretch my legs forward."

She then pouted like a small child. As if on cue, there was a crack of thunder, and the heavens opened. Flora huffed loudly, opened the passenger door, and climbed into the back seat.

Marcy climbed delicately into the car, making wincing noises as she placed her pillow carefully behind her neck. She turned her head toward her driver and fluttered her eyelashes, saying feebly, "Thank you, Dan."

His hand was resting on the gearstick, and she reached out and grabbed it. Dan responded by pulling it quickly away and starting the car.

Annie lived on a remote part of the island. To reach her farm, they had quite a trip through the rain and the wind. In other parts of the world, wind was not a big deal, but in a place covered with hundreds of thirty- to forty-foot evergreen

trees, wind was not only frightening but also dangerous.

The storm was really starting to ramp up as the rain lashed down hard on the windshield. Dan's wipers could barely keep up with the deluge, which was accompanied by significant wind gusts that blew loose branches and limbs across the road in front of the headlights.

Flora gripped tightly on the sleeve of her cardigan for comfort as they wound their way through the darkest parts of the island. They were all more than a little relieved to see Annie's cheerful little farm sign swing into view as it rocked back and forth in the wind.

Dan drove carefully up Annie's long, winding driveway, which was also lined with huge fir trees, and parked next to the long line of cars that signified that the rest of the main cast and production team were already there.

Dashing from the car, Flora raced to the farm door, accompanied by Dan. Marcy refused to budge until Dan returned from Annie's with an umbrella to shelter her.

Inside was a hive of activity. Everyone had gathered in Annie's front room. They all discussed different ideas to move forward now that the theater was not useable. The room was filled with an air of urgency, given the enemy looming so close in their bulldozers. With the storm, the workers had left for the night. The

picket line had been keeping them at bay, but everyone realized it was only a matter of time before the court would rule in the developer's favor and have the ladies removed by force. Doris ended the meeting by telling Annie that they were going to do everything they could to help her keep her home.

I was glad when the meeting was over, as I really wanted to get Stacy home. She had insisted on coming with me but had been unusually quiet the whole evening. We were just winding up when Ernie returned from putting something out in his car.

"It sure is windy out there. We should probably get ourselves home quickly," he said with a shudder as he entered the house and started all the dogs barking again.

I hurried to pack up my things and made my way into the hallway. Grabbing one of Annie's umbrellas, I accompanied Stacy to the front door. She had been complaining about a backache all day, and I had wanted to take her to the doctor, but she was having none of it. She insisted she was okay and just needed to rest. At thirty-four weeks pregnant, she was flying back to San Francisco in the morning. Chris had called the night before to tell her he was finally home to take care of her again after visiting his mother and taking an overseas trip.

The storm was whipping up into a frenzy as we stepped out into the night. Placing my arm around her shoulders, I pulled her close to me and guided her quickly to the car. She flinched as she seated herself in the front seat, and I informed her in my most superior motherly tone that if she was still in pain in the morning, I was taking her to the doctor.

I joined her in the car and drove slowly down Annie's long, winding driveway, trying not to jostle Stacy. She seemed to wince at every pothole in the drive. I carefully wove around the tree limbs that littered our path, trying to control my rising panic at the weather and Stacy's condition. I decided to concentrate on the long trail of red lights in front of me that belonged to the other cast members' cars.

About halfway down the driveway, the line of cars stopped in front of me. I waited apprehensively and looked out my side window. The wind was roaring around us, and it had started to rain again with a vengeance. All I could think of was getting Stacy home as soon as possible and settling her comfortably in her bed.

James, who had been ahead of us at the end of the driveway, approached me. He was wearing a yellow sou'wester and slicker, and as he clung on desperately to his hat, any strands of hair that worked themselves loose in the wind whipped around his face in a candy-flossed frenzy. The

side gusts were so forceful, he was having to walk with his head cocked to one side just to get to us. As he reached the car, he used his spare hand to gather his yellow slicker tightly around himself.

I opened the window just a crack to talk to him.

"Hey," he yelled over the escalating clamor of the storm. "We've got a problem. An enormous tree fell and cut off the driveway, and I can see another one down on the road too. There's just no way around it. You're going to have to drive back to the farm so we can call the authorities."

I nodded and backed the car up the driveway. Soon we were all parked back outside the farmhouse. I looked at the trees closest to Annie's house, and it appeared we would be safe inside. She had apparently kept up on limbing the low, heavy branches and topping off the high trees. As I looked through the driving rain, my thoughts matched the weather exactly—dark and dreary. To my left, the pasture was practically a lake, and to the right, the dense forest loomed ominously as the lightning periodically lit up the trees.

There was a knock on my side window, and James was back. "Can I help you inside with Stacy?" he shouted over the raging storm.

I looked over at my daughter, who was unusually quiet and pale. She nodded, which made me ever more apprehensive. Very independent and

self-assured, she normally didn't accept help from anyone.

I thanked James as he came around and held an umbrella over her car door. Opening it, he hooked her arm gently into his and pulled her to her feet before escorting her swiftly inside.

I followed, making a run for it. Once inside, I looked around as we all gathered in the main hall. I couldn't believe how wet and completely windswept we appeared after only being exposed to the storm for an instant.

Making our way into the main room, we gathered around Annie's roaring fire to dry off as James went to call the sheriff's department to let them know we were cut off at the farm. With no cell phone service this far out on the island, James withdrew to Annie's office to use her landline. When he came back to us, his face showed his concern.

"I have good news and bad news," he stated plainly. "The good news is I was able to get through to the sheriff's department and let them know we're trapped up here. The bad news is they're already dealing with many power outages and a couple of serious accidents, so we're a low priority. It may be hours before they can get to us."

There was a universal moan from everyone, and Doris took control.

"I suggest you all call home from the office

phone to let people know you're okay and will be here until we can get through. At least we have power at the moment, but that could change at any minute with the way this storm is raging."

Going into emergency mode, Doris organized people to gather flashlights and blankets as Annie pulled out her emergency supplies and placed her first-aid kit on the table.

James organized a group to fill bottles of water in the farmhouse kitchen, knowing that if we lost power, we would also lose the electricity that pumped the well on the property.

I had just put the phone down with Martin, who had informed me the power was already out at our house, when the lights around me went out as well, and I was plunged into darkness. I sat motionless at Annie's desk, feeling vulnerable. I didn't know Annie's house well enough to get myself safely back to the group in the main room. As I sat there, trying to figure out what to do, the office door opened and a beam of light illuminated the desk in front of me. It was Ernie. I knew his shuffled walk, even silhouetted in the darkness.

"Your knight in shining armor is here," he joked, "though I seem to have lost my horse."

He came over and guided me to the door.

As we made our way carefully down the hallway, we heard Flora call out from one of

the bedrooms. Ernie went in and found her too.

"Come on, princess," he said with a toothy grin that I could actually see in the shadows. We both linked arms with him, and he laughed. "Must be my lucky day, a woman on each arm," he joked. He then broke into a song-and-dance number as he promenaded us to the main room.

Just as we reached the door of the kitchen, Annie passed us in the hallway on a mission. She went to the sink and tugged at Dan's arm.

"Miss Marcy," Annie said, breathlessly, "I think she's had a turn."

Dan sighed and shook his head. He followed Annie into the main room. The three of us were right behind him. He walked over to Marcy, and as if on cue, Marcy appeared to pass out. Dan reached out and just managed to catch her before she rolled off the sofa and onto the floor.

"We should get her into one of the spare bedrooms," stated Annie.

I grabbed one of the flashlights now piled on the table, and as Annie led the way, I helped Dan carry Marcy. She sighed pathetically, and her eyes fluttered slightly. We lifted her onto the bed as Annie lit a couple of candles in the room. As he bent forward, she seemed to miraculously revive and reached out to grab his hand, saying, "Don't leave me, Dan."

Dan, red-faced and obviously very unhappy, reluctantly pulled a chair toward the bed, and I

355

gave him a look that said *That girl is working you.*

Annie said, "I'm going to see if anyone has any first-aid training."

"Don't bother," said Olivia, who had just appeared in the doorway. "I can check her out. I used to be a nurse for an elderly lady in Paris. I'm sure I can handle a fainting, healthy young woman."

She walked into the room, lifted Marcy's legs up, placed them onto a pile of pillows, and started to take her pulse.

A blinding flash of lightning illuminated the whole bedroom, followed by a deafening crack of thunder. Marcy started screaming and clung to Dan's arm like it was a life raft.

As soon as Marcy was settled, I made my way back to the kitchen to check on Stacy and found Doris and Ethel handing out hot chocolate and crackers as snacks.

"Thank goodness for a gas stove," said Lavinia as she boiled kettles of water for drinks. Lottie spooned cocoa into cups.

"This is hardly going to keep us going," said Ernie, chuckling as he took a cup and plate of crackers from Doris.

"We have to be smart," said Doris. "We could be here for days, and we have a lot of mouths to feed."

I hoped that wouldn't be the case.

I took a cup of cocoa over to Stacy. I found her

bent over, breathing in a labored way, her face flushed.

"What is it?" I asked, setting the drink down on the floor.

"I don't know," said Stacy. "The pain in my back is much worse, and it feels like I might be having contractions again."

"It's probably all the excitement," I said, trying not to panic. "We should find a place for you to lie down."

I grabbed Annie, who was just coming back from Marcy's room. "I need to get Stacy to a bed."

James saw what was going on and came over. "Do you need some help?" he asked.

"We need to get Stacy up into bed."

Between the three of us, we carried her upstairs. I knew she was sick because she didn't complain once. On the way, I told James in a hushed tone, "We should call the sheriff again and tell him we have an emergency here."

James took another look at Stacy, nodded, and went off to the office.

As we reached the top of the stairs, Stacy's water broke. We all heard it and knew what it meant, but no one spoke for a moment.

Stacy burst into tears, wailing, "I want Chris."

We got Stacy inside the bedroom, and I watched Olivia quickly come into the room and examine Stacy. She informed us as she worked

methodically that she had nearly become a midwife in her twenties. She determined that Stacy was already seven centimeters dilated and that the babies would probably be born soon.

I clung to Stacy's hand and tried to think clearly.

James arrived in the room and announced he had delivered a baby when he had been on a stint in the Peace Corps and told Stacy softly that she was in good hands and that soon she would be holding her sweet babies.

Stacy cried out, her eyes wild with panic, so Olivia taught me how to work through breathing exercises with her. I just sat there, helplessly holding her hand, breathing in and out like a pair of bellows, trying to control my own panic and Stacy's.

News traveled quickly through the house, and pretty soon we got a visit from all the book club members.

Doris was the first to arrive in the room with a pile of towels, Ethel by her side with a pile of sheets.

"Ethel and I are here with supplies," she said. "What else do you need?"

"Maybe some ice?" answered Olivia. "And more light, if you can spare it."

"Yes, ma'am," said Doris. "I'm on it." She and Ethel bustled away to do Olivia's bidding.

Ruby came floating in with a bag she had fetched from her car.

"I have crystals, essential oils, flower essences, and whale music."

"How about drugs?" wailed Stacy as she cried out in pain from another very difficult contraction.

"You won't need any of that," answered Ruby confidently as she started to hang her crystals from long strings around the bed. "You will be amazed how much good a few herbs and some music can do to help."

I looked at Stacy, who rolled her eyes and shook her head, saying, "I know exactly where I would like to stick it all, and that would definitely help."

She turned over and groaned as another racking contraction took hold of her body. It was so difficult to see my girl in so much pain, but I kept reminding myself—and her—that childbirth was a natural thing, and soon it would all be over.

"The essential oils might help," I said as we blew air in and out together, following the breathing exercises Olivia had given us.

Gracie arrived in the doorway with a bowl of ice.

"Doris sent this up," she said. She was dressed in her favorite pink fairy costume. She scooted over to the bed and sat, doll-like, on the other side of Stacy. She gently took Stacy's hand

and stroked it tenderly. She started to tell Stacy one of her rejected World War II stories, and somehow this sweet, gentle creature seemed to quiet Stacy, who was already exhausted. Her breathing relaxed as she listened to Gracie's calm and lilting words.

At Olivia's request, Annie arrived with her first-aid box and Doris with more light.

Olivia started to pull out the first-aid supplies she needed as James helped her, placing things on a tray. They worked incredibly as a team, as if they had been doing this together for years.

The twins arrived in the doorway with Ernie, and they all stood agog, hands placed on chests, brows, and cheeks, looking like a comedic version of the three wise monkeys.

"We heard," said Ernie, his eyes wide, "but we had to see it to believe it. Those babies sure know the perfect night to make their entrance."

"I'm off to pray," stated Lottie with strong conviction.

"And I'm off to boil water," added Lavinia. "I'm not sure what the water's for, but in every movie I ever saw where a baby was born, people boil water."

"And I think I will go and eat something," stated Ernie firmly, apparently not wanting to be left out of the labor preparations.

I kept rubbing Stacy's back with the essential oils as Ethel crept in, seated herself in a corner,

and took it upon herself to time the contractions with her show stopwatch. She updated us mechanically on how close they were getting over the dirge of the whale music.

Flora arrived with more supplies and a pot of herbal tea, saying, "Lavinia said to tell you she thinks she has found out what all the hot water is for and is making tea."

Flora stepped forward, set the cup down, and placed her hand on Stacy's arm. It suddenly struck me that they were very similar in age, yet so different.

"I brought you my iPod if you need some other music," she said quietly. "I hope it helps."

Stacy nodded her thanks. I was actually really glad, as the whale music was starting to hit a difficult Neptunian crescendo, and Ruby had entered into some sort of goddess ritual event. She waved her arms around, turning in small circles as she spiraled wafts of the red chiffon sari she was wearing and clanged together her finger symbols. I wasn't sure if any of what she was doing was helping, though she was an interesting distraction for me to watch between contractions. Stacy seemed to be too out of it from the pain to notice, though Ruby did have her practical uses. She took over for me while I went to the bathroom, and when I came back, she had taken Stacy through some sort of yoga breathing technique that had actually seemed to calm her a little.

About an hour later, Olivia announced that the babies were indeed about to be born, and Stacy sobbed, saying over and over again, "I want Chris. Where is Chris? Is it too early? They can't come just yet. I want to leave right now and go home. I'm not staying here one more minute."

I looked at Olivia, who just nodded knowingly, saying, "She is in transition. She will be ready to push soon."

Chapter Thirty-Nine

CANDLELIGHT CONFESSIONS & A WALK ON THE WILD SIDE

Flora had just finished getting another washcloth for Stacy when she decided to go and find Dan. She hadn't seen him for a while, and she was pretty sure that Marcy would be attempting to monopolize his time.

As she walked toward the spare bedroom, the flashlight Flora had been holding suddenly died. She slammed it hard against her palm a couple of times but nothing happened, so she reached out to feel for the wall. She knew she was just a few feet from the bedroom.

As she reached the doorway, she could hear Marcy sobbing, and she could see her silhouette in the bed reflected off the wall of the bedroom, captured by the candlelight. Unknown to both of them, Flora had entered the darkness and was about to communicate her presence when she was stopped in her tracks by Marcy's words.

Through a whimpering whine, she spluttered, "Please, Danny, I know we've had our differences over the last few weeks, but you still love me, right?"

Flora brought her hand to her chest.

She heard Dan seeming to struggle to find the right words. Then he said clearly, "Of course I love you."

Flora felt the shock in his words as that now-familiar icepick sliced its way into her heart again. The emotion was followed very quickly by anger. It was really clear to her now that he had just been playing with her emotions. She knew she hadn't imagined it this time; she had heard the words quite clearly. Dan had just told Marcy he loved her. And there was no way he would be able to play this one down.

Marcy responded to his words. "I always knew it. You've been playing hard to get with me, haven't you? We've known each other for such a long time. We were just meant to be. So what are you going to do about that other girl?"

Flora held her breath.

Dan's tone was measured in response. "My relationship with Flora is very different."

Marcy interrupted him. "You mean you just feel sorry for her, right?"

She wasn't going to wait to hear Dan's answer. Her whole life, people had felt sorry for her, and she didn't want to give him a chance to confirm her suspicions.

So she blurted out into the darkness, "I thought you should know Stacy is about to have her

babies." She knew her tone was harsh and flat, but she didn't care.

And with that, she turned on her heels and fled, dropping the flashlight on the floor as she went. Flora didn't know what had possessed her. She ran down the darkened corridor and straight out the front door. The weather that greeted her was wild. The heavy rain and wind was creating a river of dancing trees in the darkness. It reflected how she was feeling inside completely, and being out in the wildness of it all actually felt somehow comforting to her. She took in a long, deep breath of the cold, damp air, and forcing her body against the wind, she made her way toward Annie's woods.

Dan jumped to his feet when he heard Flora's voice behind him. He focused on the dark doorway, but no one was there. He was sure it had been Flora. *How much had she heard?* He tried to think about the last thing he'd said to Marcy that would have made her disappear like that. By the hasty way she'd exited, it was obvious he'd said something wrong.

He rewound the conversation in his mind. He had just been about to tell Marcy that his relationship with Flora was different, and even though he had love for Marcy, it was a friendship love. He was actually "in love" with Flora. *What was the last thing she would have*

heard? Hadn't he just said he loved Marcy? He could see how easily it would have been to misinterpret it. He needed to find her and let her know it wasn't the way it sounded. He rushed into the corridor, but she'd disappeared completely.

Grabbing a flashlight from the main room, Dan searched carefully through the farmhouse. It was large, and in the darkness, it took him a while to cover all the rooms. After searching everywhere twice, he realized that Flora was nowhere to be found. Suddenly a gripping thought overtook him. What if she'd gone outside?

Maybe she was sitting out in a car or out in the barn with the dogs. Dan pulled the collar of his jacket up around his ears and opened the door. The storm was on the move, but there was still a pretty serious driving rain, accompanied by the distant rumble of thunder and the flash of lightning that illuminated the sky. *Surely she wouldn't have come out here.*

He scoured around the farmhouse, looking in cars and opening the barn door. Inside, Annie was cooing to all of her dogs as Bruiser followed obediently by her side. Annie confirmed that she hadn't seen Flora, and as Dan closed the barn door, he looked around him.

Even in the darkness, he could see a few miles across the pasture, which appeared empty. That meant the only other place Flora could have gone

was up into the woods. Surely she wouldn't have done that.

From behind him, he heard a voice. He moved toward it. Someone was walking toward him with a flashlight. As he drew closer, he was disappointed to see it was two men. When they got close enough, Dan saw they were para medics.

One shouted out to Dan, "Is there someone here in labor?"

"Yes," Dan answered.

"Can you show us where?"

"This way," responded Dan, who made his way back up toward the farmhouse as they followed him. "How did you get here?" asked Dan as they all arrived at the door.

"By foot, from the road," answered one of them ruefully. "The ambulance is way back, behind the trees."

Dan was anxious to eliminate places Flora could have gone.

"Did you see a girl on your way up here?" he asked hopefully.

They looked at one another and shook their heads. "Sorry, nothing on the road but trees."

Dan nodded and opened the door to the farmhouse. They entered just in time to hear Doris shout from the top of the stairs, "It's a boy!" followed by the faint snuffling cry of a newborn baby.

In the main room, the rest of the group cheered. Ernie met the new guests in the hallway.

"Looks like you guys didn't need us after all," one of the paramedics commented.

"Oh, there's one more," stated Ernie. "You'll get your chance."

Ten minutes later, the paramedics delivered the second baby, with Olivia and James helping. It was a little girl. Stacy was exhausted but happy as they placed the babies on her chest to greet her. They decided to move her and the babies to the hospital. The babies were premature and needed to be in special care. The paramedics secured all three of them in the hallway. The wind started to calm down, and they waited for the helicopter to take them to the hospital.

Dan was walking around the farm one more time when he saw Flora. She appeared like a ghost at the edge of the woods. She was completely soaked from head to foot. Dan ran up the hill toward her.

"Flora," he cried, "where have you been?"

"I heard you," she shouted, stiffly. "I heard every word about how you're in love with Marcy. So where do I fit into all of that, may I ask?"

He looked into her face, grief-stricken. "We can talk about it once I've got you inside and got you warm."

"No," she said, refusing to move. "You need to

tell me now. What is going on between you and that girl?"

He took hold of her shoulders gently, and she responded by pulling sharply away from him, tripping backward over a fallen branch, and collapsing in a heap on the ground.

Instead of getting up, she shouted out to no one in particular, "I'm such a klutz!" And then, sitting there in the mud, she began to weep, mumbling, "I will never fit in. I'm just an oddity, something that people feel sorry for."

Dan knelt beside her quickly and pulled her into his arms. "You fit," he said, and he pulled her close. "You fit right here, next to me." He rocked her gently. "I'm sorry you heard that with Marcy. But what you heard was innocent, however you interpreted it. And if you had waited to hear the rest of the conversation, you would have heard me tell Marcy exactly how much I really love you."

"How do I know that for sure?" Flora spat out, attempting to push him away.

"Because," he said, pulling her face gently toward him and looking deep into her eyes, "because you're the woman I want to spend the rest of my life with. Being here and being part of those babies being born tonight totally confirmed it for me. You're the only person I want to have that experience with."

Through her tears, Flora looked up at him and

stopped fighting as he took both her hands in his. He looked deep into her eyes and said something to her.

But Flora never heard him, as the roar of a medical chopper landing drowned out his words. So he repeated the words again, shouting at the top of his lungs,

"Flora, will you marry me?"

Flora's crying slowed as she blinked away the rain in her lashes, appearing to see for the first time the genuine look of complete contentment and love on his face.

"What?" she shouted back, swiping wet, lank hair from her eyes and revealing a look of shock and incredulity.

"I asked you to be my wife," he stated. Then softly into her ear, "Please say yes."

Flora softened as her sobs subsided to short, sharp, gasping breaths. "You want to marry me?" she stammered as she gulped for air. "What about Marcy?"

"Well," he said in mock seriousness, "I asked her, and she said no, so I thought I'd ask you." Then he beamed, revealing his joke. He added resolutely, "There is no me and Marcy, only me and you. I have been in love with you since the very first day you appeared in my garage. There could never be anyone else. I see only you, and I love only you. Please say you'll marry me and make me the happiest man alive."

She swallowed back her last sobs and smiled through the raindrops that were rolling in a steady stream down both of their faces. Then, before she had a chance to stop it, her heart answered for her.

"Yes, I will."

Chapter Forty

GLADYS TO THE RESCUE

When I arrived at the usual table, I looked around at all the faces. Only Flora was missing from the group. She had informed us that she and Dan had something important to buy and would be off-island for the day.

This was one of Doris's emergency meetings. The day before, the sheriff had been by Annie's farm. Sheriff Brown had let her know that the land developers had paid him a visit. The sale was pending and all their paperwork was in order. And even though he didn't feel the way they had gone about it had been very honest, the house would soon belong to the developers, and there was nothing he could do about it. Then he had informed Doris and her crew that they couldn't keep up the picket line forever.

Now, as I looked around at all their faces, Doris looked the most despondent of them all. She just sat there, staring at the menu, oblivious to everything around her. Gladys arrived at the table.

"You lot look a sight for sore eyes. Who died?"

No one responded. We all just sat, hunched around the table, looking at the menus in front of us.

She continued her usual rant. "So, no jolty movements or jumping around the table today, then? Is it safe to send over the busboys? Are you practicing a death scene, or is this one of these center-yourself-and-focus-on-your-belly-button exercises? Personally, I have never seen the need to be centered. I like to be a little off-kilter. It keeps me shrouded in mystery."

Shrouded in mystery, I thought to myself. She was definitely shrouded all right, but "mystery" was not the word I would use. It smelled more like mothballs.

Doris didn't even have it in her to bite back. "Cup of coffee," she said and pushed the menu toward the end of the table. We all added our own drink orders. None of us felt much like eating.

Gladys shook her head as she gathered them up. "Never a dull moment with this crew," she said and went off to place the order.

I noticed that Annie hadn't arrived yet. Doris took a drink from a glass of water and cleared her throat. The twins just sat nervously. Suddenly, Lottie broke the silence.

"I prayed," she said. "I prayed that God would show me what all of this is about, because I'll be honest with you, I can't see what the point of all this is. I know it's all part of his plan, but it's some sort of odd, mess of spaghetti-type plan."

From out of nowhere, Gracie piped up. "Ice

373

cream," she said, "and pie. We all need ice cream and pie. That will make everything better."

I grabbed her hand and gave it a squeeze.

Annie arrived. She actually looked kind of upbeat. She sat down and everyone watched her carefully, taking their lead from her mood.

"Good morning," she said, brightly. In her hand, she held little bouquets of flowers. She started to give them to each of us. "I know we all feel kind of down," she said, "but you know, I've gotten used to the fact that I'm moving on. I don't know where to right now, but I've talked to a couple of pet shelters, and they've all agreed to help me in any way that they can."

"You know you can move in with us," said Lottie, stretching a hand across the table to Annie.

"That goes without saying. You could even bring a couple of those pooches," added Lavinia.

"Thank you," Annie said. "That's a lovely thought, and I may do that and bring my little family of five, but I do need to look for somewhere new." She fought back tears as she continued handing out the bouquets to each of us. "These are just a way of saying thank you. These are flowers from the farm. Deep in the forest, we have these beautiful plants that I don't see anywhere else, and I wanted to make you all bouquets of them."

Gladys arrived back at the table and stopped

short. She picked up one of the bouquets and sniffed, saying, "Why, those are *Lupinus sabinianus Fabaceae.* You're not supposed to pick those, you know."

Doris came to life, angrily.

"What does it matter," she said, "whether we pick flowers or don't pick flowers? That's all immaterial. Why don't you just serve us pie and coffee like you're supposed to?"

Gladys tutted. It appeared to be like water off a duck's back for her. "I would love to," she said, "if you weren't always so dramatic. You can't just be simple customers; there's always some fire going on you have to fight."

Doris was about to burst, but I jumped in fast.

"What do you mean about the flowers?" I asked Gladys, cutting through the contentious atmosphere, which was building up like a traffic jam on game day.

"Well, these are endangered," she said. "You can't just pick them willy-nilly."

"Endangered?" I inquired. "Does that mean that they're protected?"

Gladys nodded her head. "I'll go and get my book," she said, and she ambled away.

Doris continued to boil over. "I don't know why we even come here. Every time, we just get insulted, and the food isn't that good anyway—"

Lottie cut Doris off as she looked at me. "What are you thinking, Janet?" she asked.

I said thoughtfully, "If it's endangered, there may be a protection order on it. If there's a protection order on it, then people can't disturb that land, and you know what that means."

The penny suddenly dropped for everyone, including Doris. She slammed her hand down on the table so hard that all the condiments popped up in the air and clattered onto the floor, rolling in every direction. "That means that we can stop this going through, or at least we can slow it down," she said. "Quickly. Give me a pen."

She started to make hasty notes. "I'm going to go straight over to see the sheriff. Then I'm going over to the fish and wildlife people. I know exactly who to call. I'll see you all later."

She jumped to her feet and disappeared out the door, Ethel scurrying behind her.

Gladys came back with everybody's drink order and a huge book about plants under one arm. She looked around at the smashed condiments on the floor. "I see that the belly button contemplating didn't last long, then. Back to your usual crazy old selves." She placed down the drinks, passed the book to me, folded her arms, and added, "I would assign your very own busboy to clean up after you, but they're all scared you'll make them sing and dance, and no tip is worth all that malarkey."

Everyone was looking at Annie. I thumbed through the book till I came to the page Gladys

had dog-eared and showed it to Annie. "Do you understand what this means?" I said excitedly.

Annie shook her head. "I have no idea what's going on."

"It may be the way to save the farm. If we can at least slow down what's going on, it might give you a chance to get some money to be able to pay off the bank. Also, they may not be able to build on land where there are endangered plants."

EPILOGUE

Annie had the letter propped up on her farmhouse table, in pride of place, and informed us that she read it at least twice a day to remind herself it was real. She handed it to Doris, Ethel, and I to read when we arrived.

> Dear Ms. Thompson,
> The bank is delighted to inform you that it has a new repayment scheme available and is willing to work with you to help repay the back mortgage payments and costs on your account. We like to think of ourselves as a customer-friendly bank and like to be able to work with our members whenever we can. Please call us with any questions you have.

"A customer-friendly bank?" I inquired, lifting an eyebrow to reiterate my lack of belief.

"Oh yeah," said Annie, who was casting on a new row to start yet another set of woolen booties for Stacy. "Friendly, apparently, means being mean to you for months, then scaring you half to death as they try to throw you out of your lifelong home with the help of a bunch of heavy moving equipment."

She had called us the day before to inform us that a representative from the bank would be visiting her that morning to finish the paperwork. Both Doris and I had wanted to be there to support her, just in case she needed the help, and Ethel, of course, had come along for the ride too.

As if on cue, an uproar of barking from the barn heralded the entrance of said bank official. I accompanied Annie as she went to open the door.

"It's you," she said with clear animosity.

It seemed to make no impression on the person on the doorstep. As he walked in, Bruiser started to growl.

"I should have listened to you the first time," Annie said, rubbing the dog's ears and walking back toward the main room, leaving the front door wide open as she shouted over her shoulder, "You had better come in, then."

As he entered the house, the three things that sprang to my mind were gray suit, blue eyes, and aftershave. This clean-cut, dazzlingly handsome man was apparently the bank's best asset for breaking bad news to unsuspecting homeowners. He had a disarming presence and a friendly and pleasant demeanor.

Following us into the main room, he introduced himself as John Meyers, offering us an open palm, full eye contact, and a beaming smile. I could see how Annie had been duped into believing this person had her best interests at heart.

Annie, very uncharacteristically, didn't offer him a drink or a chair but just went back to her knitting, leaving him abandoned in the middle of the room. Not looking up from her needles, she said, "Did you bring the paperwork?"

As he pulled out a file from his briefcase, he didn't seem at all fazed by her abruptness and instead diverted all his charm in Doris's direction.

"We at the bank are so glad to be able to work with Ms. Thompson and help her stay in her home. It's the best for all parties when we can make that work."

"Yes, funny that ever since you found out that there are not only one but many endangered plants on Annie's land, your bank wants to work with her," Doris grunted.

"We obviously want to protect the lovely wildlife that is so prevalent on this beautiful island," he answered.

"Sure you do," added Doris harshly. "Your charms and fancy words won't work on us here. So why don't you get on with the business at hand so you can be on your way to 'help' out someone else?"

He shrugged his shoulders, as if he knew we were calling his bluff and that he was all out of high cards. He pulled out the paperwork, and this time we all read it before Annie signed it. He moved to leave.

We accompanied him to the door, and as he

walked outside, he turned to Annie. There seemed a genuine sadness about his eyes. "I get paid a lot for the job I do, and generally, nine times out of ten, I'm going to be the one to tell someone they are being evicted. You can believe this or not, but I'm actually genuinely glad you get to stay on this beautiful farm."

He seemed to want to say more, but by the scowls we returned, he didn't push it and started to walk toward his red sports car.

"The devil in a Sunday hat," spat Ethel as he drove away. We all nodded in agreement.

That same afternoon, we gathered at Annie's farm for a celebration. The whole cast was joining us, and we had much to do. Ethel and Doris had commandeered Annie's kitchen and were in the process of cooking up "a backyard banquet," as Doris called it.

Flora arrived, all sweetness and light, with Dan by her side. They seemed overjoyed to be in each other's company. As we gathered in the kitchen, I asked if Marcy would be joining us, and Flora shook her head.

Dan licked a spoon that Doris had handed him as he spoke. "I went over a couple of days ago to talk to her about something"—he paused and shared a knowing look with Flora—"and she informed me that because there is not going to be a show, she will be making her own way back

to Medford. Apparently a guy she met in town, Jeremy, is traveling down, and she's going back home with him."

Interesting, I thought, but not surprising in the least. I hadn't seen Flora since the birth of the twins a week before, but she was now positively glowing.

Dan and Flora helped Annie and me decorate the farm. We placed bunches of balloons around the garden, and Dan pulled out hay bales for people to sit on around the pond that was teeming with new spring life.

I looked across at Flora as we strung up a line of fabric flags together in an old apple tree. "You look happy, Flora," I said. "I'm glad things are working out between you and Dan."

She giggled as she said coyly, "Yes, things are going really well."

An hour later, we all came together on one of those wonderful warm spring days that was a nice early reminder that the sun would soon be returning for the summer. We ate Doris's famous baby back ribs, skillet potatoes, grilled asparagus, wilted spinach salad, her grandma's recipe of spicy sweet corn relish, and homemade bread, all followed by one of her notorious lemon cakes.

After lunch, the cast decided to act out an impromptu performance of *The Merlin of Ooze*, except everybody played each other's parts. Ernie placed a heap of straw on his head and played a

very convincing Dorothea as Flora giggled at his interpretation of her character.

Suddenly, we got an unexpected surprise. Martin arrived, and in tow were Stacy, Chris, and the babies, one cradled in each parent's arms. I threw up my hands in jubilation, saying, "They're out of the hospital. How wonderful."

Stacy was still a little pale but was content and glowing with that earthy maternal look that motherhood can sometimes bring, and Chris looked as if he were fit to burst with pride.

"We can't stop long," Stacy said. "We're just on the way home from the hospital with the babies but couldn't resist stopping by to let you all see them."

The assembled group quietly and carefully surrounded the couple as they cooed and offered their heartiest congratulations.

"What are you going to call them?" asked Lavinia. "I hear that Lavinia is a fabulous name."

"We had names all picked out before the birth," Stacy answered as she flashed her eyes at Chris, who nodded in response. "But after the amazing way these two came into the world, we felt we wanted to honor the people that helped give them life."

"So we would like to introduce you to Olivia and James."

Behind me, I saw James's eyes well up. I knew he had no children of his own, and I couldn't

think of a more fitting way to honor the man who had quietly been our rock over the past few weeks.

Olivia pressed her hands together and closed her eyes tightly; she was also obviously very moved. "I think the names are perfect," she purred, beaming.

"Welcome, Olivia and James," said Doris with gusto, "newest members of the Rejected Writers' Book Club."

From behind the barbecue, someone tapped their glass. We all turned around to see Dan smiling. "This seems like a good time," he said. "I, too, have something to announce. Flora, can you join me here?"

Flora moved swiftly to be by his side, and I noted a more distinct air about her. Normally, she would have hunched her shoulders and slunk forward, but as she joined him, she positively swished. As unpleasant as Marcy had been to her, I thought to myself, it was as if, in confronting her, Flora had acquired a new boldness that was all her own.

Dan gestured to Flora to make the announcement herself. She held out her left hand, and sparkling on her finger was an exquisite diamond cluster ring in a white gold Victorian-style setting. She declared with a confident air, "Dan and I are getting married."

The cacophony of sound that followed this announcement started all the dogs barking in the

barn and woke up poor little James in Stacy's arms. He mewed plaintively as she rocked him gently on her shoulder.

As the crowd died down, Flora added a little more thoughtfully, "As most of you know, my parents died a few years ago, and since then, the thought of getting married was always something sad for me, without my mom to help me or my dad to give me away. But when I look around at all your faces, I feel as if I don't have one but many moms. The Rejected Writers' Book Club has been like a family to me."

Her eyes started to brim with happy tears, so Dan picked up her thread. "Flora has decided that she would like a Christmas wedding, and she wants all of the Rejected Writers' Book Club to help her with it."

With that, the whole writers' group cheered and crowded around Flora and Dan, enveloping them both in a group hug.

Doris was the first to pull away, saying, with her barbecue tongs still in her hand, "And we'll make it the best dang wedding that Southlea Bay has ever seen."

We all laughed and hugged again before Stacy and Chris left to take the babies home to our cottage.

Later that evening, Martin and I sat side by side in the warm environment of our cozy cottage. Up

in our bedroom, Stacy was feeding the twins, and Chris was keeping her company. Martin and I had opted to sleep in the guest room to give them more space in our king-sized bed.

I snuggled up next to Martin, enjoying the pleasant ambience all around me. Stacy and Chris would stay another couple of days before heading back to San Francisco, as soon as they had the all-clear from the pediatrician.

We had waved good-bye to Annie early in the evening, and she had wept tears of joy as we left the farm. She had cried a lot of those tears most of the day. Just before we left, Doris had informed us all that, even though there was no dire financial need, she still intended on staging a production of *The Merlin of Ooze* to help Annie out with expenses while she was getting back on her feet.

I told Martin about this as he listened benevolently.

"If she thinks I'm going through all that again," I said, "she has another think coming."

Martin jumped to his feet and said, "Don't worry. I have the very thing to deal with it."

I watched him slip on his shoes and race out to his shed. I hadn't the foggiest idea of what he had up his sleeve. Two minutes later, he returned with a small plastic bottle and handed it to me.

"What is this?" I asked, reaching for my reading glasses.

"The answer to all your problems," he said, smirking.

"Is it anti-Doris cream?" I inquired, sarcastically.

"Almost. It's leftover flash powder from the show. Now you can blow up Doris anytime you want to," he stated dryly.

I punched him on the arm as I laughed heartily. "So it *is* anti-Doris cream. You'd better hide it from me. I don't want to be too tempted."

Just then, Chris crept down the stairs with a sleeping infant in his arms. Baby James was full and content from being fed, his little, downy head cradled in his father's palm as he blew out milk bubbles from his sleeping lips.

"Stacy thought you might like to hold your grandson while she finishes up with Livy," he said as he handed the tiny bundle to me.

I noticed that James was dressed neatly in all of Annie's knitwear. I held the tiny boy to my chest and mused that he was hardly heavier than a little bird as Martin stroked his miniature hand. I rocked him gently back, placing my hand behind his head. I looked into James's tiny face, and I realized that I had never been happier in my life.

Acknowledgments

I would like to thank the many people who helped make this book possible. First, my incredible team at Lake Union Publishing. To my editorial director, Danielle Marshall, and acquisitions editor, Miriam Juskowicz, thank you both for your encouragement and continued faith in my writing. Also a big thank you to my hardworking copy editors and development editors. To my wonderful agent, Andrea Hurst and Associates, for all your incredible support, advice, and wisdom and especially for your friendship. Thanks go to my personal cheering squad, my husband, Matthew, and my son, Christopher, who have to sit and listen to endless readings of scenes and still manage to laugh in all the right places. And lastly, to my sisters who have both encouraged me and to my mother, Anne Drummond, in England, who is a one-woman book marketing force of nature. Thank you for telling me I could do anything in life I wanted to. Unfortunately, I believed you.

Book Club Questions

1. Is the book engaging? How interesting do you find the story?
2. Discuss the role of comedy in the story. Does it add to your enjoyment of the book? How so?
3. Have you, like Janet, ever found yourself in way over your head when trying to help a friend?
4. Who is your favorite character? Why?
5. How well-depicted do you find the characters? Are they believable?
6. Describe the dynamics between the characters.
7. Do any of the characters remind you of people you know?
8. What is your favorite part of the story?
9. Do you enjoy the small-town setting? How does it contribute to the story?
10. What kinds of themes does the story explore?
11. Is the ending satisfying to you? Why or why not?
12. Does this book inspire you to read other books by the same author?

About the Author

Suzanne Kelman is the author of the Southlea Bay series and an award-winning screenwriter. Born and raised in the United Kingdom, she now lives in Washington in hcr own version of Southlea Bay with her husband, Matthew; her son, Christopher; and a menagerie of rescued animals. She enjoys tap dancing, theater, and high teas, and she can sing the first verse of "Puff, the Magic Dragon" backward.

Center Point Large Print
600 Brooks Road / PO Box 1
Thorndike, ME 04986-0001 USA

(207) 568-3717

US & Canada:
1 800 929-9108
www.centerpointlargeprint.com